HE
KNOWS
WHEN YOU'RE
AWAKE

HE KNOWS
WHEN YOU'RE AWAKE

A Naughty or Nice Novel

ALTA HENSLEY

An Imprint of HarperCollinsPublishers

hc.com

FIRST AVON A TRADE PAPERBACK PUBLISHED 2025.

Interior text design by Diahann Sturge-Campbell

Candy cane illustration © Marina/Stock.Adobe.com
Snowflake and skull illustration © Cintia; Pictandra/Stock.Adobe.com

Library of Congress Cataloging-in-Publication Data has been applied for.

ISBN 978-0-06-346285-4

25 26 27 28 29 LBC 5 4 3 2 1

*To Tony . . . for having the courage to make
the move and follow my wanderlust.*

Content Warning

This book contains some dark elements:

Stalking
Forced ice skating
Dominance & submission
Forced proximity
Painfully cute Christmas puppies
Voyeurism
Exhibitionism
Hidden cameras
Possessive love
Graphic sex with BDSM elements
Wearing of light-up Christmas sweaters

Proceed with caution . . .

HE
KNOWS
WHEN YOU'RE AWAKE

Chapter One
COLE

Three months of watching her every move, and she still manages to surprise me.

I leave my scotch untouched on top of quarterly reports, watching the security feed from Moth to the Flame instead. The image quality is shit, but it's enough.

From my penthouse office, it's possible to see half of Manhattan. But I'm focused on the wall of screens, their glow reflecting off the mahogany panels and marble floor. I built this room to keep tabs on my investments. Not just the jewelry lines that made the Asher name synonymous with luxury, but the entire portfolio. The chain of five-star hotels stretching from New York to Dubai, the private airline that caters to the ultra-wealthy, and the three exclusive members-only clubs in the most influential cities in the world. I've transformed my modest jewelry business into a luxury lifestyle empire.

Now I spend most of my time watching one jewelry designer work.

"Another female entrepreneur gets screwed by the banking system." Knox drops an iPad on my desk, helping himself to my scotch. The Chase Bank rejection letter glows on the screen—standard corporate bullshit about risk factors and lack of collateral. "That's the third one this week. Though I gotta say, this one's different from our usual finds."

He's right. I started monitoring loan rejections from major banks after noticing a pattern—brilliant women with innovative ideas getting shut down by old, outdated men too stupid to see past their own biases. It became almost a hobby, finding these diamonds in the rough, proving the banks wrong.

But Sloane . . . Sloane Whitmore was something else entirely.

Her long crimson hair is always the first thing I notice, falling past her shoulders when she lets it down. Today it's pulled back in that neat bun she wears at work, revealing the delicate curve of her neck, the subtle arch of her brows over those piercing green eyes. Even in her carefully curated wardrobe—tailored black blazers, high-waisted trousers, and those impossibly high heels she navigates Manhattan in—there's an elegance to her movements, a quiet confidence that commands attention. Pure New York sophistication with an edge that matches her designs.

"Tell me about Julian's plans again," I say, not taking my eyes off the feed. "His supposed 'luxury line' launch date."

Knox flips through documents on his iPad. "Still set for February. Using those mysterious 'newly discovered designs' of Claire's he's been teasing. Industry insiders are already calling it the event of the season." He pauses, scrolling further. "He's been meeting with Bergdorf and Neiman Marcus. Word is he's promising them exclusive rights to certain pieces. And I heard he's secured rare colored diamonds from South Africa."

I feel my jaw tighten. Claire. Even now, five years later, the thought of how Julian exploited her talent, how he plans to continue exploiting her name after her "accident"—it makes my blood boil.

"And our timeline?" I ask, forcing myself to focus on strategy rather than rage.

"If Whitmore says yes, and if she works at the pace her portfolio suggests she can . . . We beat him to market by two weeks. Just enough time to steal all his thunder and expose his 'Claire collection' for the fraud it is."

"Run her numbers again."

Knox snorts. "You've got them memorized."

"Humor me."

He flicks through the file on his iPad. The security feed shows Sloane at her desk, lost in her work. Even with Moth to the Flame's garbage cameras, I can see the moment inspiration hits.

"All right," Knox says. "Graduated top of her class at Parsons. Sells more than anyone else at her level but keeps getting passed over. Went to Moth to the Flame thinking she could push their look." He looks up from the iPad. "But they've got her making the same cookie-cutter crap as everyone else." A pause. "You know, this is usually where you tell me how you're going to prove the bank wrong. But that's not what this is, is it?"

I pull up her latest design. "Take a look."

"Jesus." Knox leans in. The necklace on-screen is all sharp angles and fractured metal. "It's not your average necklace. I'll give you that."

"This is what they're too stupid to understand." I zoom in on the detail work. "Everything else this company makes belongs on a grandmother."

"And Chase won't touch it." Knox hands me a drink and tops off his own. He's been with me through enough deals to know where this is going. "Bet that just makes you want it more."

I just raise an eyebrow. Knox knows me too well for lies.

"There's more than just profit riding on this investment," I say, studying the lines of her newest sketch. "If Sloane's designs are as revolutionary as I think they are, they'll completely overshadow anything Julian launches."

"And that's why we're keeping this so quiet?" Knox asks. "The confidentiality agreements, the security protocols?"

"Julian has sources everywhere. If he gets wind that I'm backing a competing line—"

"He'd do what he always does," Knox finishes. "Find a way to destroy it before it begins."

"Their loss." I turn back to the screens. "Banks keep making the same mistakes. Makes my job easier."

"Sure." Knox's voice is dry. "That's why you hacked every camera in the building. The camera in her apartment building, and her computer. Because it makes your job easier."

On-screen, Sloane runs her hands through her hair in frustration, destroying her usually neat bun. She does this when her boss shoots down her ideas. I've cataloged all her tells by now. The way she talks to herself while working, how she sketches on cocktail napkins at bars when she thinks no one's watching, her secret stash of peppermint tea hidden in her desk drawer.

"The arrangements at Tonic tonight?" I ask, changing the subject.

"Everything's set. Though I still think staging a collision is overthinking it. You could just approach her like a normal person." Knox's tone suggests he knows exactly how likely that is. "But since you're determined to be extra about this, the bartender will direct her to the right spot, your scotch will be perfectly positioned, and your ridiculously expensive suit is ready to be sacrificed to the cause."

I check my watch. Through the cameras, I see Sloane pack up for the day. She also reaches for a sweater she had delivered to her office a couple of days ago.

"So she's still wearing that sweater tonight? Christ, it's got actual antlers," Knox says.

"Battery-powered lights too." I don't mention how I know this. That I watched her open the package, saw her face light up like the ridiculous sweater itself. "Cost her nearly a day's pay."

"How would you even know—" Knox stops himself.

"Annual tradition with her friend Chloe." I tap the screen where Sloane's grinning at the sweater. "They hit Tonic every December. Ugly sweaters, expensive drinks they can barely afford. Been doing it since college."

"You could've just followed her Instagram and saved all this stalking time." Knox scrolls through his phone. "Look, there they are last year. Same bar, same ridiculous sweaters."

"That's the cleaned-up version." I turn back to the feed where Sloane's now shoving prototypes into her bottom drawer. The ones her boss would hate. "People show what they think others want to see. She's guilty of that."

"And you prefer the unfiltered version." It's not a question. Knox has watched me build and break enough empires to know how I operate.

Knox sighs, the sound of a man who's seen me go down obsessive rabbit holes before, but never on one person. Never like this.

"There's something about her that's already getting under your skin."

He's right, though I'm not ready to examine why. I've built my empire on finding undervalued assets, on seeing potential others miss.

But Sloane . . .

"Time to go," I say instead of answering, standing to adjust my cuffs in the window's reflection. The Manhattan skyline spreads out behind me, a glittering empire of steel and glass. "The scotch needs to hit my suit at precisely the right moment."

"You know normal people just ask women out for coffee, right?" Knox follows me through my office, past walls of awards and acquisitions that suddenly seem meaningless compared to the portfolio Sloane carries everywhere. "They don't orchestrate elaborate meet-cutes involving property damage."

"Since when have I ever been normal?"

The elevator doors slide open silently to my private garage, where a sleek black Bentley waits. The car's interior smells of leather and power, everything as I like it. Everything controlled.

I check my watch one last time as Knox slides behind the wheel. In exactly thirty-seven minutes, Sloane Whitmore will walk into Tonic wearing that ridiculous sweater, looking out of place among the suits and cocktail dresses. My guess is she'll try to make herself smaller, less noticeable.

But I'll notice.

Through the tinted windows, I watch my tower recede into the Manhattan skyline. I can imagine on the screens we're leaving behind, Sloane stepping into a taxi. She'll be trying to figure out her next move after another rejection, another setback. What she doesn't realize is every closed door has been leading her exactly where I want her.

To me.

Chapter Two

SLOANE

I'm already regretting this sweater.

The reindeer's nose blinks accusingly as I squeeze through Tonic's crowded entryway, feeling like a walking Christmas tree in a sea of sleek cocktail attire. A guy in an impeccable suit gives me a look of barely concealed disdain as I accidentally jostle his martini. I mumble an apology, not that he hears or would care.

The bartender catches my eye and nods toward an open spot at the far end of the bar. I silently thank whatever Christmas spirit guided me here as I make my way over, the blinking reindeer nose on my sweater creating a small red beacon in the dim light.

I'm early, and I know Chloe won't be here for another ten minutes at least. I scan the room, searching for a familiar face, but find only strangers. The contrast between their polished appearances and my garish sweater makes me want to sink into the floor.

Which frankly is unlike me. I'm normally confident in who I am and what I do, but ever since I started this process of starting my own jewelry line, I've felt like a fish out of water. Every rejection letter, every condescending meeting with potential investors. It's all chipped away at the certainty I once had in my self-worth.

I flag down the bartender, desperately in need of liquid courage. "Peppermint martini, please."

As he nods and turns to make my drink, I pull out my phone, needing something to do with my hands. No new emails. No missed calls. Just the same deafening silence that's followed every pitch and proposal I've sent out.

I'm so focused on my screen that I don't notice the man approaching until it's too late. I take a step back, right as he's moving forward with a glass of amber liquid. There's a moment of suspended time where I see it all happening but can't stop it—my elbow connecting with his arm, the arc of expensive scotch as it flies through the air, the look of surprise on his face.

Then time catches up, and I feel the splash of liquid against my chest, soaking through the ridiculous sweater.

"Oh my god, I'm so sorry!" I exclaim, mortified. I grab for the cocktail napkins on the bar, dabbing ineffectually at his perfectly tailored suit jacket. "I wasn't looking where I was going, I—"

I look up, and the words die in my throat.

He's gorgeous. Tall, with dark hair and eyes that seem to look right through me. But it's not just his looks. There's an aura of power around him, like he's used to commanding every room he enters. And right now, those penetrating brown eyes are fixed solely on me.

"No harm done," he says, his voice a low rumble that I feel in my chest. "Though I think your reindeer might need resuscitation."

I glance down to see that the scotch has shorted out the battery pack for my sweater's lights. The nose blinks weakly a few times before going dark.

"Rudolph, nooo," I deadpan. "He was so young."

The man's lips quirk up in a half-smile that shouldn't make my heart skip a beat but does. "A tragic loss. I feel partially responsible. Maybe I can make it up to you with a drink?"

I should say no. I'm here to meet Chloe, to commiserate over peppermint martinis about the state of my life and career. I don't have time for distractions, no matter how devastatingly handsome they might be.

But something in his gaze holds me there, makes me want to say yes to whatever he's offering.

"I suppose it's the least you can do, considering you've ruined my favorite holiday attire," I find myself saying.

He signals to the bartender, who appears with two glasses of scotch—instead of my peppermint martini, but who am I to criticize—before I can even blink. I raise an eyebrow at the efficiency, wondering if this man has the entire bar staff at his beck and call.

"To new beginnings," he says, raising his glass. "And sweaters that die heroically in the line of duty."

I smile as I clink my glass against his. The scotch burns pleasantly as it goes down, warming me from the inside out. It's easily the most expensive thing I've tasted in months.

"I'm Cole," he says, those intense eyes never leaving mine. "And you are?"

"Sloane," I reply, suddenly very aware of how ridiculous I must look in this damp, no longer light-up sweater. "Sloane Whitmore."

Something flashes in his eyes at my name, gone so quickly I wonder if I imagined it.

"Sloane Whitmore," Cole repeats, as if savoring the sound of my name. "A pleasure to meet you, despite the circumstances."

It's then that I notice that it's not just my sweater that has the drink on it. Cole's expensive suit jacket is also stained with scotch, a dark patch spreading across his chest.

"Oh god, your suit," I say, mortified all over again. "I'm so sorry. I'll pay for the dry cleaning, of course."

Cole waves off my concern with a dismissive gesture. "It's just a suit. Easily replaced." His eyes lock onto mine again, intense and searching. "I'm curious about the woman brave enough to wear a light-up reindeer sweater to Tonic on a Friday night."

A blush creeps up my neck at his scrutiny. "It's a tradition," I explain, fiddling with my now-dark reindeer nose. "My best friend and I do this every year. Ugly sweaters and peppermint martinis to kick off the holiday season."

"Ah, so there's more to the story," Cole says, leaning in slightly. The scent of his cologne, something woodsy and expensive, makes my head spin. Or maybe that's the scotch. "Tell me, what does Sloane Whitmore do when she's not electrocuting reindeer?"

I hesitate, unsure how to answer. My job at Moth to the Flame feels increasingly like a cage, while my dreams of starting my own line seem further away than ever. But something in Cole's gaze makes me want to be honest.

"I'm a jewelry designer," I say finally. "Or at least, I'm trying to be. Right now I mostly design what other people tell me to create."

Cole's eyes light up with interest. "A creator, then. What kind of jewelry do you design when left to your own devices?"

The question takes me by surprise. It's been so long since anyone asked about my personal vision rather than what will sell or what fits the brand.

"I . . . I create pieces that tell stories," I say, surprising myself with my candor. "Not the pretty, delicate things most people expect. My designs are about contrast. Beauty with an edge. The interplay of light and shadow, strength and vulnerability."

I pause, realizing I'm rambling. But Cole is watching me intently, genuinely interested. It emboldens me to continue.

"My latest collection, the one I'm trying to launch, it's called Midnight Frost. It's inspired by those moments just before dawn in the dead of winter, when everything is still and silent and dangerous. One slip on the ice can break everything. The way ice can be both breathtakingly beautiful and lethal. To be frank, my designs have a BDSM vibe, but I can't exactly tell possible investors that."

What. The. Fuck?!?

Why did I just include that last part? What the hell is wrong with me?

Cole's eyes seem to darken as I speak, a hint of something hungry in his gaze.

Needing to recover fast, I add, "I actually have some sketches with me," I reach for my phone where my ever-present portfolio is saved. "I always carry them, just in case I run into someone who—"

"Sloane!" Chloe's voice cuts through the moment. I turn to see her weaving through the crowd, her own ugly sweater a riot of tinsel and blinking lights.

I glance back at Cole. This man is clearly out of my league, probably just being polite to the clumsy woman who ruined his expensive suit. But there's something in his eyes that makes me hesitate to dismiss our encounter so easily.

"I should go," I say reluctantly. "My friend . . ."

Cole nods, understanding. "I won't keep you from your tradition."

But as I start to turn away, he catches my hand. The touch of Cole's fingertips sends an electric current up my arm. His skin is warm, his grip firm but gentle.

Our eyes lock for a moment, and I feel like I'm standing on ice, about to slip and fall. Then Chloe's hand is on my arm, tugging me away, and the spell is broken.

"Oh my god, what happened to Rudolph?" she asks as we make our way to a table.

I glance back over my shoulder, but Cole has already melted into the crowd with a grace that seems impossible for someone of his size.

"It's a long story," I say, unable to keep the wistfulness out of my voice. "Involving a very expensive scotch and a very handsome stranger."

Chloe's eyes widen with interest. "Ooh, do tell! Was he hot? Rich? Both?"

I laugh, settling into our usual booth. "Definitely both. But it doesn't matter. He was just being nice after I ruined his suit."

"Sure, sure," Chloe says, clearly not buying it. "That's why you look like you've been hit by a truck. A very sexy truck."

I roll my eyes, but I can feel heat rising up to my cheeks. "Can we just order our drinks and pretend I'm not a walking disaster?"

The waitress arrives, and we place our usual order of peppermint martinis. As she walks away, Chloe leans in, her expression turning serious.

"So, how did it go today? Any word from the banks?"

I sigh, the brief spark of excitement from my encounter with Cole fading. "Another rejection. Apparently, my 'lack of collateral' and 'unproven market potential' make me too risky."

Chloe reaches across the table to squeeze my hand. "Their loss. Your designs are amazing, Sloane. Someone's going to see that eventually."

"Maybe," I say, not entirely convinced. "But right now, it feels like I'm screaming into the void. No one wants to take a chance on something different."

Our drinks arrive, and I take a long sip, letting the cool peppermint wash away the taste of disappointment. The familiar flavors remind me of past Christmases, of the excitement and hope I used to feel at this time of year. Now, it just feels like one more reminder of dreams deferred.

"I've been thinking," I say slowly, tracing patterns in the condensation on my glass. "Maybe it's time for a change. A big one."

Chloe leans forward, intrigued. "What kind of change are we talking about here?"

I take a deep breath, finally voicing the idea that's been growing in my mind for weeks. "I'm thinking of leaving Moth to the Flame. Diving off the cliff with no safety net. I need to do something drastic to make this dream of mine happen."

"Wow." Chloe breathes. "That's . . . that's huge. Are you sure?"

I nod, feeling a mix of terror and exhilaration at the thought. "I'm suffocating there, Chlo. Every day, I'm forced to create things that don't represent me, that don't challenge anyone or anything. If I stay, I'll lose myself completely."

Chloe studies me, her brow furrowed in concern. "I get it, I do. But how will you support yourself? You said the banks won't give you a loan."

I take another sip of my martini, steeling myself. "I've been saving every penny I can. It's not much, but it's enough to get started. I figure I have about three months of runway before I'd have to start waiting tables or something."

"Three months isn't a lot of time," Chloe points out gently.

"I know," I admit. "But I have to try. If I don't do this now, I never will."

Chloe nods slowly, a smile spreading across her face. "You know what? You're right. It's time for Sloane Whitmore to take over the world with her badass jewelry."

I laugh, feeling some of the tension leave my shoulders. "I don't know about taking over the world. I'd settle for making enough to pay rent and keep designing."

"Oh please," Chloe scoffs. "Your stuff is incredible. Once people see it, you'll be the next big thing. I can see it now—'Sloane Whitmore: The Dark Rose of the Manhattan Jewelry Scene.'"

I nearly choke on my drink. "The Dark Rose? Really?"

Chloe grins. "Hey, every designer needs a dramatic nickname. Might as well claim yours early."

"I think the nickname needs work." I laugh, shaking my head at Chloe's enthusiasm.

But beneath the amusement, I feel a spark of something I haven't felt in months—hope. Maybe she's right. Maybe this is my moment to finally show the world what I can do.

As we finish our drinks, I can't resist the urge to scan the bar, wondering if I'll catch another glimpse of Cole. But the crowd has thinned, and there's no sign of his commanding presence.

"Earth to Sloane," Chloe says, waving a hand in front of my face. "You're thinking about Mr. Expensive Scotch, aren't you?"

I feel my face heat. "No, I was just . . . okay, maybe a little."

"I knew it. Spill. What exactly happened before I got here?"

I recount the collision, the ruined sweater, and our brief conversation. As I describe Cole's interest in my designs, I find myself wishing I'd had the courage to show him my sketches.

"Sounds like you made quite an impression," Chloe says, wiggling her eyebrows suggestively.

I roll my eyes. "Please. He was just being polite after I ruined his suit. Besides, men like that don't go for women who wear light-up reindeer sweaters and can't afford their own scotch."

"Don't sell yourself short," Chloe insists. "You're brilliant, talented, and gorgeous. Any man would be lucky to have you spill drinks on him."

"Thanks, Chlo. But right now, I need to focus on my career, not some random encounter with a handsome stranger."

"Fair enough," she concedes. "So, what's the plan? How are we launching the Sloane Whitmore collection?"

I take a deep breath, suddenly feeling the weight of my decision. "First, I need to give notice at Moth to the Flame. Then I'll need to find a small studio space, maybe sublet something in the Garment District. I've got some contacts from fashion week who might be interested in featuring a piece or two . . ."

As I outline my fledgling plans, I feel a mix of excitement and terror. This is really happening. I'm really doing this.

"You've got this," Chloe says, squeezing my hand. "And I'll be here every step of the way. Even if that means modeling your pieces in my pajamas at three a.m."

I laugh, picturing Chloe draped in my edgy designs while wearing her favorite fuzzy cat pajamas. "I might take you up on that." Changing the subject, I ask, "Do you and Jack have any big holiday plans this year?" I love that my friend is in a happy relationship, but a small part of me is envious. Jack is exactly the kind of supportive partner I've always dreamed of having.

"Staying put since he'll have to work. But I'm actually looking forward to another Christmas at the fire station this year. What about you? Are you going to Montauk?"

I shake my head, feeling a familiar pang of loneliness. "Not this year. I really need to focus on my line."

Chloe's brow furrows again. "Sloane, you can't work through Christmas. Your family will be devastated."

I shrug, trying to seem nonchalant. "They'll understand. This is important."

"So is family," Chloe counters gently. "Promise me you'll at least take some time off on Christmas Day?"

"Of course," I assure her, though the thought of explaining my decision to my parents over the phone fills me with dread. They've never quite understood my passion for jewelry design, always pushing me toward more "practical" career paths.

"One more for the road?" Chloe asks, signaling the waitress.

I hesitate, glancing at my watch. It's getting late, and I should probably head home to start working on my resignation letter. But the warmth of the bar and Chloe's company are comforting, a buffer against the uncertainty that awaits me.

"Sure," I say, smiling. "One more."

As the waitress brings our final round, I scan the bar one last time. No sign of Cole. I try to push away the disappointment, reminding myself that I have bigger things to focus on.

"To new beginnings," Chloe says, raising her glass. "And to the soon-to-be-famous Sloane Whitmore, the Dark Rose of Manhattan."

I laugh, clinking my glass against hers. "I think that nickname is growing on me."

We finish our drinks, chatting about Chloe's latest freelance gig and her plans with Jack for the holidays. As we gather our things to leave, I'm both relaxed from the booze and energized by the possibilities of what's ahead.

Outside, the cold December air hits me like a slap, making me acutely aware of my still-damp sweater. I pull my coat tighter around me as Chloe hails a cab.

"Text me when you get home," she says, hugging me tight. "And let me know if you need anything, okay? I mean it. Anything at all."

I nod, grateful for her unwavering support. "I will. Thanks, Chlo. For everything."

As her cab pulls away, I decide to walk for a bit, needing to clear my head before heading home. The streets of Manhattan are alive with holiday spirit—twinkling lights, the scent of roasted chestnuts, the faint sound of carols drifting from storefronts. The city is bustling with early holiday shoppers and tourists, and I weave my way through the crowds, my mind still preoccupied with thoughts of my resignation.

It all feels surreal, like I'm watching someone else's life unfold. But as I walk, something shifts inside me. Maybe it's the festive atmosphere or the sight of families bundled up and laughing together. Or maybe it's just a moment of clarity brought on by Chloe's words at the bar.

Either way, I find myself questioning my decision to leave my job without a backup plan.

Am I insane . . . ?

Yes, my boss is difficult to work for and the company culture stifling, but it's a steady paycheck and steady clients. My heart sinks as I realize that this may all be coming to an end. My dream of becoming a successful independent jeweler may not be as realistic as I had hoped.

I find myself stopping in front of a jewelry store window, drawn in by the glittering display. The pieces are beautiful but safe. Predictable. Nothing like the edgy, boundary-pushing designs I dream of creating.

"Is this really what you want?" I whisper to my reflection in the glass. The woman staring back at me looks uncertain, her ridiculous sweater a stark contrast to the polished luxury behind the glass.

But then I see something else in my reflection. A spark of determination in my eyes. I straighten my shoulders, lifting my chin. Yes, this is what I want. More than anything.

Chapter Three

SLOANE

The morning after my drink with Chloe, I wake to find my reindeer sweater draped over my desk chair, still faintly smelling of expensive scotch. The events of last night flood back. The handsome stranger, the ruined suit, the way his eyes seemed to see right through me. I push the thoughts away. I have more important things to focus on today.

Like quitting my job.

My resignation email sits open on my laptop screen, cursor blinking accusingly at the end of a sentence I've rewritten twelve times. How do you politely tell your boss that their creative vision is suffocating yours?

My phone buzzes with a text from Chloe: Still going through with Operation Freedom? Need moral support?

I smile, typing back: No turning back now. Letter's almost done.

Almost being a relative term. I've been staring at this same paragraph for an hour, trying to find the right words. Professional but firm. Grateful but determined. The kind of letter that won't burn bridges but also won't leave any doubt about why I'm leaving.

My tiny studio apartment feels even smaller this morning, cramped with the weight of this decision. Sketches and material samples cover every surface, the physical manifestation of dreams that have outgrown this space. A half-finished piece sits on my workbench—another design that pushes the boundaries of what Moth to the Flame considers "marketable."

The sun streaming through my window catches on a crystal I use to study light refraction, sending rainbow patterns dancing across my walls. It reminds me of that moment in Tonic, when Cole's scotch caught the light just before disaster struck. I wonder what he—

No. Focus, Sloane.

I turn back to the resignation letter, forcing myself to finish it before I lose my nerve. The final version is diplomatic but clear:

Dear Jasmine,

I am writing to formally tender my resignation from my position as Senior Designer at Moth to the Flame, effective January 15th. While I deeply appreciate the opportunities for growth and development that Moth to the Flame has provided over the past three years, I believe it is time for me to pursue my own creative vision.

I will ensure all current projects are properly transitioned and documented before my departure. Please let me know how I can best assist in making this transition as smooth as possible.

Thank you for your mentorship and guidance.

Best regards,
Sloane Whitmore

Before I can second-guess myself, I hit Send. The letter feels both too formal and not formal enough, but it will have to do.

My phone buzzes again. This time it's my mother.

"Sloane, honey," she says when I answer, her voice carrying that particular tone that always makes me feel like I'm sixteen again. "I got your message. Are you sure you can't make it to Christmas?

Your father's already planning his traditional oyster roast, and your brother's flying in from Seattle."

I close my eyes, guilt gnawing at my stomach. "I'm sorry, Mom. I just . . . I can't this year. I'm making some big changes with work, and I need to focus on getting everything set up."

"Changes?" Her voice sharpens with interest. "What kind of changes? Did you finally get that promotion?"

"Not exactly." I bite my lip, debating how much to tell her. "I'm actually leaving Moth to the Flame. I'm going to start my own line."

The silence that follows is deafening.

"Your own line," she repeats slowly. "Sloane, honey, is that wise? In this economy? What about your health insurance?"

Classic Mom, going straight for the practical concerns. "I've thought it through," I say, trying to keep the defensive edge out of my voice. "I've been saving, and I have some potential investors interested." A slight stretch of the truth, but better than telling her about all the rejection letters.

"But you have such a good position now," she persists. "Stable income, benefits, a clear career path. Why risk all that?"

I stand up, pacing the small confines of my apartment. Through my window, I can see the Manhattan skyline, a reminder of why I came here in the first place. To create something bold and daring. "Because I have to, Mom. Because if I don't try now, I never will."

She sighs, and I can picture her expression. The same look she wore when I announced I was going to Parsons instead of following Dad into medicine or her into law. "I just worry about you, sweetheart. New York is so expensive, and the jewelry business is so competitive . . . As it is, you're in an industry that's so volatile."

"I know," I say softly. "But I have to try. This is my dream."

"Dreams don't pay the rent," she reminds me gently. "Just . . .

promise me you'll be careful? And that you'll reconsider coming home for Christmas? You shouldn't be alone during the holidays, especially with all this change happening."

"I promise I'll be careful," I say, dodging the Christmas question. "I have to go. I need to get to work."

After hanging up, I stare out the window—dazed. Am I determined, maybe, or just desperate? Lost? Confused? Have I lost my freaking mind? The conversation with my mother has left me feeling . . . feeling . . . hell if I know.

I look at my phone as if Jasmine will have already responded, then tuck it and my portfolio into my bag. The weight of the unanswered email feels like a bomb waiting to go off.

The subway ride to work is a blur of nervous energy. I clutch my portfolio closer, drawing comfort from the familiar leather texture. Inside are the sketches for Midnight Frost. My vision, my future. I flip it open, studying the designs I know by heart. Each piece tells a story of transformation, of beauty found in darkness.

Moth to the Flame's offices are located in the heart of Manhattan. The brick walls and exposed pipes on the inside usually feel inspiring, but today they feel oppressive. I make my way to my desk, noting how Jasmine's office door is already closed—a sign she's in one of her "creative visualization" sessions.

"You look like you're either about to throw up or take over the world," Maya, my assistant, observes as I sit down. "Possibly both."

I manage a weak smile. "Let's go with option two."

She leans in, lowering her voice. "Seriously, are you okay? You've got that look you get before a big presentation."

I glance around to make sure no one's within earshot. "I'm giving notice today."

Maya's eyes widen. "Holy shit. You're actually doing it? The independent line thing?"

I nod, pulling out the envelope. "As soon as Jasmine finishes her morning meditation."

"About time," Maya says, grinning. "This place has been holding you back. Your stuff is way too edgy for their 'delicate feminine aesthetic.'" She makes air quotes around the phrase we've both heard in countless meetings.

"Thanks for the vote of confidence," I say, trying to ignore the flutter of panic in my stomach. "But maybe hold off on celebrating until after I survive this conversation."

"You've got this," Maya assures me. "And hey, when you're a famous designer, remember who supported you before it was cool."

I laugh, some of my tension easing. "You'll get an employee discount for life."

The morning crawls by in a haze of anxiety. I try to focus on my current projects—a spring collection that's all soft pastels and butterfly motifs—but my mind keeps drifting to the envelope in my drawer. To Cole's intense gaze when I told him about my designs. To my mother's worried voice.

Finally, around eleven, Jasmine's door opens. She emerges in a cloud of essential oils, her silk caftan floating behind her as she moves through the office. I wait until she's settled at her desk before gathering my courage.

"Jasmine?" I knock lightly on her open door. "Do you have a moment?"

She looks up, her reading glasses perched on the end of her nose. "Sloane, yes, come in. I was actually hoping to discuss the spring collection with you. I'm not feeling enough lightness in the butterfly wings. They need to almost float off the metal, you know?"

She clearly hasn't seen my email yet. She's been in her "creative visualization" session all morning. I step inside, closing the door behind me. My heart is pounding so hard I wonder if she can hear it. "Actually, I needed to discuss something else with you."

She gestures to the chair across from her desk, and I sit, staring at the desk between as if it's a bridge I'm about to burn.

"I've given this a lot of thought," I begin, my voice steadier than I feel. "And while I'm incredibly grateful for everything I've learned here, I believe it's time for me to move on." I take a deep breath and add, "I emailed you my letter of resignation."

Jasmine's perfectly sculpted eyebrows rise. She hits a few keys on her keyboard, my assumption that she's unlocking her screen. "Move on? To where?"

"I'm starting my own line," I say, lifting my chin slightly. "I have a vision for pieces that are different from what we do here. More experimental, more . . ."

"Edgy?" she supplies, a hint of disapproval in her tone. "Yes, I've seen your personal work. Very . . . interesting. But surely you understand that's not what the market wants? Women come to us for beauty, for delicacy."

"With all due respect," I say, gripping the arms of my chair to keep my hands from shaking, "I think there's room in the market for different interpretations of beauty. My designs speak to women who want something sharper, something that reflects the duality of their own nature."

Jasmine sighs, finally pulling up my email. She scans the letter quickly, her expression unreadable. "I see you're giving me plenty of notice," she says finally. "But given the sensitive nature of our designs, I think it's best if we make this effective immediately."

The words hit me like a physical blow. "Immediately? But my projects—"

"Maya can take over the spring collection." She cuts me off smoothly. "HR will process your final paycheck, including any unused vacation days." She stands, signaling that the conversation is over. "I wish you luck, Sloane. I hope you find what you're looking for."

I rise on unsteady legs, feeling like I've just been hit by a bus. This isn't how I expected this to go. "Thank you for the opportunity," I manage to say, my voice sounding distant to my own ears.

The walk back to my desk feels as if I'm walking underwater and there is a slight ringing in my ear. Maya takes one look at my face and knows. "That bad?"

"She's making it effective immediately," I say, my voice barely above a whisper. The reality of what just happened is starting to sink in. "I'm supposed to clean out my desk and go."

Maya says something . . . I think. Others come into my office to say goodbye and wish me well . . . I think. I sit, I stand, I pack. I'm not really sure if I know what is mine and what belongs to the company. Everything is a blur.

An hour later, I'm back in my tiny apartment, surrounded by the box of belongings from my desk and a stack of bank rejection letters I've been collecting over the past few months. Even a cup of peppermint tea can't shake the surreal feeling that my life has completely imploded in the span of a morning.

The rejection letters mock me from their pile on my coffee table. Chase's latest "regret to inform you" is still crisp, the corporate letterhead seeming to glare under my apartment's harsh lighting. Five different banks, five variations of "your lack of collateral and untested market make you too high a risk."

I pull out my sketchbook, needing to lose myself in design work. The foggy brain from the chaos of quitting my job and then essentially being fired lingers just enough to fuel my creativity. Either that or lose my mind. My fingers move across the paper almost of their own accord, sketching elements of my Midnight Frost collection—pieces that are too dark, too impossible for Moth to the Flame's uptight sensibilities.

The laptop sitting next to me pings with a new email. Probably another rejection, or maybe Jasmine with some passive-aggressive feedback about project handover. But the subject line makes me pause:

Your Vision for Midnight Frost—Investment Opportunity

I open it, curiosity overriding my usual skepticism about unsolicited business emails.

Dear Ms. Whitmore,

Our firm specializes in identifying and nurturing unique talent in the luxury goods sector. Your vision for the Midnight Frost collection, particularly the translucent collar piece with its innovative use of negative space and asymmetric gemstone placement, has captured our attention.

I go still. The collar piece. I've never shown that design to anyone except Chloe. It's not even on my private Instagram. How could they possibly know about it?

We believe your interpretation of beauty's duality—the interplay of submission and dominance, frost and fire—deserves proper backing. We would like to invite you to present your ideas for your line to our CEO in Gstaad, Switzerland.

Plane tickets and accommodation arrangements are attached. The meeting is scheduled for tomorrow night at the Alpina Gstaad.

We look forward to discussing how we can help bring your vision to life.

Regards,
Lawrence Blakely,
Senior Investment Manager, Asher Industries

My hands shake as I open the attachments. Sure enough, there's a ticket to Switzerland, hotel reservations at what looks like an absurdly luxurious resort, and a detailed itinerary.

"This has to be spam," I mutter, but something makes me hesitate before deleting it. The language is too specific, the details about my work too accurate.

I spend the next hour verifying everything I can. The email domain checks out. It's definitely from Asher Industries. The flight and hotel reservations are real.

My fingers hover over my phone. I need a reality check.

"I think I'm being courted by a potential serial killer," I say when Chloe answers.

"Ooh, fun! Wait, what?"

I explain about my final day at my job, the email, the tickets, and the mysteriously detailed knowledge of my designs. "It's too perfect," I finish. "And too creepy. How do they know about designs I've never shown anyone?"

"Maybe they have really good research teams?" Chloe suggests. "Look, what's the worst that could happen?"

"Um, murder? Organ trafficking? Ending up in some billionaire's underground dungeon?"

"Okay, yes, but also—what if it's legitimate? This could be your chance, Sloane. The universe literally just dropped a ticket to Switzerland in your lap right when you need it most."

I glance at my portfolio, then at my sad box of office supplies. "It does seem like extremely convenient timing."

"So go! What do you have to lose?" There's a pause. "Oh yeah . . . potential body parts."

"Not helping, Chlo."

"Sorry. But seriously, this is a legitimate company. You need this. Like, really need this."

After hanging up, I do what any rational person would do—I

google "Asher Industries." The results lead me to their CEO, Colsen Asher. Articles paint him as a brilliant but ruthless businessman who specializes in finding undervalued assets and turning them into gold. There aren't any pictures of him online, but I suppose old dudes who rule empires aren't worried about their social media presence.

Before I can stop myself, I type: "How to tell if a billionaire is a serial killer?"

The search results are not reassuring.

An hour later, my suitcase is open on my bed, winter clothes piled around it. My portfolio sits ready on my desk, containing every sketch, every design that's ever mattered to me. I still can't quite believe I'm doing this.

I check my phone one more time. The email is still there, still real. The plane ticket is still valid. And my Google search history still asks the question I can't quite answer: Is this a Christmas miracle or a very elaborate trap?

But as I pack my warmest sweaters (none with working lights, thankfully), I realize Chloe's right. In this economy, with my dreams on the line and my savings dwindling, I'll have to take my chances.

Besides, I reason as I zip up my suitcase, if he really is a serial killer, at least I'll go out in style.

Chapter Four
COLE

The Gulfstream's engines hum steadily as Manhattan disappears beneath the clouds. Knox sits across from me, iPad in hand, monitoring our elaborate plan's next phase.

"Whitmore's through security," he reports after hours of us working in silence, scrolling through real-time updates. "First class lounge at JFK. She's been staring at her phone for twenty minutes, probably second-guessing everything."

I swirl the scotch in my glass, remembering how it felt to orchestrate our "accidental" meeting. The way her eyes lit up when she spoke about her designs, that spark of defiance beneath her uncertainty. "Show me the surveillance."

Knox taps his screen, bringing up the lounge's security feed. There she is, curled in a leather armchair, her ever-present portfolio clutched close. No ridiculous sweater today. She's dressed for business in a charcoal blazer that speaks of carefully curated professionalism. Even through the grainy footage, I can see her nervous energy, the way she keeps checking her boarding pass as if reassuring herself this is real.

"You know," Knox muses, "most people would consider flying to Switzerland just to arrive before someone else a bit excessive. Even for you."

"Most people lack vision." I set down my glass, studying the flight path displayed on my cabin screen. "Everything has to be perfect. The timing, the setting, the first impression of Asher Industries."

"Because the first impression at Tonic wasn't enough?" There's a hint of challenge in Knox's voice. "She's already intrigued. Why not just—"

"Because Sloane Whitmore isn't looking for a man," I say and cut him off. "She's looking for someone who believes in her vision. Someone who sees what those shortsighted banks missed." I stand, moving to the window. Below, the Atlantic stretches endlessly, a dark mirror reflecting the winter sky. "The man she met at Tonic was a stranger who ruined her sweater. The CEO of Asher Industries is someone who can make her dreams reality."

"And the fact that they're the same person?"

"Is a detail she'll discover when I choose." I turn back to him, letting a rare smile surface. "After all, timing is everything."

Knox sets down his iPad, leaning back in his leather seat. "Walk me through the Gstaad arrangements. And please tell me you didn't book the entire hotel this time."

"Just the east wing." I return to my seat, pulling up the blueprints I've memorized. "The Alpina's discrete enough for our purposes." I chose it carefully. Old money, old walls, the kind of place where privacy is understood without being discussed.

Knox shakes his head, but I catch the glimmer of admiration in his eyes. "You've orchestrated this like a military campaign."

"This isn't war, Knox. It's courtship."

"Could've fooled me." He swipes through another set of reports. "Security detail's in place at the Alpina. And the jeweler's workshop in your penthouse has been set up exactly to your specifications."

I nod, satisfaction coursing through me. Every detail matters— the lighting, the tools, the rare gems I've sourced from across the globe. All arranged to show Sloane that someone finally understands what she sees.

"Jasmine Walsh did us a favor," I say. "Every time she forced Sloane to compromise her vision, she only strengthened her resolve."

"Speaking of Walsh," Knox interjects, "our sources say she's already trying to take credit for Sloane's spring collection designs. Telling buyers it was all her all along."

Something dark flashes through me. "Make a note. Moth to the Flame might need a change in leadership soon."

"Already ahead of you." Knox's smile is sharp. "I've had our analysts reviewing their financials. Several . . . interesting discrepancies in their books."

"Good." I turn back to the window, watching clouds roll beneath us like waves. "What's Sloane doing now?"

Knox checks the feed. "Still in the lounge, but she's sketching now. That portfolio hasn't left her hands since she arrived."

I think of that portfolio, how she'd started to reach for it at Tonic before her friend interrupted. Soon I'll see every design, every idea she's poured onto those pages. But more than that, I'll give her the means to transform them from paper into reality.

"Sir?" The pilot's voice comes through the cabin speaker. "We're beginning our approach to Zurich. Weather at Gstaad is clear for the helicopter transfer."

I check my watch. Perfect timing. Sloane's flight won't leave for another hour. By the time she lands in Zurich, I'll have everything in place at the Alpina.

"Knox," I say, my thoughts turning back to business, "what's our latest intel on Julian's suppliers?"

"We've identified three key factories he's contracted for the Claire collection. Two in Italy, one in Belgium. My contacts tell me he's been meeting with high-end department store buyers, promising exclusivity."

I nod slowly, pieces falling into place. "And Bergdorf's? Are they still interested in our New Year's reveal?"

"More than interested. Salivating is more like it." Knox scrolls through his notes. "Their luxury division director called twice this morning asking for preview details. I stalled, as instructed."

"Good. The less anyone knows about Sloane's collection, the better. If Julian gets wind that I'm backing her—"

"He'll try to destroy both of you," Knox finishes grimly. "Which is why I've tripled security for this operation. No one—and I mean no one—sees those designs until the reveal."

If everything goes according to plan, Julian's "Claire" collection will be exposed for the fraud it is, and Sloane Whitmore will be the new star of the luxury jewelry world.

And Julian Voss will finally begin paying for what he did to Claire. Well . . . it will never be enough, but at least it's something.

I check my watch, anxious for what's to come. "Let's focus on the penthouse renovations and how they're progressing."

Knox pulls up new blueprints. "They're ahead of schedule. Top-of-the-line security system. Though I still think the surveillance coverage is excessive. Do you really need four different angles of her workspace?"

"Eight," I correct, marking additional camera positions. "I want to see everything."

"This is either going to be brilliant or disastrous." Knox shakes his head, but he's already noting the new locations. "Though I guess those are the same thing with you."

"I need to understand her process. How she creates. What inspires her."

"You know this is insane, right?" But he's already pulling up the jet's manifest, checking security protocols. "The whole thing—the surveillance, the manipulations, bringing her into your world when Julian's circling . . ."

"Since when has 'insane' ever stopped me?"

The plane touches down in Zurich with characteristic precision.

On the tarmac, a helicopter waits to take us to Gstaad. I check my phone one last time before we transfer. Sloane's still in the JFK lounge, but she's moved to the window now, watching planes take off into the winter sky.

"Final preparations at the Alpina?" I ask as we board the helicopter.

"Your suite has been prepared according to specifications. Security confirms the east wing is clear of other guests."

"The dinner menu?"

"Chef Maurice is preparing a seven-course tasting menu. Wine pairings have been selected from the cellar." Knox's expression turns knowing. "Though I notice you've requested peppermint tea be available as well."

I ignore his implied question. "And the weather?"

"Snow forecast for the evening. The kind that makes everything look like a fairy tale." He pauses. "Or a trap, depending on your perspective."

"It's not a trap if she wants to be caught." The helicopter lifts off, banking toward the mountains.

I watch the Alps grow larger, their snow-covered peaks piercing the clouds like nature's own version of Manhattan's skyline. "Most acquisitions don't have Sloane's potential, Knox. Speaking of . . . has her severance package been processed?"

"Along with some interesting adjustments to her final paycheck. Seems several unauthorized deductions were made."

"Document everything. Add it to the file on Walsh's creative accounting."

The helicopter begins its descent into Gstaad, the Alpina's elegant silhouette emerging through lightly falling snow. In a few hours, Sloane will land in Zurich, still uncertain what she's walking into. By the time she reaches the Alpina, everything will be perfect—a stage set for the next act in our carefully choreographed dance.

"One last thing," Knox says as we touch down. "The background check on her friend Chloe came back. She's clean, but chatty. High risk for asking uncomfortable questions. She's in a relationship with a firefighter who also checks out."

"Leave Chloe alone," I instruct. "Sloane needs at least one person in her life who isn't part of this. Besides," I add, "she makes Sloane happy."

The helicopter's rotors slow as we step onto the Alpina's private landing pad. Snow swirls around us, transforming the world into something out of a winter's tale. Soon, Sloane will see this same view, not knowing that every snowflake, every crystal of ice, has been arranged just for her.

"Sir?" One of the hotel's staff approaches with a clipboard against his chest. "Everything is prepared according to your specifications. Would you like to see for yourself?"

I check my watch. Still hours before Sloane's flight lands. Time enough to ensure every detail is perfect.

"Show me."

Chapter Five
SLOANE

The private jet gleams in the early morning light, its sleek silhouette a stark contrast to the utilitarian JFK terminals surrounding it.

The itinerary hadn't listed an airline. I guess I should have known that meant private. Dear lord.

I grip my portfolio tighter, frozen at the base of the airstairs. Everything about this feels surreal—from the white-gloved flight attendant waiting to escort me aboard to the way my boots leave prints in the light dusting of snow on the tarmac.

"Welcome aboard, Ms. Whitmore." The attendant's smile is practiced perfection. "May I take your coat?"

"I . . . no. I mean . . . yes, I . . . sure."

Real eloquent, Sloane. Way to act like you've done this before. Though when exactly would I have done this before? My biggest splurge on transportation was upgrading to Economy Plus on a flight to Chicago.

The interior stops my breath. Honey-colored wood panels gleam against cream leather seats wide enough to curl up in. Crystal glasses catching sunlight through oval windows send prisms dancing across the ceiling. I take a hesitant step forward, terrified I'll somehow break something that I couldn't possibly afford to replace.

"Please, make yourself comfortable." The attendant gestures to what looks less like an airplane seat and more like a throne. "We'll be taking off shortly."

I sink into the leather, immediately panicking that my slacks—while my nicest pair—might somehow damage it. Do rich people even wear slacks on private jets? Should I have worn a ball gown? Do I own a ball gown?

My phone buzzes—Chloe, keeping her promise to text until takeoff: Don't forget the pepper spray! And if he turns out to be serial killer, at least get his Wi-Fi password first so you can live-stream your last moments.

I snort, then quickly try to turn it into a cough when the attendant looks my way. If I die, be sure to empty my bedside drawer. Do not, I repeat, DO NOT let my mother open that drawer.

The flight attendant appears with a steaming cup that fills the cabin with a familiar scent. My fingers close around the delicate porcelain, and I freeze. It's peppermint tea with a hint of vanilla—the exact blend I've been obsessed with this week. The one I just switched to after two weeks of chamomile, which followed my green tea phase. I can never stick with one type for long, but somehow they've managed to catch my current favorite.

"Everything all right, Ms. Whitmore?"

"Fine!" My voice comes out an octave too high. "Just . . . admiring the cup. Very . . . cuppy." Oh god, please stop talking.

The coincidences are starting to feel less coincidental, and my brain helpfully starts playing every true crime podcast I've ever listened to. Though surely serial killers don't waste this much money on their victims?

Hours later, Switzerland unfolds beneath us like a living Christmas card. I press my face against the window like a kid, probably leaving nose prints on the crystal-clear plexiglass. I can't bring myself to care. The view is too spectacular.

Snowcapped Alps pierce through cotton-wisp clouds, their jagged peaks catching the late afternoon sun. As we descend into Zurich, tiny villages appear, their church steeples and red-roofed houses dusted with fresh powder. The landscape seems to hold its breath, pristine and untouched.

"We're beginning our descent," the attendant announces, probably judging how I'm practically climbing into the window. "Please return to your seat, Ms. Whitmore."

Right. Dignity. I have that somewhere.

A sleek black car waits on the tarmac, its driver holding a sign with my name in elegant script. I nearly trip down the airstairs, catching myself at the last moment. The driver doesn't even blink, which makes me wonder what kind of training they go through. "How to Maintain Stoic Professionalism While Escorting Disaster-Prone Americans" must be a required course.

The drive to Gstaad winds through valleys that make my artist's soul ache. Pine forests march up impossibly steep slopes, their branches heavy with snow. Wooden chalets straight out of fairy tales cling to mountainsides, warm lights glowing in their windows against the gathering dusk.

"Is this real?" I whisper, mostly to myself. "Like, actually real?"

The driver—whose name is Stefan, and who finally cracked a smile when I nearly face-planted getting into the car—actually answers. "Very real, Ms. Whitmore. Though many find Gstaad rather like a dream."

We pass through villages that look frozen in time—ancient stone churches, window boxes still bright with winter flowers, boutiques displaying watches worth more than my student loans.

The road climbs higher, each switchback revealing new vistas that have me pressing closer to the window. My phone has zero bars up here, which means Chloe is probably already planning my funeral. "Died in the Swiss Alps," I mutter. "Hopefully not buried in an avalanche."

The Alpina emerges as we round the final bend—a massive yet elegant structure of wood and stone that seems to grow from the mountain itself. Most windows are dark against the twilight, except for a few that glow softly, suggesting occupied rooms within. Old brass lanterns line the curved drive, their light catching the billowing snow as we approach. The building commands the mountainside, its steep roofs and weathered timbers standing against the elements. Wooden balconies extend from the facade, their railings now thick with fresh snow.

"Holy shit," I breathe, then immediately clap a hand over my mouth. Pretty sure you're not supposed to swear at fancy Swiss hotels. But Stefan just chuckles as he opens my door.

"Wait until you see inside, Ms. Whitmore."

The lobby steals what's left of my breath. Soaring timber beams frame walls of windows that showcase the valley below. A massive stone fireplace with flames that cast flickering shadows across plush seating areas done in cream and chocolate leather. The scent of pine mingles with something spicy—mulled wine, I realize, spotting crystal glasses being served to guests who look like they've stepped from the pages of *Vogue*.

I glance down at my travel outfit, suddenly very aware of my sensible boots. The woman nearest to me is wearing what appears to be actual diamonds in her hair. Who wears diamonds in their hair? To a hotel lobby?

"Ms. Whitmore." A man in an impeccable suit appears at my elbow, making me jump. "Welcome to the Alpina. If you'll follow me, your suite has been prepared."

Suite is an understatement. The space he leads me to is bigger than my entire apartment, with a sitting room dominated by a wall of windows showcasing the Alps. The bedroom features a bed that could sleep six, draped in linens that probably cost more than anything I own.

"This can't be right," I stammer. "This is like . . . this is presidential suite level."

"Indeed," the man says smoothly. "The presidential suite. Will this be satisfactory?"

I make a sound that might be a laugh or a wheeze. "Satisfactory. Right. Totally normal. Just another Tuesday in the presidential suite."

But it's the bathroom that nearly breaks me—a freestanding copper tub positioned to watch the sunset over the mountains while soaking. I stare at it, wondering if it's possible to live in a bathtub.

Just move in permanently. Send for my things.

On the bed, an outfit has been laid out—a winter white ensemble that looks both elegant and intimidating. The note beside it reads simply: *For dinner. -C.A.*

I run my fingers over the fabric, its softness betraying its astronomical cost. "No pressure," I tell myself. "Just a mysterious meeting in Switzerland with someone who knows your tea preferences and clothing size. This isn't a setup to a horror movie at all."

My phone finally catches signal, immediately buzzing with Chloe's backlog of panic: SLOANE WHITMORE IF YOU DIE IN SWITZERLAND, I WILL KILL YOU.

I laugh despite my nerves, moving to the windows to watch night settle over the Alps as I send a reassuring text that all is well. I snap a quick photo of the breathtaking view and send it to Chloe with the caption: If I'm about to be murdered, at least the last thing I'll see is this.

The mountains are disappearing into darkness, but lights are appearing—chalets and hotels dotting the slopes. It's the most beautiful thing I've ever seen.

And possibly the most dangerous. But I could stand here and stare for hours if I had the time.

A discreet knock announces dinner in an hour. I eye the white outfit, then my portfolio filled with designs that somehow this mysterious firm already knows intimately. Everything about this situation is pure insanity. The coincidences too bizarre. The rational part of my brain is screaming to run back to Manhattan and my safe, predictable life.

But as I pick up the dress, another thought hits me: My safe, predictable life was slowly killing my creativity. And here I am, in a suite bigger than my apartment, about to meet someone who seems to actually understand my vision. Someone who went to ridiculous lengths to get me here.

I slip into the dress, trying to steady my nerves. The fabric feels like smooth butter against my skin, the cut perfect in a way that's starting to feel unsettling rather than flattering. My fingers move to the delicate silver necklace at my throat—one of my own pieces, a small reminder of who I am and why I'm here.

Through the windows, the lights of Gstaad twinkle like fallen stars caught in the valleys between mountains. Everything about this place feels like a fairy tale. But I've read enough of the original Brothers Grimm to know that fairy tales aren't always sweet. Sometimes they're sour.

Nightmarish.

I gather my portfolio and head for the door. Time to find out what kind of story I've walked into. Dream or nightmare?

Chapter Six

COLE

S now falls in thick curtains outside the Alpina's private dining room, turning the Alps into a ghostly landscape. The timing couldn't be better. By morning the storm will clear, leaving everything fresh and new for our swift return to Manhattan.

"Jesus Christ." Knox shakes his head, watching me adjust the table settings for the third time. "I haven't seen you this invested since Paris."

Paris. We both remember that gallery, the artist whose work had awakened something in me. I'd been too slow then, too caught up in the numbers. By the time I'd made an offer, my old business partner Julian had already swept in and buried her career. Another lesson in the price of hesitation.

"The penthouse preparations are complete," Knox continues, perhaps sensing my darkening mood. He consults his iPad, scrolling through updates. "Everything arranged exactly as you specified, though the contractors think you've lost your mind with some of the requirements."

I almost smile at that. Let them think what they want. They don't understand that some things require perfect conditions. The right pressure. The right moment.

"What about Claire's biometric case?" Knox asks, lowering his voice. "You still plan to move it to the New York studio?"

"Yes. It's the most secure option we have," I reply, straightening a fork that's barely out of alignment. "And it needs to be where I can monitor it."

Knox frowns. "Julian knows you have it. He's been trying to get his hands on it for years."

"And he's failed every time," I remind him.

Knox looks at me for a long moment, then pulls up a new screen on his iPad, clearly dropping the subject.

I turn away from the window, deliberately casual. Julian Voss had been more than a mentor when I was building my empire—he'd been the first person to see potential in the hungry kid from Brooklyn. The first to show me how power really worked. First person to see my value and work with me. And now he's just another part of my past I prefer not to discuss.

"He won't get to the case," I say with a certainty I don't entirely feel. "The penthouse security is impenetrable."

"No security is impenetrable, Cole." Knox's voice drops lower. "And you're getting personally involved. I can see how you watch *her*. This isn't just about protecting Claire's designs anymore."

The implications hang in the air, but I'm already distracted by movement on the security feeds. Sloane has arrived at her suite. Through the cameras, I watch her explore the space, taking in her unguarded reactions. There's something compelling about seeing her like this, away from the careful persona she presents to the world.

I remember finding her file buried in Chase's rejection pile— another dreamer deemed too risky. But where their analysts saw uncertainty, I saw hunger. The same drive that had pushed me from a Brooklyn walk-up to a Manhattan penthouse. The need to prove everyone wrong.

A discrete knock announces the hotel manager with security reports. I scan them quickly—every angle covered, every possibility accounted for. The east wing secured, no guests or staff except those cleared by Knox.

"Sir?" The manager hovers, awaiting further instructions. "The dining room is prepared according to your specifications. The vintage you requested is breathing."

I nod, satisfied. Through the screens, I watch Sloane prepare for dinner. The white dress suits her, but it's her composure that catches my attention—the way she squares her shoulders like she's preparing for battle.

"It's time," I tell Knox, adjusting my cuffs. A habit from my younger days, when secondhand suits needed constant attention. Now my closet costs more than my father's house did, but some habits die hard. "What's Julian's current position?"

"Still in Moscow, according to our sources. But Cole . . ." He hesitates.

"Drop it." I cut him off. "Our security is the best in the business. Focus on what matters—tonight."

Because tonight isn't about Julian or the past or anything else. Tonight is about Sloane, and the way she makes me want things I'd forgotten existed.

"Sir?" The manager again. "Will you be requiring anything else?"

I check my watch one final time. In minutes, Sloane Whitmore will walk into this room, and this Christmas story of ours will begin.

"No," I say. "Everything is perfect."

Chapter Seven

SLOANE

The maître d' leads me through the Alpina's empty restaurant, my heels clicking against ancient wood floors that give an elegant character. Crystal chandeliers cast intimate pools of light, each table its own private island in a sea of luxury. But we pass them all, heading toward a separate dining room.

I clutch my portfolio closer, wondering if I'm walking toward my big break or my elaborate doom. The white dress moves like water around me, making me feel both powerful and exposed. Kind of like being naked, but fancy.

"Mr. Asher is waiting," the maître d' says, pausing before massive wooden doors that look old enough to have witnessed the signing of peace treaties. Or murder conspiracies. My imagination really needs to pick a lane here.

The doors open to reveal a private dining room that makes me forget how to breathe. One entire wall is glass, showcasing the snow-covered Alps now lit by a nearly full moon. The other walls are aged wood panels that glow warmly in the light from iron chandeliers. A single table sits in the center, set with what has to be antique silver and crystal that catches the light like diamonds.

But it's the man standing at the window that stops my heart.

He turns, and the world shifts beneath my feet. I know that profile, those shoulders, that way of owning every molecule of space around him. I've seen them before, stained with expensive scotch in a Manhattan bar.

Cole.

"Hello, Sloane." His voice is exactly as I remember—that low rumble that seems to bypass my ears and go straight to my spine. "I believe we've met."

I open my mouth, close it, try again. "You're Colsen Asher?"

"Yes." No apology, no explanation. Just that intensity I remember, now cranked up to about a thousand.

I blink, my brain struggling to reconcile the stranger from the bar with the billionaire who's apparently been orchestrating my life. The room suddenly feels too warm, too small. "I don't . . . I mean, you're . . ." Words fail me completely.

Cole stays perfectly still, watching me process with those unnervingly intense eyes. The same eyes that had studied me so carefully at Tonic, that had shown such interest when I described my work. Oh. OH.

"The scotch," I say suddenly, the memory hitting me like a physical blow. "At the bar. You were so interested in my designs. You kept asking questions about Midnight Frost . . ."

His lips curve slightly, and there's something almost proud in his expression, like he's pleased I'm putting it together. But that means . . .

"How did you . . ." I stop, my hand tightening on my portfolio. Another realization slams into me. "The collar piece. In the email. I never showed that to anyone except . . ." My voice trails off as implications start stacking up like building blocks, each one more unsettling than the last.

Chloe was the only person who'd seen those designs, but somehow he knew about them in detail.

"That night at the bar . . ." I finally manage, though I'm not even sure what I'm asking. "That wasn't an accident, was it?"

"No." He moves toward me, and I instinctively take a step back, my spine hitting the doorframe. "Very little in my world happens by accident."

My heart pounds so hard I can hear it. This isn't happening. This cannot be happening.

"You've been watching me." My voice shakes with a mixture of fear and anger. "Following me. For how long?"

He doesn't answer, which somehow makes it worse. I clutch my portfolio to my chest like a shield, mind racing. I should run. I should absolutely run right now. Call Chloe, call the police, call anyone.

"Would you like some wine?" He gestures to the table as if this is all perfectly normal. As if he hasn't just revealed himself to be exactly the kind of stalker I'd joked about with Chloe.

Oh my god. I have a billionaire stalker.

"I'd like an explanation." I'm surprised by the steel in my voice. "Because right now I'm trying to decide whether to run screaming or just start throwing things."

"You won't do either." His certainty makes my blood boil.

"Oh, really? And why's that?"

"Because you want to know why." He takes another step closer. I hold my ground this time, anger overtaking fear. "Why I chose you. Why I've gone to such lengths. Why I know about designs you've never shown anyone."

"How do you know about those?" The question bursts out before I can stop it. "The collar piece—I never showed that to anyone except my friend. If you've done something to her—"

"Your friend is fine." His voice stays maddeningly calm. "Please, sit. Let me explain what I'm offering."

"Offering?" I laugh, and it sounds slightly hysterical even to my own ears. "You manipulated me. Stalked me. Lured me to another country. And now you want me to sit down for a friendly chat?"

"Yes." Still so calm, so controlled. It makes me want to scream. "Because despite your very justified anger, you're curious. You want to know how I knew about your midnight sketching sessions. About the designs you hide from Jasmine Walsh. About the darkness you keep trying to contain."

My hands shake. He's right. I do want to know. And I hate that he knows that about me too.

"Sit," he says again. "Stay. Let me show you what I'm offering. If you still want to run afterward, I won't stop you."

I should leave. Every true crime podcast I've ever listened to is screaming at me to get out now. But as I slowly sink into the chair he holds, I realize I've already made my choice. God help me, I have to know what this is all about.

A server appears silently to pour wine—something red that probably has its own Swiss bank account. I don't touch it. Rich psychopaths are still psychopaths, and I've seen enough movies to know better.

"Your work," he says without preamble, "is unique."

"My work that you've been spying on?" The words come out sharp enough to cut. "How exactly did you get access to my private designs?"

He takes a sip of wine, apparently unruffled by my hostility. "The same way I knew your loan application would be rejected by Chase. The same way I knew Jasmine Walsh would make your departure effective immediately." His eyes lock onto mine. "I pay attention to things that interest me."

"That's not an answer." My fingers clench around my portfolio. "That's just admitting to more stalking."

"Would you prefer I lie?" The question catches me off guard. "Tell you I happened to notice your talent through normal channels? That this meeting is just a fortunate coincidence?"

"I'd prefer you stop playing games and tell me what you want."

Something darkens in his expression. "I want to give you everything you've been denied. A fully equipped workshop. Complete creative freedom. Financial backing that will let you create without compromise."

The first course arrives—something that looks like winter elegance itself plated in silver. I ignore it.

"And in exchange?"

"You work exclusively for me. From my penthouse, where I've already prepared a studio space. The collection must be ready by New Year's Eve."

"Your penthouse?" I stare at him, wondering if I've heard wrong. "You want me to move in with you? A man who just admitted to stalking me?"

"I want to give you an opportunity." His voice stays frustratingly level. "The kind that comes once in a lifetime."

"The kind that comes with eight million red flags," I counter. "Why should I trust anything about this?"

"Because deep down, you know I understand your work in a way no one else has." He leans forward slightly. "The banks see risk. Jasmine sees a liability. But I see what you could become if someone would just let you embrace your instincts."

The man is saying all the right things. Damn him. Because he's right. No one has ever understood my work. And yet, *he* claims to. The question is how much that understanding is worth.

"Show me," he says quietly. "Show me the designs you've been hiding."

I look down at my portfolio, then back at him. The smart thing would be to walk away. Get a normal job. Create normal, safe jewelry that doesn't make people uncomfortable.

But I've spent my whole life being smart. Being safe. And where has it gotten me?

Slowly, deliberately, I open my portfolio. "Just so we're clear," I say, meeting his gaze, "if this turns out to be some kind of elaborate murder plot, I will absolutely come back to haunt you."

For the first time, a real smile crosses his face. It transforms him from merely handsome into something devastating. "I would expect nothing less."

I turn the first page, and we begin.

As I explain the concept behind my winter collection, Cole surprises me by asking actual intelligent questions. Not the usual "can you make it prettier" feedback I'm used to, but specific queries about technique and symbolism.

"The negative space here," he says, pointing to a particularly complex piece, "it mirrors your work from your second year at Parsons. The ice dagger series."

I freeze with my fork halfway to my mouth. "How did you—"

"I particularly liked the professor's note about your 'disturbing but brilliant use of sharp angles.'" He takes a sip of wine, watching me over the rim. "Though I disagree about the 'disturbing' part."

"Okay, this has to stop." I set down my fork. "The designs you somehow know about, fine. Creepy, but fine. But you can't just casually reference my college work like—"

"Like I've thoroughly researched everything about your creative evolution?" His smile is infuriating. "Would you prefer the Tribeca gallery showing where they called your work 'too aggressive for the bridal market'?"

We spend the next few minutes eating in a strange, loaded silence. I'm torn between being impressed by the food and unnerved by how much this man knows about me. By the time our empty plates are cleared away, I've had enough time to collect my thoughts.

"I'd prefer to discuss actual business." I try to steer us back to safer ground. "The timeline you mentioned—"

"Tell me about the first real piece you ever sold." He cuts me off smoothly. "The silver pendant with the hidden blade design."

"That's not relevant to—"

"Everything about you is relevant."

The intensity in his voice makes me pause. We stare at each other across the table, the air suddenly thick with something I can't name.

Between our appetizers and main course, I notice at least twenty minutes have passed. We've been talking through each dish, the servers hovering discreetly, never rushing us. I've nearly finished my first glass of wine when Cole reaches for the bottle to refill it. Our fingers brush as I move to stop him, and that same electric current from the bar shoots through me, stronger this time.

I jerk back like I've been shocked. "I can pour my own wine."

"Is that something you feel you have to announce?" His voice holds a hint of amusement. "Or do you just prefer to keep your distance?"

"I prefer professionalism." I straighten my spine. "This is a business meeting."

"I agree."

Before I can respond, the door opens and a man appears. His expression is tense.

"Sir, we have a situation. Julian's people have been—"

"Not now." Cole's voice turns to steel.

"But the security protocols—"

"I said not now."

They exchange a loaded look that makes me feel like I'm missing volumes of subtext. The man exits as silently as he appeared, but the interruption has changed something in Cole's demeanor. There's an edge now that wasn't there before.

"Perhaps we should continue this discussion somewhere more

comfortable," he says, standing. "The bar here makes an excellent Manhattan."

"I should probably get some rest." I don't want to admit how much this evening has rattled me. "It's been a long day of being stalked and manipulated."

That gets an actual laugh from him. "Just one drink. We still need to discuss the specifics of your contract."

Somehow, I find myself walking with him, his hand resting on the small of my back. The touch should feel presumptuous. Instead, it feels . . . claiming. Like he's already decided I'm his, regardless of whether I've agreed to anything.

The really disturbing part? Some traitorous part of me likes it.

"You know this is insane, right?" I say as we near the bar. "This whole situation is completely insane."

He leans close, his breath warm against my ear. "Wait until you see what I have planned next."

Every instinct I have screams that I'm walking into a trap. But like a moth drawn to a particularly dangerous flame, I follow him anyway.

Chapter Eight

SLOANE

The hotel bar is exactly what you'd expect from a five-star establishment in Manhattan—all dark wood paneling and strategic lighting that makes everyone look like they have secrets worth keeping. The evening crowd is starting to filter in, executives with loosened ties and women in designer suits who look like they eat quarterly reports for breakfast.

I choose a corner booth that lets me keep my back to the wall—a habit I've apparently developed in the last hour of realizing I'm dealing with a sexy but possibly unhinged billionaire. The leather upholstery is butter-soft, probably flown in from some exotic location. A single candle flickers in a crystal holder on the table, and somewhere behind the curved bar, a pianist is playing something that sounds expensive.

Cole slides in next to me—not across the table, where normal business associates would sit. No, he positions himself close enough that our knees could touch if either of us shifted slightly. A leather portfolio appears in his hands, different from my own. The contract, I realize.

"Let me guess," he says, studying me in the low light. "Another peppermint martini?"

"Not a chance. I need all my wits about me for whatever's in that portfolio you're clutching."

His laugh is warm, genuine. "Smart girl."

"You've figured me out already?"

"Always." He signals the bartender with a subtle gesture. "Though you're proving more challenging than most."

"I live to disappoint."

The drinks arrive. He's ordered a Manhattan for both of us. I raise an eyebrow at his presumption but take a sip anyway. It's perfect, damn him.

"Now then," he says, opening the leather portfolio with deliberate care. "Let's talk about your future."

I pride myself on being able to parse contracts—a skill hard-won from years of freelancing and knowing every business vulture is out there to get you. This one is different. The language shifts and weaves, precise yet somehow elusive. Every time I think I understand a clause, there's a subtle reference to another section that changes the whole meaning. Like the contract itself is a piece of jewelry, each facet reflecting and refracting light differently depending on how you look at it.

The numbers, though—those are crystal clear, and they make me dizzy. The kind of figures that could change everything. Complete creative control, something unheard of for a designer my age. A fully equipped workshop with tools I've only seen in industry magazines. Resources I've only dreamed about, materials I've never dared request from clients before. A chance to actually create the collection that's been burning in my mind for years.

"Impressive, isn't it?" Cole watches me read, and I notice he's paying close attention to my eyes—tracking how I navigate the document, which sections make me pause.

"Impressive is one word for it." I flip back three pages to cross-reference a clause. "Labyrinthine would be another."

His smile widens. "Most people don't catch the subsection dependencies on first read."

"My mother's an attorney—I grew up hearing about the 'devil in the details' at the dinner table."

I keep reading, fighting to maintain my professional expression as the figures climb higher.

But then I hit the living arrangements clause, and my blood turns to ice. I read it again, slower this time, making sure I haven't misunderstood. The language here is suddenly crystal clear.

"Required residence in your penthouse?" I look up sharply. "That's not happening."

"You'll have your own room in the east wing of the penthouse level. Private bath, study area—"

"Wait." I set my glass down. "I don't even know you, and you want me to live with you?"

His eyebrows lift slightly. "Worried I snore?"

"Worried you're a serial killer with excellent taste in jewelry."

He laughs, a genuine sound that transforms his face. "If I were a serial killer, I'd have much better pickup lines than 'Come live in my tower and make pretty things.'"

"That," I said, pointing at him, "is exactly what a serial killer would say." I narrow my eyes. "For all I know, you have a collection of artist pelts somewhere."

"Artist pelts?" He looks both amused and appalled. "Is that what you think of me?"

"I think you're a man who's used to getting his way. Who's offering a completely insane living arrangement to a stranger, and who's yet to deny the serial killer accusation."

"Fair points." He leans back, still smiling. "I hereby formally deny any involvement in serial killing, artist-pelt-collecting, or other nefarious activities. I simply want the best designer under my roof where she can work without distraction. Though I do have an extensive collection of designer scarves that might look suspicious to the right detective."

I can't help but laugh. "You're ridiculous."

"And yet here you are, considering my ridiculous offer."

"It says there will be camera surveillance at all times. With how many cameras?" I press back to the serious issue at hand.

"You'll be working with pieces worth millions, Sloane. Rare gems, proprietary designs, materials that never leave the building."

"And you protect your assets." I meet his gaze. "Is that what I am? Another precious stone to keep under lock and key?"

Something flashes in his eyes—I can't read him. "I protect what matters to me."

"Who watches the feeds?" I press. "How many people get front row seats to the Sloane Whitmore show?"

"A highly vetted security team who couldn't care less about your creative process. Their only concern is ensuring our work stays secure." He leans closer, his knee brushing mine. "Your private quarters will remain camera-free. But I need you there, especially given our timeline."

I scan the document again. "New Year's Eve? You want an entire collection designed, prototyped, and ready for production in a month? A month!"

"Cartier's pulling out of their New Year partnership with Bergdorf's." His voice drops lower, conspiratorial. "Their new creative director is taking them in a different direction. It leaves a gap—one we're uniquely positioned to fill. If"—he taps the deadline clause—"we can deliver."

My mind races with the implications. A first-of-the-year launch at Bergdorf's would be . . . "That's impossible."

"For most people, yes." That dangerous smile again. "But you're not most people, are you?"

I take another sip of my Manhattan, buying time to think. The practical part of my brain is screaming about red flags—the control, the monitoring, the impossible deadline. My bank account whispers about rent past due and maxed-out credit cards. But there's something else, something that has nothing to do with money or desperation.

"You still haven't explained why me."

"Because when I look at your work, I see something rare." He pulls out my portfolio. His fingers trail across the pages in a way that makes my skin prickle. "On the surface, these pieces are exactly what the market wants. Safe enough for the society women who lunch, creative enough for the young executives climbing the corporate ladder. You understand people—what they want, what they think they want, what they're afraid to want."

He pauses, turning to a specific sketch. It's one of my darker pieces, one I usually keep buried in the back. A necklace that's more weapon than jewelry, gothic with shadowed spaces. His thumb traces the edge of the design, almost intimate. "The way it wraps around the throat . . . there's nothing timid about this piece. A woman with dark secret desires would wear this piece."

"Most women don't want to wear their secrets so openly," I counter, watching his reaction.

"Don't they?" His smile suggests otherwise. He flips to another design, a ring that seems to writhe around the finger like smoke made solid. "These pieces? They're savage. Untamed." His voice drops lower. "Like you're trying to crack open the world and reshape it." He leans closer, and I catch the subtle scent of his cologne. "These are the ones you don't show clients. The ones that live in the back of your sketchbook, that keep you up at night." He pauses and then adds, "They represent dominance and submission, even if you don't know it yet yourself."

I feel exposed, seen in a way that makes me want to squirm in my seat. "Those are experimental pieces."

"They're honest pieces." His eyes lock onto mine, and there's something dark and knowing in his gaze. "Everyone sees in you the polished New York designer—ambitious, talented, ready to take on the world. But there's something else under that carefully curated surface, isn't there? Something that doesn't care about market trends or buyer demographics. Something that wants to create beauty so sharp it draws blood."

"You seem very interested in what's beneath surfaces," I say, aiming for professional but landing somewhere closer to breathless.

"Only certain ones." The way he says it makes heat crawl up my spine.

I hate how well he sees me. Hate that he's right about both sides—the professional who knows how to work a room, and the artist who sometimes scares herself with what emerges on the page at midnight. Hate even more how his assessment causes my pulse to quicken.

"And which designer are you hoping to hire?" I ask, my voice steadier than I feel. "The one who knows what sells, or the one who makes beauty that bites?"

His smile is slow, predatory. He leans back, but his eyes never leave mine. "I want both." There's a delicious emphasis on *want* that makes my throat go dry. "The question is: Are you ready to let me see all of you?"

This isn't just about jewelry anymore . . . or at least I don't think it is. I take a too-large sip of my Manhattan to break the moment and nearly choke. *Real smooth, Sloane.*

"So," I say, clearing my throat and trying to reclaim some semblance of professionalism. Having your potential boss look at you like that should not be this unsettling. Or appealing. Focus. "About these living arrangements. Ground rules."

Cole's expression shifts seamlessly from smoldering to amused, which somehow makes it worse. I straighten my spine and put on what my brother calls my "business bitch" voice.

"No cameras in my room," I say firmly, proud that I sound like someone who hasn't just been mentally undressing their future employer. "I don't care about your security concerns. My private space stays private. And I'm not just saying that because of what you probably think I'm saying that for." *Oh god, stop talking.* "I mean, because of privacy. Normal privacy. Professional privacy."

His lips twitch. "Professional privacy."

"Yes." I lift my chin. "Exactly."

"Of course." He's definitely trying not to laugh now. "Completely professional."

"Don't look at me like that. I'm serious about the cameras."

"Done."

"And I want full access to the workshop, day or night. If you want this done by New Year's, I'll be pulling a lot of late hours."

"Already planned for."

"Also, you don't enter my workshop or my bedroom without my express permission. I need to know my space is mine. Consider it a creative sanctuary. I can't work if I'm constantly wondering when you'll appear."

He raises an eyebrow but nods. "Understood."

"One more thing." I meet his gaze steadily. "Creative control means exactly that. You can have opinions, but final decisions are mine."

He studies me for a long moment, then nods. "As long as you're willing to defend your choices."

"Oh, I always am."

"Let me add these conditions to make them official." He takes the contract and, with a sleek Mont Blanc pen, begins writing in the margins. His handwriting is precise and architectural as he notes each point: "No cameras in private quarters. No entry to workspace or bedroom without express permission. Creative control rests with designer for all pieces."

He initials each addition, then slides the contract and pen back to me.

"These amendments are now legally binding," he says, his expression serious despite the slight curve of his lips. "I always honor my contracts to the letter."

I stare at the pen, acutely aware that I'm standing at a crossroads. The smart choice would be to walk away. But there's a part of me—the part that's always pushed boundaries, always reached for more—that wants to see just how deep this rabbit hole goes.

I pick up the pen.

"I'll need help moving."

"I'll send a team tomorrow." He lifts his glass. "To new beginnings?"

I clink my glass against his. "To not regretting this."

As I sign my name, I know I'm doing more than agreeing to a job. I'm stepping through a door that will change everything. The real question isn't whether I'm ready—it's whether I'll be able to find my way back.

Chapter Nine
COLE

S o that's it?" Sloane asks, her finger tracing the rim of her glass. "We leave for New York in the morning?"

We're still in the bar, the contract signed and tucked away. She's relaxed now, the wariness from earlier softened by good drinks and the satisfaction of negotiation well done. But there's something wistful in her voice that catches my attention.

"Disappointed?"

"It seems silly," she admits. "Coming all the way to Switzerland just to leave without seeing any of it. Though I suppose that's not very professional of me to say."

I study her in the low light. The white dress makes her look like winter itself, her fiery red hair a stark contrast against the pale fabric, but her eyes give away a spark of adventure beneath all that careful composure.

"Put on your coat," I say, standing.

She blinks. "What?"

"Your coat. Though you'll need something warmer for where we're going."

Her eyes narrow with suspicion. "Cole . . ."

I guide her to the hotel entrance where Knox waits with a sable fur coat. Of course I'd planned for this. I'd known the moment she accepted the invitation that I'd want to show her Switzerland properly.

"Oh," she breathes as I help her into it. The dark fur sets off her skin perfectly, just as I'd known it would.

A sleigh waits outside. An actual horse-drawn sleigh, because if you're going to do something, you do it right. Sloane stops dead at the sight of it.

"You're insane," she says, but she's fighting a smile.

"So I've been told." I offer my hand. "Coming?"

She hesitates longer this time, something cautious flickering across her face. "This feels . . . not like business anymore."

"Just an hour or two," I say, keeping my voice neutral. "Then back to contracts and deadlines tomorrow."

She studies me for a moment, clearly weighing professional boundaries against the lure of adventure.

She hesitates only a moment before taking it. Her fingers are warm despite the cold, fitting perfectly into mine. I help her into the sleigh, where white, fur blankets already await us. The driver, carefully vetted and briefed hours ago, clicks to the horses.

"Let me guess," she says as we start moving. "You have the entire route planned down to the minute."

"Give me some credit, Sloane." I pause for dramatic effect. "Down to the second."

She laughs. "And if I wanted to go off-route?"

"Chaos. Devastation. The complete collapse of Western civilization."

"You really don't handle unpredictability well, do you?" she asks, a teasing note in her voice.

"I prefer the term *structured*," I correct her.

"In other words, you need to control everything."

I glance at her, surprised by the astuteness of her observation. "Not everything."

"Just most things," she says, but she's smiling. "Seems reasonable." She tucks the blanket closer. "Good thing I like your route then."

The sleigh follows a path through snow-laden pines. Fresh powder crunches beneath the runners, and the horses' breath circles in white plumes against the dark. The mountains tower over us, tall and silent.

"This is . . ." She shakes her head, at a loss for words.

"Better than a conference room?"

She laughs again, the sound clear in the crisp air. "Slightly."

The sleigh winds through the sleeping village. Right on schedule, we pull up to a small café. The owner emerges immediately, carrying a silver tray.

"Hot chocolate?" I offer as she approaches with two steaming cups.

"You don't strike me as a hot chocolate kind of man."

"I'm full of surprises. Though if you tell anyone, I'll deny everything."

She grins. "Then I might need photographic evidence. For leverage."

The chocolate is rich and dark, served in elegant silver-trimmed cups, along with traditional Swiss pastries—buttery Spitzbuebe with jam centers and delicate Zimtsterne dusted with powdered sugar. The café owner beams with pride as she explains these are her grandmother's recipes, passed down for generations. Because once again, some things are worth doing properly. We stay nestled under the blankets, the warmth of the drinks mixing with the bite from the mountain air.

She takes a slow sip, closing her eyes briefly. When she opens them, she catches me watching her. "What?" she asks.

"Just curious if it meets your standards."

"I don't have hot chocolate standards," she says, but there's something guarded in her expression. A memory, perhaps, but not one she's sharing.

"Everyone has standards," I reply. "Even for the small things. Especially for the small things."

Her eyes narrow slightly, studying me. "You know, you're surprisingly difficult to read."

"I could say the same about you."

She raises an eyebrow. "Me? I'm an open book."

"With half the pages torn out," I counter, and she laughs, though it doesn't quite reach her eyes.

We sit in comfortable silence for a moment, the horses' breath creating clouds in the cold air.

"You don't talk about yourself much," she observes finally.

"There isn't much to say."

She looks away, taking another sip. "There's always a story to tell." Her gloved hand wraps tighter around her silver cup, and she glances at the café's warm interior, then back to where we sit in the sleigh. "The owner probably thought you were crazy, insisting we stay out here in the cold to drink this. But that's the point, isn't it? Hot chocolate doesn't taste the same indoors."

Something flickers across her face, and I wonder what memory I've accidentally unearthed. She doesn't share, and I don't ask.

"You planned this," she adds after a moment, her voice gentle but not pitying. Her eyes are bright with something more than just pleasure now.

"I plan everything."

"Everything?" She takes a sip of chocolate, leaving a tiny smudge on her upper lip. Without thinking, I reach out to brush it away. Her breath catches at the touch, and she pulls back slightly, a flush spreading across her cheeks that can't be blamed on the winter air.

"Sorry," I say, not feeling sorry at all.

"We should probably maintain some boundaries," she says quietly, though her eyes linger on my lips a second too long. "I'm going to be working for you, after all."

"With me," I correct. "Not for me."

"Still." She takes a deliberate breath and straightens her shoulders. "I want this opportunity to be about my work, not . . . this."

I nod, forcing myself to lean back.

We fall into an easy conversation as the sleigh carries us through the night. She tells me about growing up in Montauk, about summer jobs at the marina where she learned to curse like a sailor. I share stories about my early days in Manhattan, sleeping on friends' couches while trying to land my first investors.

"Did it work?" she asks.

"Eventually. Though I had to wear the same suit to every meeting. It was three sizes too big. The shoulders were stuffed with newspaper."

"No."

"Yes. The trick was not raising my arms. Ever."

She laughs. "And now look at you. King of Manhattan in designer suits."

"I do own more than one now."

"I never would have guessed."

The sleigh carries us past ice-glazed waterfalls and through forests where snow weighs down the branches. She tells me about her first apartment in New York—a sixth-floor walk-up with a radiator that spoke in Morse code.

"It was trying to tell me something important, I'm sure of it," she insists.

"Probably 'Pay more rent.'"

"More likely 'Your neighbor is definitely running a cult.'" She shakes her head. "There were a lot of people in robes."

"And here I thought my first place in Brooklyn was bad. At least my neighbors stuck to normal illegal activities."

"Like what?"

"Pretty sure they were running an underground poker ring. Badly, I might add. I learned everything not to do by listening through the walls."

She laughs. "Is that where you developed your poker face?"

"That implies I gamble."

"Please. Everything about you screams 'calculated risk.'"

"What about you?" I ask. "You don't strike me as someone who particularly likes structure."

She raises an eyebrow. "What makes you say that?"

"Your designs. They're controlled chaos. Beautiful, but unpredictable. Unfinished. You move on to the next design without completing the one before that."

"Is that going to be a problem?" There's a hint of challenge in her voice now.

"Not a problem per se," I say carefully. "Just . . . different from how I work. Although I do value deadlines."

"Maybe that's why you need me," she says with surprising confidence. "To shake things up a bit. And I've never missed a deadline, regardless of if I'm a hot mess getting there. The orderly way is not always the best way."

The idea of this woman and how she works both intrigues and unsettles me. I'm not used to being read so easily. Nor am I used to the suggestion that my way might not be the only way.

We stop at a viewpoint high above the valley. Below us, the village sits quietly between the mountains, untouched beneath the fresh snow. Sloane leans forward to take in the view, and I find myself watching her instead of the scenery.

This isn't part of the plan.

She turns to look at me, her cheeks flushed from the cold. A snowflake lands on her lip, and for a moment I can't look away.

She doesn't brush it off. Just watches me watching her, her breath coming faster now. The space between us seems to shrink, charged with something that has nothing to do with contracts or business arrangements.

I lean forward, drawn by the warmth of her, the way her eyes darken as I move closer. She tilts her head slightly, and I can feel her breath against my skin. One more inch and—

She places a hand against my chest, stopping me. "We shouldn't," she whispers, though her eyes say something different. "I need this to be . . . professional."

I can feel her pulse racing beneath my fingers where they rest against her wrist. For once in my life, I'm not sure what to say.

"I have to focus on the opportunity," she continues. "I can't risk complicating things."

The rejection stings more than it should. I'm not used to being denied anything I want, and I want her more than I've wanted anything in a long time.

I catch myself, gripping the edge of the sleigh. This isn't how this is supposed to go. Not yet. Not here.

I can't risk scaring her away.

"You're right. We should head back," I say, my voice rough. I have to clear my throat before adding, "Early flight tomorrow."

She nods but holds my gaze for a moment longer. "This doesn't mean I'm not . . . I just need to be smart about this. About this entire situation. Whatever this is."

"Of course," I say, keeping my voice neutral though my mind is already spinning, recalculating. I've never been good at accepting 'no' for an answer.

The wind carries the scent of pine and snow, and somewhere in the distance, a church bell tolls midnight.

Tomorrow we'll return to Manhattan, to cameras and contracts and complications. But tonight I've glimpsed something in Sloane Whitmore I didn't expect—a woman who values her work above all else, who sets boundaries even when it costs her. Someone who won't be easily figured out or controlled. The realization doesn't disappoint me. Instead, I find myself more intrigued than ever.

Chapter Ten

COLE

The elevator doors slide open, and I watch Sloane's first reaction to my penthouse. Her sharp intake of breath is barely audible, but I catch it. Through the wall of windows, Central Park stretches below us, its trees wrapped in thousands of white lights that make the snow glow.

"Welcome home," I say, guiding her forward with a light touch at her back.

Sloane steps away from my touch, putting a deliberate few inches between us. She takes in the subtle holiday touches my designer integrated into the modern design—white amaryllis arrangements, crystal decorations that catch the city lights. The great room spreads before us, all clean lines and perfect symmetry. A massive fireplace anchors one end, its marble surround stretching floor to ceiling. Above it, an abstract canvas in shades of winter blue and silver draws the eye.

"This is where you live?" she asks. Her voice is carefully neutral, professional.

"Where you live as well," I correct as she continues to walk around and study the surroundings.

"This is . . ." She shakes her head, her gaze sweeping from floor to ceiling.

She wanders around the space, trailing her fingers along the leather sectionals in the sunken living room, examining the dining area that could seat twenty, peering into the chef's kitchen with its wall of copper pots gleaming in the light. Everything here was chosen specifically to impress, to show power without being gauche about it.

"The art collection . . ." She stops in front of a glass sculpture, tilting her head to catch how it plays with the light. "This is incredible."

"I'm glad you appreciate it," I say, stepping closer. She subtly shifts her weight, maintaining the distance between us.

It's turning awkward . . . chilly.

Clearing my throat, I add, "Wait until you see your workspace."

She follows me down the hall, past my private office—door firmly closed—and into the east wing. The space opens up, ceilings rising to showcase more windows, more views of the city below.

"The entire wing is yours," I explain, opening the double doors to her studio.

She freezes in the doorway. The space is exactly as I specified—floor-to-ceiling windows, custom workbenches, tools that would make master craftsmen weep. A separate area for sketching overlooks the park, and climate-controlled storage units line one wall.

"Those are beveled casting molds," she says faintly. "Those aren't even available to the public yet."

"I know people."

"Clearly," she replies, all business now. She pulls a small notebook from her bag and begins making notes, as if conducting an inventory rather than receiving a gift. "This is . . . impressive."

"Ms. Whitmore." Knox appears in the doorway, iPad in hand. She turns, and I see recognition flash across her face.

"You were in Switzerland."

"Knox Bishop, head of security." He extends his hand, his handshake firm but not aggressive. "Among other duties, I oversee all safety protocols for the building. We need to discuss the standard security measures for all residents of the penthouse level."

I watch Sloane's face as Knox outlines the restrictions—no un-authorized guests, limited elevator access, twenty-four-seven security detail. Her expression stays neutral, but I see the tension in her shoulders.

"The cameras," Knox continues, "are primarily focused on the work areas and entry points. Your private quarters remain surveillance-free, as agreed."

"And the feeds go where exactly?"

"To our security team. And Mr. Asher's private office."

She looks at me sharply. I meet her gaze without apology.

"My bedroom . . ." she starts, then stops as the doors to her private quarters swing open.

The space is larger than her entire apartment was—a proper suite rather than just a bedroom. Floor-to-ceiling windows continue the view, with automated blinds for privacy. Her belongings are arranged exactly as they were in her old place but now given room to breathe. Her favorite reading chair sits in a window nook I had custom-built to match the dimensions of her old apartment's bay window. Her books line built-in shelves, organized by color just as she had them.

The bedroom itself is done in the same colors she chose for her apartment—soft grays and deep blues—but with higher-quality everything. Her grandmother's quilt drapes across a bed three times the size of her old one. Her photographs have been arranged in the same pattern she'd had them.

A door leads to a walk-in closet where her clothes hang in perfect order, with space for the wardrobe I plan to add. The bathroom features a soaking tub positioned to watch the sunrise, and her exact brand of shampoo already waits on the marble counter.

"The kitchenette is stocked with your tea collection," I tell her as she takes it all in. "Though you're welcome to use the main kitchen as well."

She walks into the space slowly, running her fingers along the spines of her books. "How did you . . ." She opens a drawer to find her socks neatly arranged. "My apartment. You already moved everything."

"Efficiency is important." I watch her process this, wondering if this will be the final straw.

She's quiet for a long moment, studying the precise arrangement of her possessions. Then she turns to me with an expression I wasn't expecting—determination rather than anger.

"I'd like to get started right away."

Knox blinks. "You don't want to get settled in? I could arrange—"

"I'm here to work." She cuts him off. "This timeline isn't going to meet itself."

My phone buzzes—the Bergdorf's call I've been expecting.

I pride myself on not being an easy man to read but Knox catches my reaction. His expression shifts to concern.

"Bergdorf's?" he asks, voice low.

I nod once, hoping he drops it.

"Need me to handle it?" Knox asks, already reaching for his own phone.

"No." My tone ends that line of conversation, but Sloane doesn't miss the exchange.

She glances between us, that designer's eye catching every detail. "Something wrong with the launch?"

"Nothing I can't handle." I keep my voice neutral, giving nothing away. "Just some last-minute date changes."

Sloane's glance darts to Knox, who's doing a terrible job hiding his concern. I can see her mind working, filing away his reaction for later examination. She's too sharp to miss the undercurrent here, which is exactly why Knox needs to learn to keep his damn face neutral.

"Take it," Sloane says, already moving toward her work studio in the main part of the penthouse. "I'm going to be busy anyway."

"Already trying to get rid of me?" I ask, watching her unpack her tools with practiced efficiency.

"Just trying to maintain boundaries." She lines up her pliers with scientific precision. "You know, since you've already cataloged my socks."

Knox coughs to hide a laugh.

"At least I didn't upgrade them," I say, earning a raised eyebrow from Sloane.

"Yet." She pulls out her favorite set of files, arranging them by size.

Her hands still over her tools. "You're really leaning into this whole stalker thing, aren't you?"

"I prefer 'detailed observer.'"

"And exactly how long have you been 'observing' me?" She tries to keep her tone light, but I catch the undercurrent of uncertainty.

"Long enough to know you hide your best sketches in that blue folder under your desk." I pause, watching her process this. "The one you think no one knows about."

She freezes for just a second—barely noticeable unless you're looking for it. Which I am. She recovers quickly, but her smile doesn't quite reach her eyes now. "Should I be worried about what else you've noticed?"

"Probably."

Her fingers trace the edge of her workbench, and I can see her reassessing everything, wondering just how long I've been watching, what else I might know. Good. Let her wonder.

"Well," she says finally, trying to sound casual, "I suppose there are worse things than having a billionaire who knows my tea preferences."

"Many worse things."

The slight tension in her shoulders tells me she caught my meaning. She busies herself with arranging her tools, but I note how her eyes dart to the cameras in the corners, seeing them properly for the first time.

She picks up her sketchbook, angling it away from the nearest camera before catching herself. "So how many of these do you have pointed at me? Should I be waving at regular intervals? Practicing my good side?"

"Depends on the angle." I enjoy watching her try to act casual while clearly mapping each camera location.

"Let me guess. You have a favorite view already." She moves a toolbox, then moves it back, aiming for humor but not quite hitting it. "You know, most people just follow their employees on Instagram."

"You keep your account private."

She stills at that, and I see the moment she realizes I know this because I've tried to access it. A slight flush creeps up her neck, the only crack in her professional veneer. "Less creepy than hidden cameras, though."

"Nothing's hidden. They're all in plain sight."

"All twelve of them?" She tries to make it sound like a joke, but she's counting them now, eyes darting from corner to corner.

"Twenty-seven in this room alone."

She nearly drops her pliers. "You're kidding."

"Maybe. I'm going to enjoy watching you try to find them all," I tease.

"That's cruel." She picks up her sketchbook, turning it slightly. "Now I'll be paranoid about every suspicious light fixture. Every art piece. That plant in the corner looks particularly sneaky."

"The plant's innocent. Probably."

She narrows her eyes at me. "Probably?"

"I'd be a poor stalker if I gave away all my secrets." I move toward the door. "Although . . ."

"Although what?"

"You missed one." I nod toward the ceiling. My phone buzzes again. "Upper left corner."

I leave her with that, enjoying how her carefully constructed professional facade briefly cracks with a soft curse.

In my office, I split my attention between screens. On one, my Bergdorf's team outlines how we are going to launch Sloane's line, but they have concerns on the timeline. On another, Sloane begins setting up her workspace with quick, efficient movements.

"Cole." Knox's voice cuts through the CFO's droning about deadlines. "Are you going to watch her all night?"

I watch Sloane pull out her sketchbook, settling into the chair by the window. Her pencil moves across the page with sure strokes, completely absorbed in her work despite everything that's happened tonight.

"It's business," I tell him, ending the call with the CFO. "I'm investing a lot in her. I just want to watch her work."

Knox rolls his eyes but says nothing more.

I lean back in my chair, switching off the business feeds to focus on a single screen. Sloane pauses in her sketching, studying whatever she's created with that slight head tilt that means she's seeing something new. Something unexpected.

Tonight, I want to watch her create.

Chapter Eleven

SLOANE

I wake to sunlight streaming through soaring windows that stretch from the polished hardwood floors to the crown molding above. For a moment, I stare at the unfamiliar coffered ceiling, my mind struggling to place where I am. Then Manhattan's Christmas lights twinkle against the early morning sky, and reality crashes over me like a wave.

Not a dream then. I'm actually here, in Cole Asher's penthouse, in a bed that feels like sleeping on a cloud.

My hands shake slightly as I reach for my phone, pulling up my banking app before I can talk myself out of checking. My modest savings sit unchanged. But beside them gleams a new seven-figure deposit that appeared overnight. I stare at the number until my vision blurs, wondering if this is how people feel when they win the lottery. Except this isn't luck. This is Cole, systematically inserting himself into every aspect of my life.

The thought should terrify me. Why doesn't it terrify me?

My phone vibrates with a notification. A message from Maya. I tap it open, grateful for the distraction from the dizzying figure in my bank account.

Sloane,

Remember that conversation we had over coffee last month? When you told me I should stop letting fear hold me back and "take the damn leap already"? I finally did it. I left Moth to the Flame yesterday.

You were right. Life's too short to stay somewhere just because it's comfortable and safe. Watching you walk away to pursue your own designs gave me the courage I needed. I was recently approached by someone who actually sees my potential, not just as an assistant but as a creative force.

I can't share details yet, but it feels right.

Dinner soon to celebrate our new paths? I want to hear all about your line. People in the industry are talking.

You showed me it was possible.

Maya

I read the message twice, a genuine smile spreading across my face. Maya had been talking about leaving for months. The thought of her finally taking that leap makes me feel lighter somehow.

I set my phone down and stretch, feeling the delicious pull of muscles that had spent too many hours hunched over my workbench last night. The bathroom beckons with its promise of a soaking tub and rainfall shower.

The space is a study in luxury, an expanse of veined marble and polished chrome that could practically fit my entire old bedroom with room to spare. Everything echoes slightly, the space so generous it creates its own acoustics. At least in here, I'm truly alone—no cameras, as per our agreement. This should comfort me, but as I take in the array of products lined up with military precision on the counter, a different kind of unease settles in my stomach.

The expensive La Mer face cream I usually ration for special occasions sits front and center. Beside it, my favorite Ouai shampoo that's perpetually sold out at Sephora.

I find myself moving through the space like a detective, checking behind the Italian-silk shower curtain, in the walk-in closets, under the double vanity. No cameras—I believe that much.

My suite's kitchen contains my preferred coffee—the small-batch roast from that tiny shop in Brooklyn I discovered last spring. But the aroma of something more substantial draws me toward the main living area. It's only when I'm halfway down the hallway that I remember I'm wearing my oldest, most comfortable pajamas. The flannel pants have seen better days, and my ancient Parsons T-shirt has a small hole near the hem. I should turn back, should change into something more appropriate for a million-dollar penthouse. But the smell of coffee and whatever else is cooking proves too tempting.

Cole stands at the kitchen island in a suit that transforms him from merely handsome into something devastating. The dark gray Italian wool fits him perfectly, but he's not reading market reports or checking his phone like I'd expect from a man dressed for Wall Street domination at 7 a.m. His presence dominates the space, a stark reminder of exactly who owns everything around me—including, for the next few months, my time and creativity.

I freeze, acutely aware of my inappropriate attire. He looks up from his phone, his expression shifting from business mode to something I can't quite read.

"I'm sorry, I didn't realize—I should change," I manage, self-consciously tugging at my worn T-shirt.

"Don't bother on my account," he says, voice cool and professional. "This is your living space too."

But his eyes linger a moment too long, contradicting his detached tone. I break eye contact first.

"Right. Well, I'll try to be more . . . prepared . . . in the future," I say stiffly.

His eyebrow raises slightly. "No need to stand on ceremony, Ms. Whitmore. We'll be sharing this space for the foreseeable future."

The formal address feels like both a reminder and a challenge.

Heat blooms across my neck and cheeks. I attempt to slip past him to the coffee maker, but the kitchen suddenly feels impossibly narrow. Our arms brush accidentally, and I jerk away as if burned. He stiffens but doesn't move, forcing me to navigate around him. The power play isn't lost on me.

"Sleep well?" he asks, his voice neutral but his eyes following my movements with unsettling intensity.

"Like someone who just agreed to defuse a ticking time bomb. Less than a month is . . ." I reply, focusing intently on the coffee machine instead of looking at him. "This thing requires an engineering degree to operate."

He reaches past me to press a button, his chest nearly touching my back. I can feel his breath on my neck, stirring loose strands of hair. Neither of us acknowledges how deliberately close he's standing.

"Just this button," he says, voice dropping lower. "For future reference."

A throat clears from the doorway. "Cole." Knox stands there with an iPad, carefully avoiding looking at our proximity. The tips of his ears are slightly pink. "The launch projection reports are in."

Cole steps back, though his eyes remain fixed on mine. Something unspoken passes between us, heavy with promise. "We'll discuss it in my office." He clears his throat and continues, "I have meetings all day, but if you need anything—"

"I'll be fine," I interrupt, even though I have no idea if I will be. I have no idea where to start this day.

I remain frozen in place long after he leaves, my coffee forgotten. The kitchen feels different without him in it—bigger, emptier somehow. My skin still tingles where we touched, and I press my hands against the cool marble counter to ground myself.

What is wrong with me? I'm here to work, to create something fresh and exciting, not to get caught up in whatever this electricity between us means. I've fought too hard to be taken seriously as an artist to let myself get distracted now, even by a man who looks at me like that.

Gathering what's left of my composure, I retreat to my studio. The familiar sight of tools and workbenches centers me, reminds me why I'm really here. This is my space, my sanctuary, where I can focus on what matters . . . my art, my vision, my future.

The pristine equipment waits like an artist's dream made real. Every tool I've ever coveted gleams under perfect lighting. German files with handles worn to my exact grip preference, precision calipers, casting equipment that would make my old professors weep with envy.

I get down to work and two hours pass in a blink, the cameras catching my attention periodically, their tiny red lights blinking steadily. I wonder if Cole observes my work, if he's watching right now. The thought sends an unexpected thrill down my spine, followed immediately by confusion. When did the idea of his surveillance start feeling less like an invasion and more like . . . anticipation?

My phone buzzes—Chloe demanding details about everything. The screen fills with question marks and exclamation points that perfectly capture her personality. A smile tugs at my lips as I type back that I'll tell her everything in person.

After changing into a sweater and jeans, I gather my courage and my purse. I need coffee with my best friend, need to process whatever this situation is becoming.

I'm halfway to the elevator when Knox emerges from what I

thought was a plain wall panel. His sudden appearance makes me jump.

"Good morning, Ms. Whitmore." Cole's security guy. His tone is professional, but there's something assessing in his gaze as he takes in my outdoor attire. He's all military precision—crew cut silver-blond hair, impeccable posture, and the watchful eyes of someone who misses nothing. Despite the expensive suit, there's no mistaking the coiled readiness of a former Special Forces operative. "Planning to venture out?"

"I . . ." For a moment I consider lying, then realize how ridiculous that is. I'm a grown woman. I can leave if I want to. "Yes. Meeting a friend for coffee."

He nods as if this is perfectly normal, though something in his posture shifts. "I'd be happy to drive you."

The way he says it makes it clear this isn't really a suggestion. I straighten my spine, channeling some of Cole's boardroom confidence. "That's not necessary. I can take the train."

"Mr. Asher insists on certain security protocols when you leave the building." His expression softens slightly, and I catch a glimpse of genuine concern behind his professional facade. "You're not confined here, Ms. Whitmore. You're free to go wherever you'd like. We just need to ensure your safety."

The "we" catches my attention. Just how many people are involved in "ensuring my safety"? And safety from what exactly?

I weigh my options. I could argue, insist on my independence, maybe even try to sneak out later. But something in Knox's stance tells me that would only make things more complicated. Besides, part of me is curious about the layers of security Cole has wrapped around me.

"Fine," I say, adjusting my purse strap. "But I'm picking the music."

Knox's expression doesn't change, but I swear I see amusement in his eyes. "The elevator is this way, Ms. Whitmore."

"If we're doing this whole protective detail thing, you really need to stop calling me Ms. Whitmore," I say as we step into the elevator. "It makes me feel like I'm being called to the principal's office."

"Protocol dictates—"

"Protocol can handle first names," I cut in. "I'm Sloane. And you're Knox, right? Or do you prefer Mr. Bishop?"

"Knox is fine." He pauses, then adds with the barest hint of humor, "Though Mr. Bishop was my father, and he was considerably more intimidating."

"Somehow I doubt that." As we descend, I ask, "So do you drive everyone Cole keeps under surveillance, or am I special?"

The corner of his mouth twitches. "I don't usually play chauffeur."

"Not even for all the other artists Cole keeps captive?"

"You're the first captive," he corrects, but there's definitely amusement there now.

"Lucky me." I study his impassive expression in the mirrored walls. "I can see why Cole hired you. You've got the whole ex-Army thing down to an art form." The sleeve of his suit jacket shifts slightly as he checks his watch, revealing the edge of what appears to be intricate ink work wrapping around his wrist.

"Marines," he says without elaborating, adjusting his cuff to cover the tattoo again.

"Does the mysterious and stoic thing come naturally, or did you have to practice?"

This time I definitely catch a hint of amusement. "Both. There was a whole course at security school. Proper Brooding 101."

I wasn't expecting him to play along, and it makes me wonder what else I don't know about Knox. About any of this. "Let me guess. You aced it?"

The underground garage is a study in luxury vehicles, but Knox leads me to a sleek black Audi that probably has more security features than the average bank vault.

"Top of my class in looming silently." He opens the car door for me with practiced efficiency, the movement causing his collar to shift just enough to expose what looks like the tip of another tattoo climbing up his neck. "Though I did struggle with ominous staring. Too much eyebrow."

I laugh despite myself. It's oddly comforting to discover that Cole's head of security has a sense of humor, even if his massive frame and battle-hardened eyes suggest he probably knows sixteen ways to kill someone with a paper clip.

The drive through Manhattan gives me time to think. About Cole. About this whole surreal situation. About how in less than twenty-four hours my life has transformed into something unrecognizable. My mind drifts to the other night in Switzerland, the sleigh ride through snow-covered forests, the way I'd stopped him when he'd leaned in, though everything in me had wanted that kiss. The memory of my hand against his chest, feeling his heartbeat quicken beneath my palm. The struggle to put my career first when his nearness made rational thought nearly impossible.

I made the right choice, I remind myself. I can't afford to blur the lines, not when this opportunity means everything to my future. But it's harder than I expected—remembering the disappointment in his eyes when I pulled away, the roughness in his voice when he suggested we head back.

But that's exactly what I shouldn't be thinking about. This is business. Just business. Even if the memory of his proximity makes my skin tingle, even if that moment in the kitchen this morning felt charged with the same electricity as last night. I'm here to create my collection, to finally realize my vision. Not to get tangled up in whatever this pull toward Cole means.

I catch Knox watching me in the rearview mirror and wonder

what he sees—the jewelry designer Cole's invested in, or something else? The way his expression shifts makes me think he knows more than he's letting on. About Cole. About why I really need security. About everything.

"I'll wait across the street," Knox says as he pulls up to the curb. "Take your time, but keep your phone on you."

The café Chloe's chosen is a holiday explosion— "Santa's Workshop" according to the chalkboard outside. I push through the door, immediately engulfed in Christmas sensory overload. Every inch of the place is decked with garlands, fairy lights, and vintage ornaments. The air is thick with the scent of cinnamon, gingerbread, and peppermint. Oversize nutcrackers stand guard by the counter where baristas in elf hats serve drinks in mugs shaped like Santa's face.

An a cappella group in the corner breaks into "O Holy Night," their harmonized voices rising above the general hum of conversation. Families with shopping bags crowd tables adorned with miniature Christmas trees, while a line of excited children waits to meet the impressively authentic Santa seated on a throne of candy canes.

I spot Chloe at a corner table with perfect sight lines to both the entrance and the street. From here, I can see Knox standing vigilantly across the street, pretending to check his phone while actually scanning everyone who enters the café.

"Influencer perk," Chloe explains when I reach her, gesturing to the reserved table decorated with sprigs of holly and tiny wrapped gift boxes. "They just opened last week—Santa's Workshop is the hottest holiday pop-up in the city. Been booked solid, but I got us VIP access." She grins, then adds, "Plus, I needed photographic evidence that you're still alive."

I slide into the seat across from her, shedding my coat and gloves. Snowflake projections dance across our table, and tiny fairy lights twinkle from the garland wrapped around every column.

"Okay, spill. Everything," Chloe demands before even sitting down, her eyes bright with curiosity. "Did you really move in with him? Into his actual penthouse?"

A server in reindeer antlers delivers our drinks. Mine is a peppermint mocha topped with whipped cream and crushed candy canes, hers something elaborate with edible gold flakes and cinnamon. "On the house," she tells Chloe. "Perfect for your Instagram story." As she leaves, she hangs a sprig of mistletoe on the light fixture above our table with a smile.

I take a careful sip of my coffee, buying time to figure out how to explain this without sounding completely insane. How do I tell my best friend that I've agreed to live with a man who orchestrated our first meeting? That my new home comes with surveillance cameras and security details? That something about Cole makes me forget all the reasons this is probably a terrible idea?

"Let me take a quick pic of you with your drink first," Chloe says, pulling out her phone. "The lighting under that mistletoe is perfect."

"It's a business arrangement," I say finally, the words sounding hollow even to me. "I have my own wing of the penthouse. Complete creative freedom. Access to materials I could never afford on my own." I focus on the practical aspects, the things that make this sound rational rather than reckless.

Chloe's eyes narrow. She knows me too well to buy the carefully edited version I'm offering. "And?"

"And nothing." I fidget with my coffee cup, avoiding her gaze. "Actually, there is something. It's just . . . Cole seems almost obsessed with this jewelry line. Not just the quality, which I'd expect, but the timing. The secrecy. It all feels more intense than a normal business venture."

Chloe leans forward, suddenly interested. "What do you mean?"

"The security measures are extreme," I explain, lowering my

voice. "I'm not allowed to discuss designs with anyone. Everything is under lock and key. And he keeps emphasizing this New Year's Eve deadline like the world might end if we miss it."

"Well, yeah," Chloe says with a shrug. "He's investing millions in you, a relatively unknown designer. Of course he's being cautious and deadline-focused. That's how these finance guys operate—by quarters and fiscal years."

I nod slowly. "I guess that makes sense."

"Plus, luxury launches are all about timing," she continues, stirring her drink. "If he wants to capitalize on the New Year buzz, missing that window could cost him."

"You're probably right," I admit. I try to shrug off my misgivings as Chloe takes another sip of her drink. "Now, tell me about how your collection is going instead. You don't have to keep it secret from *me*, do you?" She flutters her eyelashes.

I laugh and seize on the change of subject with relief, launching into details about my designs. It's easier to talk about work than my confusing feeling for a man who's been watching me for months.

Around us, the scene is pure holiday chaos. The a cappella group has switched to "Jingle Bell Rock," complete with the classic *Mean Girls* dance. A family nearby strings popcorn garlands at their table, the youngest child more interested in eating the supplies than creating decorations.

"So, I got an interesting email," I say, remembering the message I'd received earlier. "You remember Maya, right?"

"Your old assistant?"

"She quit Moth to the Flame. Got some mysterious new opportunity." I show Chloe the message.

"No way!" Chloe's eyes widen as she reads. "Good for her. First you, now Maya . . . Jasmine must be losing her mind."

"Right? I feel kind of bad, but also proud of her for taking the leap."

"Any idea where she's going?" Chloe asks, handing my phone back.

"No clue. She's being super secretive about it."

Chloe leans in, lowering her voice conspiratorially. "You know what I heard from Darren at that Christmas party last weekend? Apparently, Moth to the Flame is in serious financial trouble. Like, might-not-make-it-to-next-quarter trouble."

"What? No way. They just opened that new showroom in Soho."

"Yeah, and according to Darren, they way overextended. Plus, Jasmine's been making some questionable investments. The place is hemorrhaging talent. First you, now Maya."

"Wow," I say, processing this news. "I had no idea it was that bad. Maya got out just in time too." I pause and shake my head. "Are you sure it's not just a rumor? I can't see Jasmine having any money issues."

"What's that saying that if there is smoke, then there's a fire," Chloe muses, stirring the remains of her drink. "Or something like that. You might have jumped ship at exactly the right time."

I glance at my phone and wince at the time. "Speaking of my own escape, I should get back. This collection isn't going to design itself, and I'm sure Cole's expecting progress by tonight."

"Of course." Chloe stands to hug me goodbye. "And Sloane? Be careful, okay? Not just with Cole, but"—she waves her hand vaguely—"all of it."

I squeeze her tight, grateful for her concern even though I can't explain exactly what she should be concerned about. "I will. Promise."

As I head for the door, she calls after me: "And text me if he turns out to be a serial killer!"

I wave without turning, my thoughts already drifting back to the penthouse, to the designs waiting to take shape under my hands.

Chapter Twelve
SLOANE

I've been at the workbench for hours, completely lost in the process. I set another tiny pavé diamond in place, fingers working from muscle memory as I complete the curved edge of what will become a statement cuff. The torch flame hisses softly as I solder another connection, the metal glowing red before cooling to silver again. I barely notice my stiff shoulders or the hunger pangs until a knock at the door finally breaks my concentration.

I set down my tools and stretch, checking the time. Wow— almost six hours without a break. No wonder my back feels like concrete.

I open the front door expecting one of the security guards or staff, but am surprised to see a small package waiting for me.

When I open the velvet-lined cases, my hands start to shake. Inside are pieces I've only seen in museum catalogs—actual historic jewels I've studied for years.

A Panthère de Cartier bracelet from the 1940s. The iconic Van Cleef & Arpels Mystery Set ruby necklace. A vintage Harry Winston diamond suite that I'm almost afraid to touch.

Cole's note is simple: *For inspiration. Handle them as much as you like. They're insured.*

My fingers trace the Panthère's articulated spine, marveling at the engineering. Each piece represents a milestone in jewelry design—innovations that changed what we thought possible with metal and stone. The Mystery Set alone revolutionized how we work with precious gems. The fact that Cole knew exactly which pieces would speak to me, would inspire me . . . I don't know whether to be impressed or unnerved. How deeply has he studied my work, my influences, my aspirations?

The enormity of my deadline crashes over me. New Year's Eve is only three weeks away. Thank god I've spent the last two years secretly designing most of this collection in my spare time, sketches hidden in portfolios and notebooks scattered around my apartment and stuffed in office drawers. I have the designs—the concepts, the sketches, the measurements—but translating them into actual pieces, perfecting each mechanism and setting? That's the real challenge now.

No pressure or anything. Just create something worthy of sitting next to actual museum pieces while my three camera friends document every time I chew my pencil or have an existential crisis. My hand flies across the paper anyway, because apparently being watched like a reality show contestant is great for productivity. Who knew? The ideas are coming so fast I can barely get them down, each one a little bolder than the last. Cole wants a show? Fine. I'll give him one worth watching.

Hours blur together. The light outside fades to darkness. I'm deep in concentration, working out the intricate mechanism of the heart-shaped lock, when a soft knock interrupts my focus.

I look up to see Cole standing at the entrance to my studio, his tall frame silhouetted against the hallway light. "May I come in?" he asks formally. Despite the polite words, there's something almost predatory in the way he watches me.

I nod, suddenly aware of how disheveled I must look after hours hunched over my workbench. "It's your penthouse," I say, but he remains at the door.

"No," he corrects me, his voice soft but firm. "It's your work-space. We had an agreement."

I'm momentarily taken aback by his adherence to our terms. "Then yes, you can come in," I say, watching as he enters with measured steps.

"You missed dinner," he says softly. Steam rises from the cup of mint tea in his hand.

"Did I?" I blink at the clock. Midnight. Oh hell. I study him, noting the subtle signs of his own long day—the loosened tie, the slight stubble darkening his jaw. Look at his jaw, not his mouth, I remind myself firmly. "Looks like I'm not the only one working late. Do you ever actually leave this place, or do you have a secret bat cave somewhere?"

His lips curve into a knowing smile, and damn it, I looked at his mouth anyway. "The perks of being the boss. No one tells you when to stop." He sets the tea beside me, close enough that his arm brushes mine. "Though I notice you don't need anyone to tell you to keep working either."

"Is it really work when you lose yourself in it?" I gesture to my sketches, to the completed necklace lying among them. "When every problem solved feels like unwrapping a gift?"

"No," he agrees, his voice warming. "It's more like breathing. Essential. Natural." His eyes meet mine. "Addictive."

I pick up the necklace, the chains sliding cool and smooth through my fingers. The design is deceptively simple—multiple delicate silver chains connected by a central ring that sits at the hollow of the throat. What makes it unique is how the chains can be adjusted, creating varying degrees of tension around the neck. It's both elegant and subtly suggestive.

"Speaking of addiction . . ." I say, looking down at the necklace in my hands.

He gets this look in his eyes when he's really interested in something. I'm starting to recognize it.

"Tell me about it."

"It's . . ." I hesitate, wondering how to explain the darker turn my designs have taken since moving into his tower. "Different from my usual work."

"I've noticed." He moves closer, his chest nearly touching my back as he studies the intricate chainwork. "The way these chains connect and flow together . . ." His fingers brush mine as he lifts the necklace. "This is something else entirely."

"Maybe you're rubbing off on me," I say, aiming for lightness but my voice comes out husky. "All those cameras, all that control . . ."

"Is that what inspired this?" He tugs gently on the chain, and they slide together with a soft clink. The movement causes the chains to shift and tighten slightly against each other. "The idea of control?"

I watch his hands work the mechanism, designed to allow the wearer or another person to adjust how the chains sit against the skin. "The person wearing it would be technically free to move, to choose . . ." I demonstrate how the chains flow through the central connecting ring. "But always aware of the potential for . . ." I let the word hang.

"Consequences?" he supplies, his voice dropping to a register that makes my pulse jump. "The engineering is flawless. The way it tightens . . ." He tests the tension, watching how the multiple chains respond to the slightest pull.

"No." I swallow hard, hyperaware of his proximity, of the heat radiating from his body.

"It's designed so that when worn, the chains rest perfectly against the skin, neither too tight nor too loose. But with just a slight adjustment . . ." I wet my lips. "The wearer would have to . . . trust whoever has control of it."

"Trust," he repeats, watching how the chains move with his touch. "Or submit."

The word hangs between us, heavy with possibility. My mouth goes dry. "Is there a difference?"

His free hand settles on my waist, and I fight the urge to lean back against him. "Why don't you tell me? This is your creation, after all. What made you design it this way?"

I should stick to technical specifications. Should discuss market trends or engineering challenges. Instead, I find myself telling the truth. "I was thinking about surrender," I say softly. "How choosing to give up control is its own kind of power."

His grip tightens fractionally. "Show me," he murmurs, the necklace dangling from his fingers. "Put it on."

I glance down at my worn T-shirt. Right. Because nothing says "professional jewelry demonstration" like the shirt I've been wearing since 8 a.m. This is where I should step back, maintain boundaries, remember he's my investor. Focus on the collection, on proving myself as an artist. Instead, I'm noticing how his voice has gone all low and rough, and how his fingers on those chains are doing things to my blood pressure.

Every rational thought I've had since meeting Cole is evaporating. Watching him handle my creation like that . . . well. My professional judgment seems to have left the building.

"This T-shirt isn't going to work." I tug at the high neckline, aiming for practical and landing somewhere between breathless and bizarre. "Can't see the chains properly."

"No?" His thumb traces one of the chains. The studio suddenly feels about as spacious as a broom closet.

"I have something better. For the necklace." Oh good, I've forgotten how sentences work. "Different neckline. To show it off." Words. I used to be good at those.

His lips curve. "By all means. I'd hate to miss any of the . . . details."

I'm a professional artist discussing my work. A professional artist who's apparently developed a sudden coordination problem, given how I nearly take out my entire pencil collection standing up.

"I'll just . . ." I wave vaguely toward my room. "Go. Change. For the necklace. The demonstration."

My brain helpfully lists all the reasons this is a terrible idea. The deadline. The contract. The fact that my investor is looking at me like he wants to devour me. Yet here I am, already thinking about which piece in my closet would work best. For the necklace. Sure. Let's go with that.

I don't do this—don't blur professional lines, don't let attraction mess with business. But something about Cole makes all my careful rules feel like suggestions. Or maybe they were doomed the moment I signed that contract, agreeing to live in his tower like some kind of jewelry-making Rapunzel.

My room is my one camera-free zone, my single slice of privacy in this gilded fishbowl. I find what I'm looking for—a black silk dress I'd optimistically packed for Switzerland, thinking there might be fancy design guild events or dinners.

I'm still adjusting the straps, trying to convince myself this is all very professional and artistic, when movement catches my attention.

He's at my doorway without warning, his large frame filling the space completely. His eyes, dark and hungry, lock onto mine. The necklace dangles from his fingers like a silent threat.

"Invite me in, Sloane," he says, his voice low and commanding. It's not a request. It's a demand barely contained by the rules we've established. He doesn't cross the threshold, but everything in his posture suggests he's barely restraining himself.

I hesitate, remembering our agreement. My space is mine. I'm supposed to be in control here. But the way he's looking at me, waiting at the door like some vampire who can't enter without verbal permission . . . it makes my blood rush faster.

"Come in," I say, the words coming out breathier than I intended. As soon as they leave my lips, I feel something shift between us . . . a power transferring from me to him.

He takes one step over the threshold. We both know what it means. No cameras here. No excuses. No going back.

"Turn around," he says softly, but it's not really a request.

I do. The metal feels cold against my throat, but his fingers are warm as they work the clasp. Each small adjustment of the chains sends a new sensation across my skin. When they finally settle into place, the weight is perfect—commanding but not confining. Not yet.

"Look," he murmurs, turning me toward the mirror.

The necklace transforms the simple camisole into something dangerous. Something powerful. Cole's fingers trail along the chains, testing the tension. "Beautiful," he says, but he's not looking at the jewelry anymore.

"The cameras—" I start.

"Can't see us here." His hands settle on my waist. "That was part of our deal, remember?"

His hand finds the chain at my throat, fingers sliding beneath the links. With the slightest pressure, he pulls me back against him. I watch in the mirror as his other hand grips my waist, holding me in place while he tests the tension of the necklace. The intensity of his gaze, the barely controlled power in his grip. My knees would buckle if he wasn't holding me up.

"Tell me to stop," he whispers against my ear.

I don't.

His lips brush against my neck, just above where the metal rests. "Last chance," he murmurs, his breath hot on my skin.

I meet his eyes in the mirror, seeing my own desire reflected back. "I don't want you to stop," I whisper.

The air between us changes.

Suffocating as if his hand is around my throat and squeezing.

But instead of restraining my breath, his hand slides up to grip the necklace, not pulling, just holding—a reminder of the control I've given him. His other hand spans my waist, fingers splayed possessively against the silk.

"Do you understand what this means?" he asks, voice rough at my ear. "What you're offering?"

I can barely breathe, caught between fear and a desire so intense it borders on pain. "I think so."

"Not good enough." His grip on the necklace tightens fractionally. "I need to hear you say it."

"I'm giving you control," I whisper, my voice trembling. "Over this moment. Over me."

A sound rumbles from his chest, something between approval and hunger. His free hand slides up my arm, fingers tracing a path to my shoulder, then along my collarbone. So light, so deliberate, making me hyperaware of each point of contact. I stare at our reflection. I look flushed, eyes wide, lips parted.

"I could make you do anything right now," he says, his mouth at my ear, breath hot against my skin. "You know that, don't you?"

I nod, unable to speak. His hand slides higher, fingers encircling my throat above the necklace. The pressure is gentle but firm, a promise rather than a threat. I feel my pulse hammering against his palm.

"This necklace makes me want to do dirty things. Raw, unhinged things," he admits, his voice barely above a whisper. "It makes me want to see what you'd look like surrendering. I think this necklace could unleash the inner beast in anyone."

With his hand on my throat, my head tilted back against his shoulder, I should feel vulnerable, afraid. Instead, I feel powerful, desired. Like I'm the one who's brought this controlled, powerful man to the edge of his restraint.

"How does it feel?" he asks, adjusting the necklace so the chains drape differently, creating new sensations against my skin.

"Like flying," I answer honestly. "Dangerous. Thrilling."

His eyes meet mine in the mirror, dark with desire. "Good. Remember this feeling when you're designing. This is what sets your work apart. You understand both sides of the power exchange. The freedom in surrender."

His hand returns to the chains at my throat. With subtle pressure, he adjusts the tension, tightening the necklace just enough that I feel the pressure increase. Not enough to restrict my breathing but enough to remind me who controls it in this moment.

"If I were to kiss you right now," he says, his lips hovering near mine, "could you stay professional tomorrow? Could you separate this"—his fingers trace the edge of the necklace—"from the business we're building together?"

The question is not what I expected. It's not what I expected. I'd been prepared for him to push further, to take more. Instead, he's offering me a choice. A way back to safer ground.

"I—" My voice breaks, and I try again. "I don't know."

His smile is knowing, almost sad. "That's what I thought."

To my shock, his hands fall away. He steps back, putting distance between us. The absence of his touch leaves me cold, aching.

"The necklace is exquisite," he says, his voice controlled again, though I can hear the strain. "It's fucking hot and perfect for the collection."

I turn to face him, confusion warring with frustration. "That's it? A design critique and good night?"

"For now." His eyes are still dark, hungry. "The collection comes first. We both know that. And crossing this line now . . ." He shakes his head. "It complicates things we can't afford to complicate."

He's right, damn him. The collection, my career, everything I've worked for. It all hangs in the balance. And yet . . .

"And if I don't want to wait?" I challenge, lifting my chin.

"That's not your decision to make." He reaches out, running one finger along the edge of the necklace, the touch so light it makes me shiver. "Not if you gave me control."

I swallow hard, hating how needy my body feels . . . how desperate.

"Keep the necklace on," he says as he turns to leave. "Think about what it means. What you want it to mean."

At the doorway he pauses, looking back at me with an intensity that steals my breath. "And Sloane? If we do revisit this conversation—I can't promise I'll have the restraint to walk away. Remember that."

The door closes behind him, leaving me alone with my reflection and a necklace that suddenly feels far heavier than before. My heart is racing, my body on fire with unfulfilled desire. I've never wanted anyone the way I want Cole Asher at this moment.

And he just walked away.

I drag a shaking hand through my hair, trying to understand what just happened. One minute we were on the verge of . . . something explosive. The next, he was gone, leaving me frustrated and confused.

But as my pulse slowly returns to normal, I realize what he did. He gave me space to think clearly. To consider what crossing that line would really mean.

I touch the necklace at my throat, feeling the cool metal warm against my skin.

Control. Surrender. Consequences.

Damn him for understanding my creation better than I do myself.

Chapter Thirteen

COLE

'Ve watched the studio footage so many times the time stamp is burned into my retinas. Not just replaying last night in my head—I'm not that far gone. Just the moments before. The way she looked at me when she realized what kind of piece she'd created. How her fingers traced those chains. The slight tremor in her hands when I asked her to put it on.

I should be reviewing the Q4 projections.

Instead, I'm remembering the shift that happened the moment we stepped into the penthouse. In Switzerland, there had been moments—the sleigh ride under the stars where I'd glimpsed the real Sloane. But the second we returned to New York, those walls came up. Professional. Distant. Polite.

I've seen her body language change whenever I enter the room—spine straightening, expression cooling, voice shifting to that carefully neutral tone. Even last night when we were working together, each time I moved too close, she'd find a reason to step away. Always maintaining that careful distance.

Until she didn't.

Something had cracked in that moment with the necklace. I saw it in her eyes when our fingers brushed, felt it in the sudden catch of her breath. For a heartbeat, those walls came down.

The intercom buzzes. Knox.

"Your girl's been in the studio since five a.m."

"She's not my—" I stop myself. I check the time—7:30. "Why didn't you alert me earlier?"

"Because watching her dance to Mariah Carey while measuring silver powder is the most entertainment I've had on night shift in months." A pause. "She's on her third coffee. Probably needs intervention before she hits four."

I pull up the studio feed. Sloane's in silk pajamas, hair piled messily on top of her head, and she's covered in metallic powder. Every surface she touches sparkles with metallic traces. The dancing has stopped, but she's still humming—"All I Want for Christmas Is You" on endless repeat—while she measures something with intense concentration. I've memorized every detail of her workspace by now, but seeing it transformed by her chaos still gives me pause.

I check my watch, frowning. She should be working on the frost series bracelet by now, according to the schedule I'd laid out. Instead, she's jumped ahead to the necklace components, completely disregarding the production timeline I'd carefully crafted.

"I'll handle it," I tell Knox, already standing.

Ten minutes later, I'm dressed in a charcoal cashmere sweater that fits exactly how I want it to—just tight enough to draw her attention without being obvious about it. My plan is to casually get coffee at exactly the same time—

"Oh shit!"

Sloane spins around, nearly dropping her empty mug. She's even more of a mess up close—the metallic powder has gotten everywhere, in her hair, on her face, coating her hands. She looks like she rolled in stardust.

"I was just . . ." She waves the mug vaguely, leaving a sparkly print on its handle. "Coffee. Need coffee. Words better after coffee."

I want to reach out and touch her, to see if the silver dust feels

as soft as it looks on her skin. But she's tense now; her eyes keep
darting to the cameras.

"If you're wondering about . . ." She gestures to herself, shimmering particles cascading from her sleeve. "I'm trying this new
technique with atomized metal. Don't worry, it's not toxic. It's a
specialized formulation with polymer coating that makes it safe to
handle. The piece needed this specific texture, but it's so fine it gets
everywhere. And I mean everywhere. Pretty sure I'm going to be
finding it in my hair until New Year's."

She stops, staring at the shimmering marks she's left on the
counter. Her eyes dart to the camera in the corner, then back to me.

"We need to talk about the production schedule," she says, squar-
ing her shoulders. "Your timeline isn't working. I can't create pieces
in the order you've specified. That's not how my process works."

"The schedule exists for a reason, Sloane," I reach past her for the
coffee beans, letting myself get closer than necessary. She smells
like metal and coffee and something uniquely her. "If you follow
it, there should be no issue meeting our deadline."

"Right." She takes a step back, bumps the counter, creates another smear of silver. She glances up at the cameras again.

"You hired me for my vision, not to be a production line worker.
My process is . . . less linear." She gestures at the surveillance equipment. "Your staff's already got enough entertainment from my
Mariah Carey performance. We don't need to add to their morning feed with a creative dispute." She pauses, then adds in a rush,
"And about last night . . . That was . . . intense. But I think we need
to keep things strictly professional from now on. The contract,
the collection, everything else . . . I can't afford distractions right
now."

I agree out loud because it's what she needs to hear, what will
keep her from running. But inside, I'm already planning our next

moment alone. I've spent too long watching her, wanting her, to let professional boundaries stop me now.

"No distractions," I say, watching her attempt to clean the counter only to spread more of the glitter across its surface. She turns, and her hand brushes my sweater, marking the cashmere with a shimmer of silver.

She stares at it for a moment. "That's probably not coming out."

"You're single-handedly redecorating the entire building for Christmas," I say, looking at the trail of silver she's left everywhere. "Though the cleaning staff might not appreciate your artistic vision."

"Speaking of Christmas . . . I need a Christmas tree," she says suddenly, looking around the stark kitchen. "Not one of those designer monstrosities with the monochromatic ornaments. A real tree. With colored lights and mismatched ornaments."

I set down my coffee mug. "Absolutely not."

"Excuse me?"

"No real trees in the penthouse." I keep my voice level, professional. "Pine needles get everywhere. They're a fire hazard. The sap damages the floors. And the smell is overwhelming."

"It's Christmas." She crosses her arms, her expression hardening. "This is my first Christmas away from my family, ever. I've never spent December without a tree, and I'm not starting now because you're worried about your precious marble floors."

Her voice wavers slightly on the word *family*, and something in me softens despite myself. But I can't afford to give in. Not when maintaining boundaries is already proving so difficult.

"You're here to work, not decorate," I remind her, my voice sharper than intended. "We have a deadline. Twenty-two days. A tree is a distraction we can't afford."

"A distraction?" Her eyes flash with indignation. "You think having some semblance of normalcy during the holidays is a distraction? Christmas has always been a big deal in my family, and I'm already missing enough traditions being stuck here. I need this one thing, Cole."

The genuine emotion in her voice throws me. This isn't just about decoration or holiday spirit. It's about something deeper. Home. Family. The things I've spent years convincing myself I don't need.

"Fine." The word comes out sharper than I intended. "The Rockefeller tree. Tonight. If you're so desperate for Christmas spirit, I'll take you to see the biggest damn tree in the city."

She blinks, blindsided by my offer. "Are you serious?"

"Consider it research for your winter collection." If I can't stop her from bringing holiday chaos into my space, at least I can redirect it.

"Research," she repeats skeptically. "For jewelry."

"Light refraction on ice. Crystal formations. Winter aesthetics." I maintain a cool, professional tone. "The collection is called Midnight Frost for a reason. You should see what you're designing for."

I reach out, brush a spot of silver from her cheek, withdrawing my hand quickly when I realize what I've done. She tenses, that professional mask slipping back into place.

"Besides, we could both use some air that isn't full of metal powder. I'll meet you in the lobby at seven."

"Seven," she repeats. "For research."

"Seven," I repeat, enjoying the way she's fighting a smile now. "Try not to get lost on your way to your front door. And Sloane? We'll revisit the production schedule tomorrow. I expect to see progress on the frost bracelet by then."

Her smile fades slightly. "We'll see."

Back in my office, I pull up the security feeds one last time. Sloane's back in her studio, still humming, still trailing glitter wherever she goes. She moves between projects with a focused grace that I've watched for hours through these cameras. Each piece she touches becomes something darker and more compelling than the last.

She picks up the design specifications for the frost bracelet, studies them for a moment, then deliberately sets them aside. I watch as she returns to the necklace components instead, her jaw set in quiet defiance. My fingers tighten around my pen.

I shouldn't want this. Shouldn't want her. I've built my life on control, on keeping everyone at a safe distance. But watching her dance around her workspace, scattering metallic particles like snow, humming Christmas carols off-key . . . She's already made herself at home in my head. Now she's making herself at home in my space, leaving her marks everywhere she goes. And for the first time in my life, someone is challenging my carefully constructed order. It's infuriating. Fascinating. Mesmerizing.

I've always known exactly how to control every variable, how to bend people and situations to my will. But Sloane Whitmore refuses to be controlled. And god help me, that might be exactly why I want her.

Chapter Fourteen

SLOANE

I sink deeper into the bubble bath, watching little sparkles swirl in the water. Even with the expensive bath products Cole stocked in my bathroom, the metallic powder clings to my skin. I've officially become a walking art installation.

But it was worth it. The pieces are coming together better than I'd hoped. The atomized metal technique gives them exactly the edge I was looking for—strength wrapped in delicacy, like armor that catches light. If I keep up this pace, I might actually meet the deadline.

Cole and I spent the day in an unspoken standoff. Me continuing work on the necklace components, him sending increasingly detailed notes about the bracelet specifications I was ignoring. Neither of us mentioned the Christmas tree again, but it hovered in the air between us all day. Silent battle lines drawn over something so ordinary. The tension had been thick enough to cut with a jeweler's saw.

"You meet every deadline," I tell my reflection in the gleaming faucet. "You always come through."

It's what I do. What I've always done. Never disappoint. Never let anyone down. Show up early, stay late, exceed expectations. Make everyone proud—my parents, my professors, my clients. Now Cole.

Cole.

I'm not supposed to be thinking about him like this.

Not when he's my boss. Not when everything depends on keeping this professional. But he's under my skin, in my thoughts, in the way my body reacts when he so much as looks at me. And worse, I think he knows.

When I finally drag myself out of my camera-free sanctuary, I stop dead in my tracks. There's an outfit laid out on my bed—a cream sweater dress I'd seen in the window at Bergdorf's but hadn't dared to try on, alongside perfectly coordinated accessories. A white wool coat hangs nearby, and when I reach out to touch it, the fabric is impossibly soft under my fingers. And then I see them— thigh-high boots in the softest leather. I've stopped to stare at boots like these a dozen times, always talking myself out of them. Too impractical for someone who spends their days in a studio. Too extravagant for something I'd probably only wear once or twice. Too much, just too much.

But right now, with the dress and coat and everything else laid out like an invitation.

He's been watching me, studying me . . . and I hate that I love it. That I crave his attention like it's oxygen. That some part of me wants to belong to him, even when I know I shouldn't.

I should be creeped out. Should be irritated by his presumption. Any reasonable person would have questions about a man who can guess their exact size down to the half-inch of a boot heel. And the old Sloane—the one who always plays it safe, who never rocks the boat—would put on the dress as expected.

I stare at the perfectly curated outfit for a long moment, my fingers lingering on the soft wool of the coat. The presumption of it all hits me like a slap. This is exactly the problem. He thinks he can just decide everything for me, right down to what I wear.

"Nope," I say aloud to the empty room. "Not happening."

I march to my closet, pulling out my favorite red-and-green plaid skirt that I save for holiday parties. Paired with a simple black sweater, some sparkly earrings, and my battle-tested ankle boots. The ones with the scuffs I've earned from years of Manhattan commutes. It's festive without being what he expects. I even add a silly snowman charm bracelet that Chloe gave me last Christmas as the final touch of rebellion.

As I get dressed, I can't help glancing at the cream outfit still lying on my bed. Part of me wants to try it on, just to see. My fingers actually twitch with the urge to reach for it.

"No," I tell myself firmly. "Boundaries. Remember those?"

The click of my boots against the marble floor announces my approach to the elevator, where Cole is waiting. He turns, and for a moment, we both freeze. He's traded his usual suit for dark jeans and a charcoal sweater that makes me want to touch him just to see if it's as soft as it looks.

His gaze travels over me slowly, confusion flickering across his face as he registers my outfit choice. A brief flash of something—disappointment? amusement?—crosses his expression before his features settle into that familiar half-smile.

"I like the snowman," he says simply, nodding toward my bracelet. "Very *in season*."

I fight the urge to smooth my hands over my skirt, suddenly feeling like I've made a childish point. "I suppose I should thank you for the thought, at least. The outfit was nice."

"The clothes don't matter." His eyes meet mine briefly before moving to the elevator buttons. "It's the person wearing them."

His eyes travel over my outfit again, lingering just long enough to make me uncomfortable.

"You do realize it's slightly unsettling that you know my exact measurements?"

"I know everything." He pauses. "That sounded less ominous in my head."

The elevator arrives with a soft ding, and I step in, laughing. "At least you're self-aware about the creepy factor."

"I prefer thorough." He follows, standing close enough that I can feel the heat radiating from him.

Outside, the city is transformed by Christmas lights and weekend crowds. Cole guides me through the sea of people with subtle touches—a hand at my elbow, fingers brushing my back. He's different here, more relaxed but still unmistakably himself.

When a group of tourists stops abruptly to take selfies, nearly causing a pileup, he mutters, "I swear tourists think sidewalks have pause buttons." He then smoothly guides me around another abruptly stopping group.

"Says the man who probably hasn't taken a single tourist photo in his life."

"I've taken plenty." He gives me a sidelong glance. "I just don't need fifty attempts to get one decent shot."

"No?" I laugh. "You probably get it perfect on the first try."

"Second, sometimes," he admits, and his mock seriousness makes me laugh harder.

"Is that how you got to be so . . ." I wave my hand vaguely at all of him.

"Devastatingly handsome? Naturally brilliant? Excellent at picking out boots?"

I bump his shoulder with mine. "I was going to say intense, but now I'm changing my answer to insufferable."

We make our way to Rockefeller Center. The Christmas tree stands seventy feet tall, strung with thousands of white lights that make the whole plaza glow. Red and gold ornaments catch the light, and the star at the top is so bright it's visible even against the night sky. Despite the crowds of people taking photos and children pointing up at the decorations, there's something peaceful about it. Ice skaters glide below, their movements synchronized to holiday music floating through the air.

"So this is your compromise?" I ask, gesturing to the massive tree. "Instead of getting our own tree, you bring me to see someone else's?"

Cole's lips quirk up at one corner. "I thought this was a reasonable middle ground."

"A reasonable middle ground would be a six-foot Fraser fir in the living room corner," I counter.

"Hardly reasonable."

I cross my arms but can't help smiling. "This isn't over, you know. I'm getting that tree."

"Not a chance," he says, but I catch the softening in his eyes.

I've walked past this rink hundreds of times, usually hurrying to meetings or rushing between suppliers. But tonight I notice things I've always missed. The way the ice seems to glow from beneath, the sound of blades cutting clean paths through frost, the laughter that rises above the music. Or maybe it's just that everything feels sharper, more vivid with Cole standing next to me. I'm hyperaware of his shoulder brushing mine, the warmth of him in the cold December air.

Cole's hand brushes my lower back. "Stay right here where I can see you," he says, his tone making it more command than request. "I'll be back in two minutes."

He disappears into the crowd, returning exactly when he said he would with two cups of hot chocolate—my favorite kind with extra whipped cream and a dash of cinnamon. I've stopped questioning how he knows these things.

We find a quiet spot overlooking the ice rink, and I catch him watching me instead of the skaters. I gesture to a small boy wobbling on the ice, his father holding both his hands. "Did you ever learn to skate?"

"Sort of. My grandfather taught me," he says, a warmth entering his voice. "Every winter on the pond behind his house in Vermont. He said a man should know how to stay on his feet in any situation, but the ice wasn't really my friend back then." His expression softens. "The weeks I spent there were . . ." He pauses, like he's weighing how much to share. "They meant everything. He'd take me skating, teach me about business, about integrity. About the importance of protecting what matters."

"Sounds like a wise man."

"He was." The tenderness in his voice makes my chest tight. "He would have liked you."

"Why?"

"Because you don't back down. Because you create beautiful things and work like hell to make them perfect." His eyes trace over my face, and I can't look away. The usual sharp edges of his expression have softened, and there's something almost vulnerable in the way he's watching me. My breath catches when his hand comes up, hovering near my cheek like he wants to touch me but is holding himself back.

Don't lean in. Don't close the distance. Don't let him break the last boundary you've been clinging to.

I clear my throat and turn back toward the rink.

"What about you?" he asks. "Do you skate?"

"Figure skated for ten years." I smile at his raised eyebrow, though the memories aren't all sweet. "Ahhhhh . . . something you don't actually know about me. Competed and everything. My mom had Olympic dreams—for me, not for her. She never quite got over missing her own shot at qualifying."

I pause, surprised by my honesty.

"Five a.m. practices, coaches who thought kindness was weakness, a diet of criticism and protein bars. I lived for the moments between the drills, when I could just . . . move. Create something beautiful on the ice. But that wasn't enough. It was never enough."

His eyes stay on mine, patient, waiting.

"I was good. Not great. Not Olympic-bound. Breaking my mom's heart was the hardest thing I'd ever done, but staying would have broken me." I gesture to the rink below, where a young girl lands a wobbly jump, her face pure joy. "Now I just do it for fun. Though these days, I spend more time in my workshop than on the ice. Trading one kind of perfection for another, I guess."

"Show me sometime?" The request is casual, but his eyes are intent on mine.

"Careful what you wish for. I might make you join me out there."

"I think I'd like that." His voice drops lower. "Watching you in your element."

A gust of winter wind sweeps across the plaza, and I pull my coat tighter. Without hesitation, Cole steps closer, shielding me from the worst of it. This close, I catch the scent of his cologne mixed with the crisp December air.

"Cold?" he asks, his voice low enough that I have to lean closer to hear him over the holiday music.

I shake my head. The temperature is the last thing on my mind right now. The space between us feels charged, like the air before a storm. He's still looking at me with that intensity that makes me forget about everything else—the crowds, the contracts, all my careful rules about keeping my distance.

For a moment, I think he's going to kiss me. His eyes drop to my lips, and my heart pounds so hard I'm sure he can hear it. Part of me, the reckless, impulsive part I've been trying to silence, screams for me to close the distance between us. But the other part, the practical artist who knows exactly how much is at stake, keeps me frozen in place.

Don't do this. Don't ruin everything you've worked for with one impulsive decision. You can't afford this. You can't survive this.

A group of carolers stumbles into our quiet corner, their enthusiasm making up for their complete lack of pitch. My hot chocolate sloshes over the rim, and I jump back with a yelp, narrowly saving my coat from certain destruction. The moment, whatever it was going to be, shatters.

"Don't worry," Cole says, his hand steadying me at the small of my back. "I know a great dry cleaner who specializes in hot chocolate emergencies."

"Of course you do." I'm trying to sound exasperated, but I'm laughing too hard.

The tipsy carolers barrel through a chaotic rendition of "Deck the Halls," but I barely hear them.

I'm too aware of Cole's hand still at my back, the slight pressure of his fingers, how close we're standing despite the crowd giving us plenty of space now.

"I think they're trying to clear the plaza," he says near my ear, his breath warm against my skin.

I laugh, trying to break the tension, but it only seems to make things worse. There's an awareness between us now, an unspoken acknowledgment of what almost happened, what we both wanted to happen.

The drive back to the penthouse passes in a blur of city lights and holiday decorations. Neither of us speaks, but the silence feels loaded, heavy with all the things we're not saying. My hand rests on the seat between us, and occasionally I feel the brush of his fingers against mine—accidental or deliberate, I can't tell.

In the elevator, I watch our reflection in the polished doors. His hand shifts to the small of my back, and there's something different in the way we stand together now, like the space between us has changed. The floors tick by too quickly, and I find myself wishing for a power outage, anything to make this night last just a little longer. Cole walks me to my door. He reaches past me to turn on the hallway light, and for a moment we're standing so close I can feel the warmth of him.

"Thank you," I say softly, trying to push those thoughts away. "For tonight. For everything."

Part of me wants to pull him into my room, to feel that delicious loss of control again.

But that's not who I'm allowed to be right now.

"I should go," I whisper against his lips. "Early morning tomorrow. Lots of work to do."

"You do need your rest." That commanding tone, the one that always leaves me breathless. He steps back, but his eyes stay dark with promise. "Sweet dreams, Sloane."

I slip inside my room and lean against the closed door, listening to his footsteps fade down the hallway.

Chapter Fifteen

SLOANE

I've been staring at the same sketch for twenty minutes. Instead of the delicate latticework I'm supposed to be designing, I keep drawing the curve of Cole's lips, the sharp line of his jaw. This is the fourth ruined page this morning. At this rate, I'll need a new sketchbook before noon.

This has to stop. I didn't spend ten years building my reputation to throw it all away because I can't keep my hands off my investor.

Cole Asher is a businessman. Everything comes down to profit margins and deadlines. This line needs to be ready for New Year's, and here I am doodling like a schoolgirl with a crush. He probably has a dozen other designers lined up if I fail. That's what smart businessmen do. They hedge their bets.

If I'm reading more into this, into him, I'm setting myself up for disappointment. And I don't do disappointment. I don't do failure. I do perfect execution and exceeded expectations.

Focus. I need to focus.

The coffee maker in my room is empty. Of course it is. I've already had three cups, and it's not even ten. Cursing my caffeine addiction, I head to the main kitchen. And stop dead.

Cole's there, fresh from his workout. His hair is damp with sweat, his black athletic shirt clings to his chest, and he's drinking a protein shake like this is completely normal. Like I'm supposed to be able to function when he looks like this.

Our eyes meet over his glass, and neither of us seems to know what to say. The silence stretches until he breaks it.

"Productive morning?" His voice is casual, but his eyes aren't.

"Not exactly." I gesture vaguely at my messy hair, still wearing my sleep tank under my cardigan. "Haven't quite found my focus yet."

His gaze trails down my body, lingering on the exposed skin above my collarbone, and suddenly the tension is back, different but just as intense. I need to handle this now, before I lose my nerve.

"About last night . . ." I start, then falter when he sets down his glass. "I could have finished the marquise design if I'd stayed in. These . . . extracurricular activities need to wait until after the deadline. I can't afford distractions right now, not when there's so much riding on this collection, and—"

"Sloane." He cuts off my rambling, moving into my space with that predatory grace that makes my breath catch. "You'll meet the deadline." His eyes lock with mine, his voice dropping lower. "And I'm not a distraction you need to manage."

Before I can respond, Knox bursts in. His face is grim. "Cole, we've got a situation. The—"

"Not here." Cole cuts him off sharply, his whole body tensing. Whatever Knox was about to say, Cole doesn't want me to hear it.

Cole shifts instantly—his stance wider, shoulders back, all softness gone. And then he's there, crowding me against the counter, close enough that I think he might kiss me. Instead, his lips brush my ear: "We're not done discussing this."

And then he's gone, leaving me gripping the counter to stay upright.

Back in my workroom, I pour everything into my designs—the

frustration, the want, the confusion. The possessiveness in his voice should frighten me. Instead, I keep replaying it, again and again.

But something about Knox's expression nags at me. The way Cole cut him off so abruptly . . .

Before I can talk myself out of it, I'm heading toward Cole's office. The hallway is empty, but raised voices leak through the heavy wooden doors. I can't make out most of it, just fragments of their argument.

". . . can't keep ignoring this . . ." Knox's voice rises.

Cole's response is too low to hear. I glance up at the security camera in the corner and freeze. What am I doing? If Cole wanted me to know about his business dealings, he'd tell me. I'm not about to get caught eavesdropping.

I hurry back to my workroom, but the questions linger. What is this morning's emergency? And why didn't Cole want me to hear it?

A knock at the door breaks my focus. A delivery. Inside an elegant black box, I find an antique jewelry case and a note in Cole's precise handwriting:

THIS PIECE INSPIRED AN ENTIRE COLLECTION IN 1957. I EXPECT YOU CAN DO BETTER. DINNER TONIGHT? I PROMISE NOT TO LET ANY CAROLERS INTERRUPT THIS TIME.

The piece inside takes my breath away—a necklace that incorporates exactly the kind of metalwork I've been struggling to perfect. He must have been watching my attempts through the cameras to know exactly what I needed for reference.

A normal person would probably have issues with the cameras, with being watched. Instead, I catch myself looking up at the one in the corner of my workroom. Is he watching now, taking a break from whatever crisis Knox brought to him?

I stand slowly, stretching my arms above my head. My sleep

tank rides up, exposing a strip of skin above my yoga pants. I can almost feel his gaze through the camera, imagining him sitting in his office right now watching this little show.

I move to my desk, purposely choosing the chair that gives the camera the best view. Leaning forward, I examine the vintage piece with exaggerated care, letting my hair fall forward. I know exactly what I'm doing when I bite my lower lip, pretending to concentrate. When I run my finger along the delicate metalwork, taking my time, imagining his reaction.

I should stop.

I won't.

My phone buzzes with a text from Cole: I can see you at your desk.

I glance up at the camera, pretending I hadn't noticed it before. Then I slowly and deliberately bite my lip again, staring right at the camera. My phone lights up.

> **Cole:** Very subtle.

> **Me:** I'm just concentrating on this piece.

> **Cole:** Is that why you keep looking at the camera?

I smile to myself, enjoying the edge in his texts.

> **Cole:** You're playing a dangerous game.

> **Me:** I have no idea what you mean.

The three dots appear, disappear, then appear again. He's choosing his words carefully.

Cole: You're changing the rules.

Me: I don't like rules. You should know that by now.

Cole: You don't know what you're asking for.

I shouldn't push this further. But something about the edge in his texts makes me want to see how far I can go.

Me: Then show me.

His response is immediate this time.

Cole: Careful what you wish for. Last warning.

I hesitate, then decide to push one more time.

Me: I'm not afraid of you.

A full minute passes. Nothing. Just when I think I've gone too far, my phone vibrates.

Cole: You should be.

I feel my pulse in my throat as I read his words. Another text follows immediately.

Cole: I've been watching you. Learning what makes you tick. What makes you nervous. What you want.

My fingers hover over the screen. Is this a threat or a promise? Maybe both.

> **Me:** And what exactly do you think I want?

> **Cole:** Things you're too afraid to admit. Even to yourself.

I swallow hard. He's right, and we both know it.

> **Me:** Try me.

I stare at my screen, shocked at my own daring. Did I really just send that? I'm practically daring him to cross the line we've been dancing around. There's something about the way he watches me, the way he always seems to be in control, that turns me inside out. The good girl who always aimed to please shouldn't take risks. Shouldn't want this so much.

His response makes my mouth go dry: Dinner. 8pm. You'll find what I want you to wear on your bed later. Bring your *completed* bracelet design as well. And Sloane? I won't ask twice.

I grin and set my phone down. So much for getting any work done today.

Professional boundaries be damned. I'm done fighting this.

Chapter Sixteen

SLOANE

Tell me again why I agreed to dinner?" I hold my phone closer to my face, watching Chloe roll her eyes on the screen.

"Because you're into him. And he's into you. And honestly? The sexual tension is exhausting just hearing about it."

"But the cameras—"

"The cameras that you were literally performing for this morning?" She raises an eyebrow. "The ones you admitted make you hot?"

"I'm actually looking forward to them now," I groan, dropping my head into my hands. "What is wrong with me?"

"You've gone full Stockholm syndrome, and I am HERE for it." Chloe's grin is wicked, but it fades when she sees my expression. "What's really bothering you?"

"I've worked so hard to get here." I sink onto the edge of my bed. "Ten years of apprenticeships, studying metallurgy, learning from masters. I don't want anyone looking at this collection and thinking I got it because I'm sleeping with the investor."

"Stop." Chloe leans closer to her camera. "Cole Asher has a reputation for being ruthless with his investments. You really think he'd risk millions on a jewelry line just because he wants to get laid? Please." She rolls her eyes. "He chose you because you're brilliant at what you do. The fact that you two can't keep your hands off each other doesn't change that."

I think about the way Cole watches me work, how he asks questions about my process, the vintage pieces he keeps finding that align perfectly with what I'm trying to create.

"Hey, have you heard anything about Maya?" I try to keep my voice casual.

"No, actually. It's weird. She hasn't posted anything in like two weeks. A few people from Moth to the Flame are starting to ask questions." Chloe tilts her head. "Why? Have you heard from her?"

"No, and that's what's bothering me. She's never offline this long. Not even when she went to Bali last year." I shrug, but my stomach tightens.

The silence is so unlike Maya. She's the person who posts every day's breakfast. Something about her silence feels wrong. Like there's a piece of a puzzle I'm missing, and it might be important. And here I am, letting myself get distracted by hot chocolate and near kisses at Rockefeller Center, designer dresses and vintage jewelry. I've read enough thrillers to know how this usually ends for the girl who ignores the warning signs because she's too caught up in the fantasy.

"Hey." Chloe's voice softens. "I'm sure she's fine. Maybe she's just doing a digital detox."

I nod. She's probably right, but I make a mental note to do some digging of my own.

"So stop overthinking and show me what you're wearing."

I turn the camera toward my bed, where another perfectly curated outfit waits. The deep blue dress catches the light, but it's what's beside it that makes me pause—a vintage diamond and sapphire necklace. The note underneath reads: *I want to watch the diamonds rest against your throat while you remember who put them there.*

"Holy shit," Chloe breathes. "That's—"

"A lot."

"Put it on," Chloe insists. "I need to see it."

I stare at the dress, torn. "I don't know. He's so controlling already. If I wear exactly what he wants, exactly when he wants it . . ." I pick up the note again. "Who does he think he is, telling me what to wear?"

"The same man you were teasing with a camera show this morning," Chloe points out. "Come on, just try it on. For me."

"It feels like giving in," I say, but my fingers are already running over the fabric. The dress is gorgeous. Exactly what I would have chosen for myself. And the necklace . . .

"*Submitting* can be fun sometimes." Chloe grins. "Besides, didn't he say something about not asking twice? On second thought, maybe *don't* wear it. I wanna know what he'll do . . ."

I bite my lip, remembering his text. The thought of pushing him further is tempting, but something tells me this isn't a boundary I want to test. Not tonight.

"Fine. Reverse psychology for the win," I say, and we both laugh.

I send Chloe a photo once I'm dressed, endure her squealing about how perfect everything is, and promise to tell her everything tomorrow. My hand trembles slightly as I fasten the necklace, the diamonds cool against my skin.

At eight sharp, Cole knocks on my door. His eyes land on the necklace, lingering there long enough that I forget to breathe.

"Turn around," he says, his voice low with something that's not quite approval. Something darker. When I do, his fingers brush the nape of my neck, adjusting the clasp. "Perfect," he murmurs against my ear. "You decided to listen after all."

I turn to face him, trying to keep my voice steady. "Was there really a choice?"

"There's always a choice, Sloane." His hand slides to my lower back, the pressure firm and possessive. "You just made the right one. Ready to see where I'm taking you?"

He leads me down a narrow staircase I didn't even know existed. The temperature drops as we descend. At the bottom of the stairs, a wine cellar stretches before us. Antique crystal sconces cast intimate light across walls lined with vintage bottles. A heavy wooden table dominates what looks like a tasting area, its surface reflecting the warm glow from above. The space feels both opulent and intimate, like a secret tucked away beneath the bustle of the city.

"Where are we?" I ask, taking in the rows of bottles that seem to stretch endlessly into the shadows.

"My private collection." Cole's voice is different down here—softer but somehow more intense. "Welcome to my favorite room in the building." He moves through the space with easy familiarity, trailing his fingers along bottle labels, at home among the vintage wines in a way I haven't seen him anywhere else.

"This Bordeaux," he says, selecting one, "took three years to acquire. The owner refused to sell until I convinced him I'd appreciate it properly." He glances at me. "I can be very persuasive when I want something."

"Three years for one bottle?" I glance at him, remembering how skillfully he'd negotiated our own deal. "I can believe it. I've seen your powers of persuasion firsthand."

His eyes darken at that. "Have you?"

"Though I'm curious what methods you used on the wine seller."

"Some secrets I need to keep." He runs a finger along the bottle's label. "For now."

He pours the wine with the precision of a man who's done this a thousand times before. Every movement becomes deliberate, practiced. His fingers brush mine when he hands me the glass. His body shifts closer as he explains the vintage, using words I've only heard on cooking shows. His eyes follow my lips as I taste it.

A bottle on the far wall catches my attention—one he mentioned earlier. I step closer to examine it, my fingers hovering near the label without quite touching. My hands feel clumsy, my movements too big for this delicate space. The wine in my glass sloshes dangerously close to the rim with each breath, and I find myself overthinking every small motion. Which of course is exactly when disaster strikes.

The wineglass slips. Time seems to slow as I watch it fall, my brain helpfully supplying a montage of every clumsy moment I've ever had. The crash when it hits the floor makes me jump.

"I'm so sorry," I gasp, mortified. "The wine—I can't believe I just—" I look at the spreading puddle of red against stone. "I need something to clean this up. Where's the—"

He catches my wrist as I start looking around. His thumb traces circles against my pulse point. "Sloane."

I try to pull away. "No, really, if we hurry we can save the—"

Cole releases my wrist, picks up his own glass, and deliberately lets it fall. The crash echoes through the cellar.

My jaw drops.

Has the man lost his mind?

But there's something about the way he's looking at me, the casual display of destruction just to prove a point.

"Stop apologizing." His hand slides to my waist, pulling me closer. "Stop trying to be perfect." His lips brush my ear, then trail down my neck. "You're more interesting when you're not."

I reach for him. "It's just . . . I'm sorry, I should be more—"

"What did I say about apologizing?" His voice has an edge that makes my skin tingle. He tilts my chin up. "Unless, of course, your goal for the night is to do exactly that . . . *please me.*" He studies my face. "Is that what you're doing, Sloane?"

I meet his eyes. Everything else falls away—the broken glass, my nerves, all my earlier doubts. There's only this moment, this man, and the way he's looking at me like I'm something precious and dangerous all at once.

A knock breaks through the tension. We both turn toward the stairs.

"Mr. Asher?" A staff member calls down. "Dinner is ready to be served."

"Shall we eat?" His voice is rough. "I had them set up down here. No cameras."

I nod, trying to steady my breathing as he leads me to where covered dishes await us on the far end of the table.

"I thought we deserved a proper meal after both working all day." He pulls out my chair. "And I need to make sure you actually take the time to stop and eat." The way he says it is both teasing and protective, like he's already learned this about me.

Cole lifts the silver covers from our plates, revealing perfectly seared steaks with roasted vegetables.

"So this is how you impress all your business partners?" I pick up my fork. "Private wine cellars and intimate dinners?"

"Only the ones who break my expensive wineglasses." He sits across from me, his eyes bright with amusement. "Though you're the first to make me want to break one too."

"I create chaos wherever I go. It's a gift." I cut into my steak. "Though usually I at least make it through the appetizer before destroying things."

"I notice you keep the French reds separate from the Italian ones." I gesture at the wall of bottles. "Some might call that obsessive."

"Some might call it respect for tradition." His lips quirk up. "Though clearly I'm not as devoted to order as I used to be."

"What gave it away?" I glance pointedly at the broken glass. He takes a slow sip from his glass.

"Let's just say my priorities are shifting."

"The steak is perfect," I say, taking another bite. "Though I'm surprised you didn't go with something more elaborate."

"You struck me as someone who appreciates simplicity." He

watches me over his new wineglass. "At least when it comes to food. Your designs are anything but."

"Says the man who spent three years hunting down a single bottle of wine." I take another sip from my glass, considering him. "I've never met anyone so determined to get exactly what they want."

His smile holds a hint of challenge. "You should look in the mirror."

I lean back in my chair, fingers absently touching the necklace. "So tell me something I don't know about Cole Asher. Something that isn't in the press releases or Forbes profiles."

"Trying to get the upper hand?" He cuts into his steak with precise movements.

"Maybe I'm just curious about the man who breaks thousand-dollar wineglasses to make a point."

"Two thousand when you count the wine inside of it." He sets down his knife with a smirk. "And what would you like to know?"

"Why jewelry?" I tilt my head. "Of all the investments you could make, why choose this collection?"

"Because you didn't try to sell me on profits or market projections." He studies me for a moment. "You showed me the pieces and let them speak for themselves. It's rare to find someone that confident in their work."

"Most people would call that arrogance." I pause, studying his face. "But I think there's more to it. Something you're not telling me."

Cole's expression shifts subtly, a shadow passing over his features. "Someone I once cared about was an incredible jewelry designer like you. She died and never got to complete her vision." His voice grows softer. "When I saw your work, I felt like it was important to support you, to show the world what you could create. And maybe . . . maybe it honors her memory too."

My heart beats faster. "Who was she?"

"Her name was Claire," he says, the words coming reluctantly.

"Claire?" I lean forward, a suspicion forming. "Wait—Claire as in Claire Voss?"

Cole's eyes meet mine, and he gives a small, tight nod. "Yes."

"Oh my god!" I can't hide my excitement. "I studied her work obsessively in design school! Her use of negative space, the way she incorporated unexpected materials—" I shake my head in disbelief. "Her pieces weren't just jewelry; they were tiny sculptures that told stories. I have her portfolio book dog-eared to death. Everyone was devastated when she died so young."

Cole nods again, his jaw tightening in a way that tells me not to push further. I can see the pain in his eyes, and suddenly a thousand questions flood my mind. How did he know her? Were they close? What really happened to her? But I don't ask. Instead, I reach across the table and briefly touch his hand.

He's quiet for a moment, turning his own glass slowly between his fingers.

His eyes drop to my wrist, and his expression shifts. "You're not wearing the frost bracelet."

I follow his gaze to my bare wrist and sigh. "It's not finished yet."

"Not finished?" His voice takes on an edge. "I thought I was clear that I needed it completed by tonight."

I set my fork down. "Look, the stones weren't working with the setting. I needed to reconfigure the entire clasp mechanism. It wasn't ready."

"Sloane." The way he says my name is both caress and warning. "We have deadlines for a reason. The frost bracelet is central to the winter collection. When I say I need something by a specific date, it's not a suggestion."

I feel my hackles rise. "That's not how creative work happens. I can't just force it because of some arbitrary deadline you've set. The piece speaks to me when it speaks to me."

"Arbitrary?" His jaw tightens. "The New Year's launch isn't arbitrary, and neither is the timeline leading up to it. Every piece needs to be completed, photographed, and cataloged. There's PR, marketing, distribution—"

"I know how a product launch works," I cut in. "I've been doing this for years. And I've never missed a deadline that actually mattered."

Cole's eyes narrow. "This one matters, Sloane. More than you know."

For the first time, I notice the tension in his shoulders, the slight crease between his brows. This isn't just business-as-usual Cole. He's genuinely stressed about the timeline.

"Why?" I press, leaning forward. "Why is this date so important? What aren't you telling me?"

He takes a slow sip of his wine. "The date is nonnegotiable. That's all you need to know."

"No, it's not." I push my plate aside. "If I'm going to be a part of this, I need to understand the business side too. I'm not just some . . . some monkey with a soldering iron, churning out pretty baubles on command."

Something dangerous flashes in his eyes. "A monkey? Is that what you think I see you as?"

"I don't know what you see me as," I counter. "But it's clearly not as a full partner in this venture. You keep me in the dark, dictate deadlines without explanation, and expect me to just fall in line."

"I brought you in for your creative vision," he says, his voice tight with controlled anger. "Your talent. Your unique perspective. I'm not looking for a business partner. I've been down that road before. I'm looking for an artist who can deliver on time."

"Deliver on *your* schedule, you mean." I stand up, my appetite completely gone. "Well, guess what? Art doesn't work that way. I don't work that way."

"Everyone works according to deadlines, Sloane. That's how the world functions."

I hate how he says my name when he's pissed.

"Not my world."

"It is now." His tone is final. "You signed a contract."

The mention of the contract stings more than I want to admit. Because he's right. I did sign it. I needed this opportunity. I needed his backing, his resources, his connections. Without them, my designs would still be sketches in a portfolio that no one would ever see.

"Fine." I toss my napkin onto the table. "I'll go work on your damn bracelet. Right now. Will that make you happy?"

"Ecstatic." His smile doesn't reach his eyes.

I turn to leave, then pause. "You know, I may need your money to make this happen, but you need my creativity just as much. Your capital is worthless without my vision to turn it into something real."

"Artistic genius that never makes it to market is just wasted potential."

His words hit harder than I want to admit. Without another word, I head for the stairs, already mentally sketching the modifications I'll need to make to that fucking bracelet tonight.

Behind me, I hear another glass shatter against the floor.

Back in my studio, I channel my frustration into creating something new. Four hours of work and the bracelet transforms into something else entirely—twin cuffs connected by a platinum chain.

I make them cold and sharp, with jagged crystals that catch light like actual frost. The silver metal has a matte finish that looks like ice against skin. The clasp I've been fighting with becomes a locking mechanism that can tighten the chain between the cuffs.

It's not just jewelry anymore. It's power. Control. The kind that makes your pulse quicken.

I'm admiring my work when the knock comes at my door. I know it's him.

"What?" I call out, not looking up.

The door opens. Cole stands in the doorway, tie gone, sleeves rolled up, tension visible in his shoulders. The argument from earlier still hangs between us, but there's something else now too.

"You shouldn't be working this late," he says, his voice low, not moving past the threshold until I explicitly invite him in.

"Deadlines, remember?" I hold up the finished pieces. "Happy now?"

His eyes focus on what I've created. "Those aren't bracelets."

"They are. Just not what you expected." I stand, moving toward him. "They're exactly what this collection needs."

"Restraints?" he asks, still not stepping into the room, though his knuckles whiten where he grips the doorframe.

"Cuffs," I correct. "Functional jewelry. Come in and I'll show you."

The invitation hangs between us.

"Are you sure about that? Once I enter . . ." Cole's voice is controlled, but I can hear the tension underneath.

I hesitate, knowing where this might lead. "Yes."

His eyes darken as he steps across the threshold, closing the door behind him.

"Put out your hand," I say, testing how far this new power dynamic will go.

"I'm the one that gives the orders." His voice drops lower, a warning that sends heat through me.

"Scared?" I challenge.

Something shifts in his eyes. He extends his hand, palm up.

I place one cuff in his palm instead of on my wrist. "You want control so badly? Here it is."

Cole studies the cuff, running his thumb over the locking mechanism. "You've been holding back on me."

"You have no idea."

His eyes snap to mine.

Without breaking eye contact, I hold out my wrists. "Go ahead."

For a second, he doesn't move. Then he steps closer, his body radiating heat. He takes the first cuff and locks it around my left wrist, his fingers brushing my skin.

"Both," I say, my breath catching.

He secures the second cuff on my right wrist. The chain between them is short, maybe six inches. Not enough to pull my arms apart.

He yanks the chain, pulling me against him. Our bodies collide. His free hand grips my hair, tilting my head back.

"This what you want?" he asks, his eyes dark.

His grip tightens. The sting on my scalp only heightens my need. I've never wanted something . . . *someone* so much in my life.

"Yes . . ."

His mouth crashes down on mine. The kiss is intense, hungry, with all the tension that's been building between us since we met. I bite his lower lip, and he pushes me backward until I hit the wall, my bound hands trapped between us.

I'm vulnerable, and I fucking love it.

He breaks the kiss, both of us breathing hard. His hand slides from my hair to my throat, not squeezing, just holding. "Once I step forward, I never step back. You better be fucking sure."

"I know exactly what I'm doing."

"Do you?" His thumb moves along my jaw. "Because once we cross this line . . ."

I answer by pressing forward against his hand, forcing him to either tighten his grip or let go.

He doesn't let go.

Chapter Seventeen

SLOANE

This is madness.

Everything about this is chaotic and reckless. And I want more.

"Tell me to stop," he breathes against my skin. It's not a request—it's a dare.

His hands slide down to my thighs, lifting me onto the workbench. Tools topple. The handcuffs at my wrists catch the light as my head falls back, his mouth trailing fire down my neck.

It should feel too fast. Too dangerous.

Instead, it feels inevitable.

I wrap my legs around him, drawing him closer. "Is that what you want? For me to stop you?"

His laugh rumbles low against my throat. "What I want . . ." His teeth graze my collarbone. "Is to take you right here, surrounded by your sketches and scattered gems. To watch you come apart on this table where you create."

My body answers before I can think. But it's not mindless lust. It's a choice.

A surrender.

Heat pools low in my stomach. But through the haze of desire, a voice in my head reminds me that this solves nothing. The secrets are still there.

I press my bound hands against his chest, creating just enough space to think. "Cole."

My next protest dies in my throat as his mouth finds that spot beneath my ear.

I should ask questions. I should demand answers.

But I don't. I tilt into him instead, chasing the only certainty I have right now: him.

God, I want this man to fuck me.

My fingers continue to curl into his shirt, torn between pushing him away and pulling him closer. Cole's lips curve against my skin, sensing my hesitation.

"Say it," he murmurs, his breath hot on my ear. "Tell me you don't want this."

I swallow hard, fighting to find my voice. "I . . . I can't."

His hand slides up my thigh, fingers teasing the hem of my dress. "Then don't fight it."

My resolve crumbles. With a low moan, I capture his mouth with mine, kissing him deeply. Cole responds instantly, pressing me back against the workbench. The remaining pliers and metal sheets crash as they hit the floor, but neither of us notices.

His hands are everywhere, setting my skin ablaze. I want to unbutton his shirt, but the handcuffs make it difficult. I fumble with the buttons, my restricted movements clumsy. Cole growls low in his throat as he sees my struggle, reaching up to capture my bound wrists with one hand.

"Let me," he says, unbuttoning his shirt with his free hand while keeping my wrists pinned above my head.

Cole hitches my dress up around my waist. His fingers brush against my inner thigh, teasing, testing. I arch into his touch, silently begging for more.

"Tell me what you want," he murmurs against my ear, his breath hot and tantalizing. "Say the words."

I swallow hard, trying to find the courage to voice my desires. "I want you," I whisper, my voice barely audible. "I want all of you."

Cole growls in response, his grip on me tightening as he captures my mouth in a searing kiss. His tongue delves deep, exploring every inch of my mouth as if he can't get enough of me. I respond in kind, meeting his passion with my own and giving myself over to the moment completely.

I want it dark. I want it dangerous. I want his hand to squeeze around my neck until I can barely inhale . . . wait . . . what the fuck? Why am I even . . . but I want. I do.

"Please," I whisper, not even sure what I'm asking for. I don't know how to voice exactly what I want. But I do know one thing. I know that I want more of him.

Cole's response is immediate and fierce. His mouth crashes down on mine once again, his hands continuing to roam my body, gripping my hips and pulling me even closer against him. The chain between the handcuffs presses against his chest, the metal warming between our bodies.

Cole's hands slide down to my thighs, and in one swift motion he lifts me up, pinning me against the wall. I loop my bound arms around his neck, the chain pressing against his nape. I then wrap my legs around his waist instinctively, gasping at the friction this new position creates.

His lips find mine again, the kiss deep and demanding. I match his intensity, pouring all my pent-up longing into the kiss. My fingers tangle in his hair, pulling him closer. I want to drown in this moment, in him.

"I don't fuck easy. I don't fuck sweet."

"I don't want easy," I breathe against his lips. "And I don't need sweet."

He rewards me with another kiss, his tongue battling with mine for dominance. I surrender willingly, melting into him.

I can tell this man likes to hurt but in the best way possible.

Cole's hands move to the hem of my dress, slowly inching it upward. "This needs to go," he growls, breaking the kiss just long enough to pull the garment over my head. He has to work around the handcuffed wrists, briefly opening one, threading the fabric through the chain before yanking my panties down.

Oh. My. God. I'm. Naked.

The cool air hits my bare skin, and instead of cowering or trying to cover myself, I embrace it. But then his hands are on me again, hot and demanding, and I forget about everything else. He cups my breasts, thumbs brushing over my nipples, and I moan at the sensation.

His mouth replaces his hands, tongue swirling around one nipple as his fingers pinch and tease the other. I cry out, my back arching off the wall.

Cole spreads his jacket across the floor beside the jewelry display and lowers me onto it with surprising gentleness. But there's nothing gentle about the way he looks at me. His eyes are dark with desire, hungry and predatory.

Cole stands over me. "Spread your legs, baby. I want to see that pussy on display."

I hesitate for a moment, a flicker of self-consciousness passing through me. But the way Cole is looking at me—like he wants to devour me whole—banishes any lingering doubts. Slowly, I part my legs, feeling exposed and vulnerable under his intense gaze.

He finishes removing his shirt, revealing a toned chest and abs that . . . fuck me . . . I knew the man would be good-looking. But Jesus Christ this is taking it to a completely new level.

Cole's eyes rake over my body, his gaze so intense I can almost feel it like a physical touch. He reaches out, tracing a finger along the inside of my thigh, inching closer to my pussy. "Wider."

I obey, spreading my legs further apart and exposing myself to him completely.

"You're so fucking beautiful," he growls, his voice low and rough. "I can't wait to feel my cock buried inside of you."

"I'm on the pill," I somehow say as he kneels between my legs.

He gives me a wicked smile as he aligns his body with mine, the heat from his hard cock pressing against my wetness. "I know."

His thumb circles my clit slowly as he pushes inside me all at once—no gentle stretching, no gradual accommodation. The burn makes me scream into his shoulder as my cuffed hands clutch at his back, unable to find purchase.

"Let's spread this tight pussy of yours," he rasps against my neck while I tremble beneath him. I don't know why I'm slightly stunned by the dirty talk coming from Cole, but it only makes me clench around him harder. His groan vibrates against my collarbone as he withdraws almost completely before slamming back in with brutal precision. "That's it—squeeze me just like that while I ruin you."

The rhythm of his thrusts builds, sharp and punishing, flesh meeting flesh in relentless tempo. He licks a stripe up my throat before biting down at the center of my chest, the pressure threatening to blur my vision. My hips rise desperately to meet his punishing rhythm, each snap of his pelvis wringing another broken sound from my lips.

"Look at me." His command slices through the haze when I obey; his gaze holds me more trapped than any chain. There's no softness there, only feral possession. "You take this cock like you were made for it."

I am. I am. The thought loops wildly as he drags a hand between us, fingertips finding my clit again and rubbing tight circles that fray my sanity.

Pleasure coils like live wire beneath my skin, every nerve alight—

until suddenly his thumb stills, denying release as he slows his thrusts to a torturous grind.

"Cole—"

"Beg." A wicked smile as he watches tears of frustration prick my eyes. "Or don't you want it bad enough?"

The words unravel me faster than any touch could. But not quite enough. I want to come. I need to come.

I arch beneath him, choking out something between a plea and a curse, my bound hands straining against his grip.

"Please." The word cracks open something feral in him. His hips snap forward with renewed force as his thumb resumes its relentless pressure.

"What do you want?" he demands, voice ragged yet controlled.

"Y-you," I stammer, my head falling back as he angles deeper, hitting a place that makes my toes curl. "Need—"

"Need what?" He punctuates each syllable with a thrust so brutal I cry out.

"To come!"

The demand explodes between us like lightning. The pressure unspools and then I'm gone, lost in a pleasure so sharp and bright it feels like breaking.

But Cole doesn't stop.

He slows only to drag his fingers lower, gathering my slick and pressing teasing circles against the tight ring of muscle just below. I freeze. My breath catches.

"Relax," he growls, his voice low and full of heat. "Let me in."

His finger presses gently until it breaches me, slow and steady. I gasp at the stretch, the unfamiliar intrusion shocking and electric.

"You're mine," he says again, his words threading through the haze of overstimulation. "Mine to claim. Mine to punish. And if you ever try to run out on me again, it won't be just my finger in your ass."

A sound escapes me—half moan, half whimper—as he begins to move, his cock still thrusting while his finger matches the rhythm. The combination is too much. Perfect. Exquisite.

I shouldn't like this. But fuck me—I do.

His other hand finds my clit and I'm spiraling again, wrecked and wrecking as he coaxes every last tremble from my body.

When I come this time, I shatter. Completely.

Cole groans into my neck and follows me over the edge, hips jerking, cock twitching deep inside me as he spills with a broken curse.

We collapse in a tangled, breathless heap on the floor. Raw. Spent. And I know I'll never be the same.

Chapter Eighteen
COLE

Control is everything until it isn't.

I watch Sloane sleeping in my bed, her breath steady and deep in the early morning quiet. She's curled into my sheets like she belongs there. No one has ever slept in my bed before—I've made sure of that, keeping this space as controlled and solitary as every other aspect of my life. But last night, when she tried to go to her room, I pulled her to mine.

I wasn't ready to let her go.

Last night changed everything—the barrier between professional and personal collapsing with the first press of her body against mine. I'd planned for every aspect of her moving into the penthouse, designing the jewelry line, even the security protocols. But I hadn't planned for this. The way she slipped past my defenses and made me want something I'd denied myself. Connection. Intimacy beyond the physical. A woman who challenges me in ways no one else dares. Now, watching her here, I realize I want her to stay.

The thought makes me uneasy.

My phone buzzes. Knox's morning briefing details Julian's latest move—an attempted break-in at one of my jewelry stores in Venice. Smart actually, as I know he's seeing if the case with Claire's designs is there. Classic Julian, testing the edges of my empire while playing this game of hide-and-seek.

I slip out of bed, careful not to wake her. The morning routine I've perfected over years feels different with her here—the silence less empty, weighted with her presence. I dress quickly, choosing a charcoal suit without having to think about it. Years of discipline have their uses.

In the kitchen, I start the coffee maker and call my usual bakery. They're used to my precise orders, my exacting standards. Today those standards serve a different purpose.

Twenty minutes later, the smell of coffee and warm pastries fills the kitchen when Sloane pads in, wearing one of my shirts. She stops at the sight of almond croissants and coffee made exactly how she likes it.

"You did all this?" She leans against the doorframe, sleep-mussed and soft in a way that makes my chest tighten.

"The bakery opens at five." I push her coffee toward her, made the way I've seen her order it countless times—one sugar, splash of cream.

She takes a sip, watching me over the rim. "So much for keeping things professional." There's amusement in her voice as she slides onto one of the barstools, bare legs crossing.

I should regret this. The complication, the risk to everything I've built. Instead, I feel strangely liberated. For once in my life, I've done something without calculating every consequence, without weighing every risk. I've simply wanted and taken, and the world hasn't collapsed.

Yet.

I lean across the counter, drawn to the mark my teeth left on her neck. "I find myself reconsidering that position."

"Clearly." Her fingers brush over the bruise, and her eyes meet mine with a heat that makes me want to drag her back to bed.

She wraps her hands around the mug, breathing in the steam. The silence between us is comfortable, nothing like last night's tension. When she finally looks up, something has shifted in her expression.

"You know everything about me," she says quietly. "My coffee order, my favorite breakfast, even what shade of lipstick I wear."

"Ask me anything." When she raises an eyebrow, I add, "I mean it. I can be an open book . . . If I try."

I watch her tear apart her croissant, scattering flaky bits across the counter. The mess should bother me. It doesn't.

She takes another sip of coffee, then looks up at me. "I wanted to ask you last night, in the cellar . . ." She traces the rim of her mug with one finger. "Why wine? I mean, you could collect anything. But you chose a private cellar of wine."

I open my mouth to give her the usual line about market appreciation and investment diversity. The words are there, polished smooth from years of use. But something in how she's watching me makes them die in my throat.

"My father . . ." The words taste bitter. I take a drink of coffee, buying time. "He was partial to whatever whiskey he could get cheapest. Used to keep bottles hidden all over the house."

Sloane sets down her croissant, going still. I force myself to continue.

"When he'd been drinking, his hands got mean. Everything got mean." I look down at my own hands wrapped around the coffee mug, knuckles white. "I promised myself back then that if I ever got out, I'd only have the finest things. Things worth savoring. Things he couldn't afford to touch."

Her hand slides across the counter toward mine, but my phone buzzes with Knox's message.

Knox: Julian's here. Board room in 30.

Of course he is. Julian's always had perfect timing when it comes to disrupting my life. I look at Sloane's hand, still inches from mine, and resist the urge to throw my phone across the room.

"I have to go." The words come out clipped, anger bleeding through despite my control. "Meeting."

Sloane withdraws her hand slowly. "Now?"

"Unfortunately." I round the counter, needing to touch her before I leave, to remind myself of what matters. My hands find her waist and I pull her close, kissing her hard. But she pulls back, eyes bright with something that looks like amusement.

"I get another question later," she says. Not asking permission.

I nod, knowing I'll tell her things I've never told anyone.

"I have a full day at the studio anyway." She stretches, my shirt riding up her thighs. "The winter collection won't design itself. I need to finish the icicle choker—the metal needs to look like it's frozen mid-drip." Her eyes light up the way they always do when she talks about her work. "New Year's Eve isn't getting any further away."

Which means she'll work straight through until midnight if I let her, forgetting to eat. Not anymore. "Dinner tonight." I run my thumb across her lower lip. "Eight o'clock. You need to eat."

"I can feed myself, you know." But she's smiling.

"And yet you don't." My fingers trail down her neck. "That's my job now."

IN THE BACK of the car, my phone buzzes. It's been less than twenty minutes since I left her.

Favorite color?

Black would be the sexy answer, right?
Though lately I'm partial to frost-blue.

First car?

Never had one. I lived in Brooklyn.

Biggest fear?

That one I leave unanswered. Some truths need wine and darkness to emerge.

I type out one last message:

Eight o'clock. I'll be ready and hungry.
Don't work through dinner.

Her reply comes instantly:

I have protein bars.

Not dinner. Don't be late.

Then I close my messages, letting the calm settle over me. The one I've perfected over years of boardroom battles. Julian mistakes my silence for weakness. His first of many errors.

The car turns onto Madison Avenue. Time to remind him why that's always been a mistake.

Chapter Nineteen
COLE

My office door opens without a knock. Julian's never respected boundaries. Not in the decade we worked together, and certainly not now.

"Making me come to you?" He drops into the chair across from my desk, sprawling like he owns it. Like he still owns any part of this. "Bit dramatic, don't you think?"

I continue reading the document in front of me for another thirty seconds before looking up. "You're the one who wanted a meeting."

"In the boardroom. With the full board present." His smile doesn't reach his eyes. "But you've always preferred to handle things . . . privately."

"Some conversations shouldn't have witnesses."

He laughs, but there's an edge to it. "Always so cautious. So controlled. It's that control I've come for today, Cole."

The morning sun catches on the steel and glass buildings outside my window. I've had this office for fifteen years, watched the skyline change, watched empires rise and fall. But Julian didn't come here to admire the view.

"I want what's mine," Julian says, his voice deceptively calm. "Claire's designs. The case."

"We've been over this," I say. "Nothing in that case belongs to you."

His jaw tightens. "She was my wife."

"Unfortunately."

"You have no reason to hold on to that case."

"How about Claire wouldn't want you to have them. She gave them to me."

"Claire is dead. I'm her husband so they belong to me."

I take a deep breath, determined to not lose my shit in this exchange. "She was going to divorce you, and you and I both know it."

"Only because you got into her head." He rolls his eyes. "The Boy Scout. Always doing what you feel is right. And then you got her on your side."

"We wanted nothing to do with blood diamonds. Smuggled goods! And you fucking knew it. You tried to taint her name and her brand. I wasn't going to allow it. And when she found out, saw you for what you are—"

"You shouldn't have gotten involved!" Julian's face turns red as sweat beads on his temples, a tell that I'm getting to him.

I lean back in my chair, letting him see how little his words affect me. "Are you done? You're starting to sound like a B-rate movie villain."

"You think this is funny?"

"I think you're a problem I need to deal with before my nine o'clock." I check my watch. "But maybe I should reconsider my priorities."

The tension in the room thickens. Julian's always had a way of filling a space with his anger, letting it seep into every corner.

"Five years, Cole," he says, his voice tight. "Five years since her accident, and you've kept her final collection locked away where no one can see it. Where I can't touch it."

"That's how it has to be."

Julian goes quiet, his eyes fixed on something distant. When he speaks again, his voice has changed, almost soft with memory.

"Remember when I found you? Barely twenty-five, brilliant but broke." His voice shifts to something almost nostalgic. "You had that pathetic little office in Brooklyn. I knew you had the eye for this business." He smiles thinly. "I made you, Cole. I brought you into our world. Into Claire's world."

"You saw an opportunity," I correct him. "Don't pretend it was charity."

Julian's eyes drift to the desk between us.

"You insisted on keeping this exact desk. The one where we made our first real deal." His gaze shifts to the right drawer. "The one where you started keeping the gun, after Moscow." He meets my eyes. "Still in there, isn't it? Still loaded?"

I don't answer. We both know it's there. The weight of it has been a constant reminder of what this business used to be. What I used to be.

"But you'd never use it, would you?" Julian's voice drips contempt. "Not the great Cole Asher. Too civilized now. Too weak." He stands, planting his hands on my desk. "I built this business with you. The real business. The one that got us here. While you were playing with spreadsheets, I was getting my hands dirty. Making the hard choices."

"You mean killing people who got in your way."

"I did what was necessary. What you couldn't stomach doing yourself." He straightens.

"I want that case, Cole. Those designs are my legacy."

"You mean you want to pass them off as newly discovered designs," I say coldly. "Profit from her name one more time."

"I know that's what *you* plan on doing! I've heard you have a top secret collection you're working on. I know what you're doing. I'm not fucking stupid. Those designs aren't yours to use as your own. They're my right. She was my wife."

"And now she's gone." The accusation remains unspoken between us.

He straightens. "You always were a self-righteous little prick."

I sigh. "Are you done? Because I am." I'm not going to give Julian even a sliver of information on what I have planned. Let him think what he wants.

I watch him pace, three steps left, three steps right. The same pattern he's followed since we were young and hungry, plotting our way to the top. Some habits die hard.

"You know I won't stop," Julian adds. "If I can't have the originals, I'll create them. The 'Immortal Claire Collection' launches in February one way or the other. Pieces she was 'working on' before her accident." His smile cuts like glass. "The world is so hungry for her genius, they'll believe anything."

"Forgeries," I say flatly.

"Call it what you want. Who could prove otherwise? You? The man who kept her final work hidden for five years? And you can *try* to beat me to the punch with her half-finished stuff, but there's no way you can beat me to February."

I keep my expression neutral despite the contempt rising within me.

"I'll have those designs, Cole. One way or another."

"The case will stay locked."

He laughs, cold and knowing. "You know . . . when Claire died"—his voice catches, a perfect performance of grief—"I needed time. And you used it against me. Turned everything I built into your sanitized corporate fantasy."

"When she went off that cliff," I say carefully, watching his face.

His face goes still, eyes cold. "Black ice. A tragic accident."

My hands stay flat on the desk. Perfectly still. But something cold settles in my chest.

He stares at me for a long moment. "When I'm done, everyone will remember Claire's genius as mine to share with the world. You'll be a footnote. A petty business rival who tried to keep her light hidden."

I stay seated, keeping my voice level. "You can try."

"Oh, I'll do more than try." He heads for the door, then pauses. "You know there are a lot of young designers out there that come close to Claire's designs. Of course, they aren't Claire, but they can try. And well . . . if they fail, there's always another one. Disposable. Everyone is disposable."

The door closes behind him. I open the right drawer, running my fingers over the cold metal beneath the files before reaching for my phone.

Knox answers on the first ring. "My office. Now."

He appears within minutes, closing the door behind him. Knox hasn't changed since he left Special Forces—same crew cut, same watchful eyes, same ability to blend into the background until needed.

"The man's unhinged." I keep my voice low. "He knows about the line and the launch but hasn't connected all the dots yet."

Knox nods once. "Does he know about Sloane?"

"No. He thinks I'm going to steal Claire's designs for this launch. Do what he wants to do." I slide the drawer shut. "He still plans to launch the fake Claire line. He mentioned he had designers trying to mimic her work. But he still has the February date. So as long as we beat him to the date . . . But—"

"You're worried about Sloane?"

"Double her security detail. But quietly. She doesn't need to know about any of this. He also mentioned 'disposable designers.' I'm not sure what that's all about, but can you look into it?"

Knox leaves without another word. He understands what's at stake. He was there when Julian started pushing boundaries, when accidents started happening to our competitors. When those accidents turned into something darker.

After Knox leaves, I stand at the window overlooking the city. The streets below are starting to fill with morning traffic. Somewhere out there, Julian's already putting his next move into play. He's too close to what I care about most. First Claire's designs, and now Sloane herself.

I grab my phone, pulling up the security feed of Sloane's studio. She's working, completely absorbed in her designs, unaware of the danger circling closer. The knife twist of guilt in my gut is unexpected. I brought her into this war with Julian without telling her the full truth. I told myself it was to protect her, but was it? Or was it to protect my chance at finally destroying him?

Five years I've waited, building toward this moment. Sloane's collection replacing Julian's forged Claire pieces, hitting him where it hurts. But watching her work, I realize with sudden clarity: If it comes down to revenge or her safety, there's no choice at all.

If he touches what's mine, I'll remind him exactly who he taught me to be.

Chapter Twenty
COLE

The sound of metal hitting the floor echoes through the studio as I enter. Sloane stands at her workbench, shoulders tight with frustration. The necklace she'd mentioned this morning lies in pieces before her.

"Damn it." She pushes away from the bench. "Nothing's working."

She blows a strand of hair from her face, nose scrunched in concentration. Even when she's frustrated, it's impossible to take my eyes off her.

I check my watch. Eight o'clock. "You've been at this for twelve hours. Time for a break."

She doesn't look up. "I should keep working—"

"You need a break. And after the day we've both had, we need a change of scenery." I take her arm, guiding her away from the bench. "And that's not a suggestion."

"If I keep having days like this, the collection won't be ready." She lets me help her into her coat anyway, still talking as I find her boots under the workbench. "The metal's fighting me on every piece. Nothing's flowing right."

I kneel down, sliding the boots onto her feet while she steadies herself with a hand on my shoulder. For someone so resistant to being taken care of, she doesn't pull away.

"The collection will be ready." I stand, straightening her collar. "You've never missed a deadline. And I've never backed the wrong horse." A ghost of a smile touches my lips. "Though you might be the most expensive bet I've made."

The roof access requires my fingerprint and a code. I watch her face as the doors open, catching the exact moment her eyes widen. The entire space has been transformed. State-of-the-art heating lamps line the perimeter, casting golden light across the dark Brazilian wood decking. White fur blankets drape over modern loungers and deep-cushioned sofas, arranged around sleek fire tables. Strings of lights curve overhead, weaving between heated glass pergolas that shelter intimate seating areas while maintaining the view.

But it's the center of the roof that draws her attention. A professional photography setup gleams under the lights—cameras with lenses that cost more than most cars, soft boxes creating perfect illumination, reflective screens positioned at precise angles. Behind it all stands a backdrop of white silk draped to look like snow drifts, with crystal icicles hanging from an ornate frame above.

In the corner, partially sheltered by a pergola, stands a massive Christmas tree. Every branch holds crystal and silver ornaments, each piece catching and fracturing the light. No colored lights, no tinsel—just pure winter elegance that matches the rest of the space. The kind of tree that belongs in a place like this, sixty stories above the city.

The view through the glass walls takes in most of Manhattan. The Empire State Building rises ahead of us, its spire bright against the night sky. The Hudson River cuts a dark line in the distance. Office buildings cluster close by, their windows still lit up despite the late hour. Central Park opens up before us, darker than the surrounding blocks and dusted with the snow that fell earlier.

"God, this view is incredible," she breathes, turning slowly to take it all in. "I've lived here ten years and I've never seen the city quite like this."

And then she sees her—Vivienne Moore, current Hollywood It Girl, sitting in a makeup chair while someone touches up her hair.

"Holy shit," she breathes, turning to take it all in. "Cole, what is this?"

"Your jewelry deserves better photos than phone shots," I say, enjoying her shocked face. "Vivienne agreed to model for a private shoot. The photographer's ready whenever you are."

She takes a few steps forward, touching one of the light stands like she can't believe it's real. "This is crazy. When did you even set all this up?"

"When I saw you were stuck," I reply. "Sometimes seeing your work on someone else helps break through the block."

"You arranged all this?" she asks, still stunned as an assistant approaches with a clothing rack—all whites and silvers that will make her jewelry pop.

"Your work deserves it," I reply. "The collection needs good photos before launch. Something that shows what you've created. The edge, the beauty, the frost effect you've been chasing."

"Fur blankets and all?" She runs her fingers over one of the blankets. Below, steam drifts up from the street vents. The low clouds suggest more snow is coming before morning.

"A frozen girlfriend would be significantly less entertaining." The word slips out before I can catch it. *Girlfriend.* Like I'm sixteen instead of thirty-five.

She smirks but doesn't comment as Vivienne walks over to us.

"Your jewelry is amazing," Vivienne tells Sloane, genuine excitement in her voice. "Those dagger earrings made me feel like an ice villainess. In the best way."

"Thank you so much! I'm thrilled you liked them," Sloane says, her smile widening. Then she turns to me, eyes bright. "I can't believe you did this."

"I pay attention," I say simply. "Even to the things you don't say out loud."

We move toward the set where the photographer gives Sloane a nod. "Ready when you are. Your vision. I'm just here to capture it."

Sloane hesitates briefly before her professional side takes over. I watch as she directs the shoot, placing pieces on Vivienne carefully, adjusting angles, suggesting poses that show off her designs.

"The necklace needs to catch the light right here." She shows Vivienne, adjusting the centerpiece. "So the diamonds break the light instead of just reflecting it."

I sit back, watching and occasionally asking questions as the shoot goes on. Despite her initial surprise, Sloane runs the set confidently, her vision clear. The photographer follows her lead, recognizing she knows what she's doing.

"Today was pure hell before this," she admits during a break while Vivienne changes. "I hate days when nothing works right."

I nod, understanding. Sloane's work is more than just jewelry; it's art. Each piece carries a piece of her soul.

"Maybe you're trying too hard," I suggest. "Sometimes, when we force things, they resist."

She looks at me, a hint of amusement in her eyes. "Is that your philosophy on relationships too?"

I chuckle, caught off guard by her directness. "Perhaps. Though I find some things are worth pursuing, even if they resist at first."

Sloane's eyes linger on mine for a moment before she looks away, her gaze drifting to the twinkling city lights beyond the rooftop. "I've never been good at forcing things," she admits softly. "In my work or . . . otherwise."

"That's not always a bad thing. Your determination but also your flexibility is what's gotten you this far."

She smiles, but it doesn't quite reach her eyes. "And what about you, Cole? What's gotten you this far?"

"Calculated risks," I reply, watching her closely. "Knowing when to push and when to step back."

Sloane nods, her fingers tracing the edge of her blanket. "And which are you doing now?"

The question hangs between us, loaded with unspoken implications. I consider my words carefully before responding. "I'm . . . assessing the situation."

She laughs softly, the sound melting into the night air. "Always the businessman."

"Not always," I murmur, reaching out to tuck a stray strand of hair behind her ear. My fingers linger, tracing the curve of her jaw. "Sometimes I'm just a man who knows what he wants."

Sloane's breath catches, her eyes meeting mine. The sounds of the city fade into the background, and all I can focus on is how her skin feels under my fingertips.

"And what is it that you want, Cole?" Her voice is barely above a whisper.

Instead of answering, I lean in slowly, giving her time to pull away if she chooses. She doesn't. Our lips meet, soft and tentative at first, then with growing intensity. I taste her lip gloss, feel the warmth of her skin as my hand cups her face.

When we finally part, both slightly breathless, Sloane's eyes are wide with surprise and desire.

"I want this," I say simply, my thumb caressing her cheek. "Us. No more dancing around it."

She bites her lip, considering. "It's risky. Isn't the saying 'You shouldn't mix business and pleasure'?"

"Some risks are worth taking."

A slow smile spreads across her face. "Well, you have always had good instincts when it comes to investments."

"Is that what we're calling this?" I raise an eyebrow, enjoying the way her smile widens.

"What would you call it?"

"Research and development?" I suggest, making her laugh.

"Just how much research are you planning to do?"

I grin, pulling her closer. "Oh, I intend to be very thorough."

As we kiss again, Sloane relaxes into my embrace. Her fingers thread through my hair, and I feel the last bit of hesitation leave her body. When we finally break apart, her cheeks are flushed and her eyes bright.

"I think," she says softly, "that this might be exactly what I needed."

I pull her closer, wrapping us both in one of the fur blankets. "Good. That was the goal."

We sit in comfortable silence, watching the photographer capture the final shots. Vivienne poses with the Manhattan skyline behind her, Sloane's diamond crown catching the city lights perfectly.

The shoot wraps up around ten. Vivienne thanks Sloane warmly, genuinely impressed with the collection. "Those frost pieces are going to be everywhere next season," she says as her assistant helps her into her coat. "Send me the pricing when they're ready. I want first pick."

The photographer and lighting crew pack up efficiently, the makeup artist trailing after them with her case. I watch Sloane thank each of them personally, her excitement visible as the photographer shows her a few preview shots on his camera.

"We'll have the full set edited by tomorrow afternoon," he promises, zipping up his equipment bag.

Within twenty minutes, they've all filed into the elevator, leaving us alone on the rooftop.

"These photos are going to be amazing," Sloane murmurs, her head on my shoulder, her breath warm against my neck.

"Tell me about your day," she murmurs eventually. "You mentioned it was rough?"

I sigh, thinking of Julian's competing line and his move to try to get a hold of my case with Claire's designs.

"Just the usual corporate politics and egos."

She shifts to look at me, her expression serious. "You don't have to downplay it, you know. I want to hear about your struggles too."

Her words surprise me. I'm so used to being the one in control, the one who listens and solves problems. The honesty in her eyes makes me want to tell her everything, but I can't risk it. Not with Julian still on my mind.

"There's a competitor of Midnight Frost rushing to market," I admit, keeping it vague. "It's annoying but nothing major . . . yet. But it's why we need to stay focused and on deadline. There's no wiggle room and that New Year's deadline is a must."

Sloane nods, her brow furrowing in concentration. I can see her mind working, probably already thinking of solutions. It's one of the things I love about her—that brilliant mind never stops.

"But that's the last thing I want to talk about right now," I say, repositioning her body so I can get a better look at her face. With her this close, work is the furthest thing from my mind.

"Oh yeah?" Her smile turns playful. "What would you like to talk about?"

I trace my fingers along her jawline, savoring the softness of her skin. "I'd much rather talk about how my cock feels buried inside of you."

Sloane's breath catches, her eyes widening slightly at my bold words. A flush creeps up her neck, but she doesn't look away.

"That's quite a change of subject," she murmurs, her voice low and husky. She swallows, her gaze dropping to my lips for a brief moment before meeting my eyes again.

My hand moves to her thigh, slowly tracing patterns on the fabric of her dress.

Sloane sucks in a breath, her pupils dilating. "Here? On the rooftop? The camera . . ."

I lean in close, my lips brushing her ear. "I told you, the cameras are only for security. No one's watching." My hand slides higher up her thigh, bunching the fabric of her dress. "Unless you want them to be."

Sloane's breath hitches. "Cole . . ." Her tone is a mix of warning and desire.

"Shhh," I murmur, nipping gently at her earlobe.

"We shouldn't," she whispers, even as she spreads her legs wider, granting me better access. "We're out in the open. Outside."

"We absolutely should," I counter, sliding her panties to the side. I trace her slick folds, reveling in how wet she already is. "God, you're perfect."

I slip a finger inside her, and she gasps, her hips bucking up to meet my hand. "Cole," she moans, her head falling back. "I'm still sore from last night."

Hearing those words hardens my cock even more, if possible. "I think you like the pain." I add a second finger, stretching her more. "You like the sting."

Sloane's eyes flutter closed as she arches into my touch. "Maybe," she breathes. Her hands grip my shoulders, nails digging in slightly.

In one swift motion, I lift her onto my lap, her legs straddling me. My fingers never leave her as I use my free hand to undo my pants, freeing my aching cock.

With a soft moan, Sloane lifts herself up and slowly sinks down onto my cock. We both gasp at the sensation—her tight heat enveloping me, stretching to accommodate my size.

"Fuck," I groan, gripping her hips. "Your pussy is so fucking tight."

Sloane starts to move, riding me with slow, deliberate motions. Her dress has ridden up around her waist, and I push it higher, exposing her breasts to the cool night air. I take one hardened nipple into my mouth, sucking and teasing with my tongue.

Her head falls back as she moans, her rhythm becoming faster and more desperate. I can feel her getting closer, her muscles tensing around me. I slide my fingers back to her clit, rubbing slow circles that make her gasp and writhe on top of me.

"Cole, I'm close," she pants, her fingers digging into my shoulders. "Don't stop."

As if I would.

I increase the pressure on her clit, my other hand gripping her hip to help guide her movements. She's so wet, so hot, and she feels incredible wrapped around me. I can feel my own release building, my balls tightening as I fight to hold back just a little longer.

Sloane's movements become erratic, her breath coming in short, sharp gasps. She's right on the edge, and I can't wait any longer. I thrust up into her, hard and deep, and she comes apart with a cry. Her pussy clenches around me as she rides out her orgasm.

The sight of her like this, completely lost in pleasure, is too much for me. With a low growl, I let go, my own release crashing through me like a wave. I buck up into her, again and again, until I'm spent and collapsing back onto the blanket, taking Sloane with me.

We lay there for a moment, panting and tangled together. The city hums below us, oblivious to our private moment high above. Sloane shivers slightly in the cool night air, and I pull one of the fur blankets over us, cocooning us in warmth.

Sloane hums in what I can only hope is satisfaction, nestling closer to me. We stay like that for a while, watching the twinkling lights of the city, our breathing slowly returning to normal.

Eventually, Sloane stirs. "We should probably head back down," she says reluctantly. "I still have work to do on that necklace."

I tighten my arms around her. "The necklace can wait until morning. Tonight, you're all mine."

She looks up at me, a glimmer of mischief in her eyes. "Is that so?"

"Absolutely," I growl playfully, rolling us over so she's pinned beneath me. "I'm not done with you yet."

Chapter Twenty-One
SLOANE

My phone buzzes again—another text from Chloe. I glance at the notifications piling up: "CALL ME!" followed by a string of exclamation points. I've been ignoring her messages for days, caught up in the intricate details of the necklace design. And if I'm being honest, caught up in Cole.

I smile, thinking of how it always starts the same way—him looking over my shoulder at whatever piece I'm working on, his breath warm on my neck. Four nights of following him to his room instead of mine. This morning, I'd curled up in his sheets while he took calls in his office, my sketchbook balanced on my knees, feeling strangely at home there.

I pick up my phone and dial Chloe's number. She answers on the first ring.

"Finally! Where have you been? I've been trying to reach you for days."

"I know, I'm sorry. I've been working on the winter collection." Not entirely a lie. "The necklace design needed adjustments."

"You never even called me after your date," Chloe says.

I sink onto the couch in my studio. "Things have . . . intensified."

"Intensified how?" There's a pause. "Sloane. Have you been sleeping with him?"

I bite my lip, glad she can't see my face. "The past four nights."

"Holy shit," Chloe breathes. "I knew you liked him, but I didn't realize it had gotten this serious. Sloane. We need to talk about him and someone named Julian Voss." The familiar last name makes my blood freeze.

"*Julian* Voss? Who's that?"

"Well . . ." Chloe lowers her voice. "This guy Julian, he used to be married to that designer Claire Voss. And he isn't just some businessman. He's got connections to some serious underground crime rings."

"What do you mean underground? Like, mafia and shit?"

"Hailey isn't sure exactly what, but she's heard rumors. Bad ones. People who cross him tend to disappear. And I don't mean they move to Florida."

"Jesus," I mutter.

"That's not all," Chloe continues.

I sit up straighter.

"According to Hailey, Claire died in a car accident five years ago, but there were always whispers that it wasn't really an accident. That Julian might have been involved somehow."

My mouth goes dry. "Why are you telling me this?"

"That's the thing, Sloane. Cole and Julian were business partners back then. They ran everything together."

I think of Cole's face when Claire's name came up at dinner the other night. The way his expression had closed off completely.

"Cole isn't like that."

Chloe is quiet for a moment. "Are you sure? I mean, really sure?"

I almost laugh, remembering my paranoid thoughts on that first flight to Switzerland. I'd googled him obsessively, convinced that any man that powerful had to be hiding something. Serial killer had actually crossed my mind—which seemed ridiculous now, but . . . oh god. Had I accidentally stumbled on to something?

No. I shut the thought down immediately. I've seen Cole with his staff, seen how he treats everyone from his executives to the cleaning crew with the same respect. The gentle way he handles my pieces, like they're treasures.

"He's not in the mob, Chloe. And he's definitely not killing people." But even as I say it, I think of how carefully he chooses his words when discussing his past. How much he leaves unsaid. And the way he spoke about Claire, like he'd cared about her deeply. Was it grief? Or guilt?

"Maybe not anymore. But Sloane, you need to be careful. These aren't the kinds of people you want to get tangled up with. And I know this isn't as important," Chloe says quietly, "but Hailey says Julian's been making moves with Bergdorf's. Word is, if this keeps up, Cole Asher might not have his hold with them for your launch much longer. Rumors of a possible delay so Julian can launch first with his line. Are you sure Midnight Frost is scheduled as—"

"Wait." Her words hit me. "Are you asking if there's still going to be a launch for my collection?"

"Is it on schedule for the first of the year like you think?"

I actually laugh at that.

"Look, I might not be able to swear the man isn't secretly storing bodies somewhere, but I can absolutely guarantee he's on schedule. The man runs a tight ship."

"Okay, okay," Chloe says, sounding convinced. "But Sloane." Chloe's voice gets serious. "What are you going to do?"

I sink deeper into the couch. "I don't know. Am I being stupid? Should I pack up my studio and run?" I pause, thinking of the winter collection, of the resources at my fingertips, of Cole's complete faith in my vision. "This is the opportunity of a lifetime, Chloe."

"Yeah, if it doesn't get you killed."

"You really think I'm in danger?"

"I think . . ." She sighs. "I think you need to be very, very careful about what you're walking into. Keep your eyes open. And most importantly, protect your heart."

My mind is spinning, my heart is sinking . . . Oh. My. God.

"Or," she adds after a moment, "you could just ask him."

I snort. "Right. How exactly do I bring that up? 'Hey, baby, amazing sex last night. Quick question—do you know anything about your business partner's wife's suspicious death?'"

"I'm serious."

"So am I. There's no casual way to ask the man you're sleeping with if he's involved in something like that."

"Look, all I'm saying is be smart about this. You're already in deep with the collection, and now you're sleeping with him . . ." Chloe trails off. "Just don't let either blind you to any red flags."

"I know." I rub my temples. "I hear you. I do."

"By the way," I ask, trying to sound casual, "have you heard anything more from Maya lately? I still haven't heard a word from her."

"Actually, that's another thing I wanted to tell you," Chloe says, her voice dropping. "She's still completely MIA. Apparently one of her friends has reached out to her family. They haven't heard anything either."

My stomach knots tighter. "That's . . . not good."

"I know. And with everything else going on . . ."

"You think there's a connection?" The suggestion sounds paranoid even to my ears, but I can't shake the uneasy feeling.

"I don't know," Chloe admits. "But the timing is weird, right? She vanishes right when you start working with Cole?"

I swallow hard. "Maybe it's just a coincidence."

"Maybe. But be careful, okay?"

"I will."

"Call me tomorrow? And I mean actually call me this time, not ghost me for days while you're getting laid."

"God, you're terrible." But I'm smiling. "I promise. Tomorrow."

"I mean it, Sloane."

"I know you do. Thank you for looking out for me."

After hanging up, I sit there for a long moment, letting everything sink in. Julian Voss. Underground crime rings. Murder. It sounds absurd. Like something out of a movie.

And now Maya, vanished after taking a mysterious new job. The timing makes me feel ill. Is it connected? Or am I letting paranoia take over?

Finally, I push myself up and return to my workstation, immediately aware of the cameras mounted in each corner of my studio.

I pick up my tools, trying to focus on the necklace in front of me, but my hands aren't steady. The cameras had taken some getting used to. I'd justified them—after all, I'm handling pieces worth more than most people's homes. Security makes sense. But now my imagination is running wild. What if this whole setup—the penthouse, the studio, the cameras—is something more sinister?

Jesus Christ, Sloane. Stop watching true crime documentaries.

I force the ridiculous thoughts away, but I can't quite shake the unease as the red recording light blinks steadily. Cole's watching. He always is. Is he in his office right now, splitting his attention between some multimillion-dollar deal and my live feed? The thought used to make me smile. Now it makes my stomach twist.

I set down my tools. The precious stones scatter across my workspace, catching the light. Just like everything else in my life right now—beautiful, valuable, and sharp enough to draw blood.

I glance around my studio, then at my room down the hall. The room that had been waiting for me when I returned from Switzerland, filled with every single thing from my apartment—clothes organized in custom closets, books arranged on built-in shelves, even my ratty old college sweatshirt folded neatly in a drawer. He'd moved it all while I was gone, an entire life relocated in a single night. No discussion, no warning. I'd been too overwhelmed by everything else to question it at the time.

I hit Redial before I can talk myself out of it.

"Seriously?" Chloe answers, laughing. "It's been like thirty seconds."

"I'm spiraling. I need to talk more . . . Quick hypothetical," I say, keeping my voice barely above a whisper, one hand cupped over my mouth. I have no idea if the cameras pick up audio, or if Cole or his security team can read lips. Better safe than sorry. "What if I needed to leave?"

"Leave as in . . . ?"

"*Leave* leave. All of it."

"Oh shit." Her voice drops. "The designs?"

I look at the necklace pieces spread across my workspace. The winter collection—*my* winter collection. Except it's not really mine, is it? None of it is. The materials, the studio, even the tools I'm using—it all belongs to Cole. I signed something about that, didn't I? Pages of legal documents I'd carefully read, too excited about the opportunity to worry about the fine print.

I try to imagine packing up, sneaking out in the middle of the night like some stupid movie scene. The thought makes me laugh out loud—partly because it's ridiculous, partly because I know I couldn't do it. Not just because of the legal mess it would create, but because . . . I don't want to.

"He's never given me any reason not to trust him," I say.

"Except the maybe-murder thing?"

"That's not him. That's Julian. And we don't even know if that's true."

"You know," Chloe says dryly, "most people wait at least an hour before calling back with their murder-related anxiety."

I think about Cole bringing me coffee in the mornings, asking questions about my design process, genuinely interested in understanding how I work. The way he geeks out over engineering specs with the manufacturing team. How he notices when I'm stuck on a design and gives me space to work through it.

Those aren't the actions of someone playing an elaborate game. Are they?

"You know . . . like I said," Chloe says after a moment, "you could just ask him."

"I told you, you can't just blurt out something like this," I hiss into the phone. "What am I supposed to say? 'Hey Cole, quick question—are you involved with the mob? Also, why are there cameras everywhere? Oh, and by the way, moving all my stuff without asking was kind of weird.' He's going to think I'm insane. Or worse, he'll be offended that I even considered . . ."

"Not exactly what I meant." I can hear her rolling her eyes. "But yeah, actually. Talk to him. About everything. That's kind of how relationships work."

"Okay, okay, I'll talk to him," I say. "I need to anyway—I'm drowning with this deadline. I could really use an assistant to help with the collection. Maybe he'll let me bring someone on."

"Oh!" Chloe's voice brightens. "You need Hailey. She's an incredible designer and I've worked with her before—she does these amazing gothic-inspired pieces. I've worn some of her stuff in my shoots. She's between projects right now."

I hesitate, and Chloe adds quickly, "Trust me, she's perfect for what you're doing. Her aesthetic is exactly what your collection needs."

I think about some of the dramatic pieces Chloe has worn in her photos—beautiful but with a dangerous elegance to them. Perfect for what the Midnight Frost collection is becoming. "Wait a minute. Wouldn't Hailey be crazy to work here after everything she found out?"

"Are you kidding?" Chloe snorts. "When I mentioned you

might need help, she literally said 'Potential mob ties and a chance to design luxury jewelry? That's literally my jam.'"

"You're kidding."

"Nope. She also said something about how the fashion industry is basically organized crime anyway, so at least this would be being honest about it."

"Oh my god." I'm trying not to laugh. "She's insane."

"She's perfect is what she is. Plus, she figures if things go south, she can always use it as inspiration for her next collection. 'Confessions of a Mob Jeweler' or something."

I shake my head. "Can you ask her? Maybe you both could come by later if Cole's security team approves it?"

"Of course. See? This is what happens when you actually call me back instead of ghosting me for days."

"Yeah, yeah." I smile despite everything. "I'll talk to Cole about all of it—Hailey, Julian, everything."

"Good. That's what normal people do, you know. They talk about things."

"I'm hanging up now."

"Love you too. And Sloane? It'll be okay."

I end the call and stare at the cameras again. Talk to him. Simple advice. Impossible execution. How exactly does one start a conversation about potential murder connections over morning coffee?

Chapter Twenty-Two

SLOANE

Late into the night, I'm still at my workstation, thinking about Hailey. I've always hated the idea of collaborating—design is personal, intimate. But with this impossible deadline looming, I don't have much choice, and getting it cleared with Cole hopefully won't be an issue. And maybe having someone else here wouldn't be the worst thing, especially someone whose work I've actually admired. The few pieces of Hailey's I've seen in Chloe's photos have that edge I've been trying to capture—that understanding that beauty doesn't always have to be vanilla in nature. Fresh eyes might be exactly what this collection needs.

Through the studio windows, I watch snow starting to fall over the city's Christmas lights. Perfect conditions for frost . . . and something a little more dangerous.

I pick up the centerpiece of what will be the signature necklace. The diamonds are arranged like icicles, but with an asymmetrical edge that makes them look almost like broken glass. Between them, black rhodium-plated thorns twist and curl. It's winter, but not the soft, dreamy kind. This is the winter that kills.

A soft knock at the door pulls me from my thoughts.

"Sloane? May I come in?" Cole's voice carries through the door.

"Yes, come in," I call out.

The studio door opens, and I catch Cole's reflection in my design mirror. He's still in his suit from work.

"You're here late," he says, resting a hand on the back of my chair.

"Lost track of time." I glance up at him in the mirror. "Board meeting run long?"

He picks up one of the sketches instead of answering, studying the way the thorns wrap around the diamonds. "The design's evolved."

"I'm getting there. I'm starting to see the light at the end of the tunnel with this line."

His fingers trail along the edge of my worktable, stopping near the intricate tangle of metal and stones. "Show me your latest."

I reach for the centerpiece, aware of his warmth at my back, his breath stirring my hair. I hold up the necklace, letting the stones catch the light. The thorns cast strange shadows, making the diamonds look like they're floating in darkness.

"It's becoming something wilder," I say, remembering our argument at dinner. "Not quite what you had in mind when you wanted me to prioritize the bracelet, is it?"

His lips quirk into a half-smile. "I was wrong. This is exactly where your focus needed to be."

I can't help the smug grin that spreads across my face. "I'm sorry, what was that? Cole Asher admitting he was wrong?"

"Don't push it," he warns, but there's heat in his eyes that makes my stomach flip. His hand slides from my chair to my shoulder, fingers working at a knot there.

Just ask him. That's what normal people do, right? Hey Cole, quick question—what really happened with Julian and Claire Voss?

His thumb works another knot in my shoulder and my eyes flutter closed. The question about Claire dissolves on my tongue.

God, that's unfair. How am I supposed to interrogate someone when they're basically turning my brain to mush?

"You like being right, don't you?" Cole murmurs, his voice dropping to that register that makes it hard to think straight.

"It happens so often, I've gotten used to it," I manage to reply, trying to sound casual despite the way his touch is short-circuiting my brain.

His chuckle is low and so deliciously dangerous. "That kind of talk might work out here, but in the bedroom . . ." He leans closer, his lips brushing my ear. "In the bedroom, it'll get you punished."

My breath catches. Julian Voss suddenly seems very distant and unimportant.

Focus, Sloane. The rumors about Claire. Julian's business connection to Cole. The whispers about what might have happened.

"What's going on in that head of yours?" he murmurs, and for a heart-stopping moment I think he's actually reading my mind. But no, he's just noticed me spacing out while having an internal crisis. Which is probably better than knowing I'm mentally rehearsing how to ask about his ex–business partner without ruining everything between us.

Just say something. Anything. Open your mouth and—

He slides my hair aside and kisses my neck.

—and apparently make a small noise that definitely isn't words because holy hell, that's distracting.

This is ridiculous. I'm ridiculous. The man's probably just a regular billionaire with regular billionaire secrets. Like tax evasion. Or a private island. Or a collection of rare sports cars he never drives.

"I should finish this," I manage, gesturing vaguely at my workspace and trying to remember what exactly I was working on. Something about winter. And diamonds. And definitely not about how good he smells or how that suit fits him or—

"It'll still be here tomorrow." His voice has that low, rough edge that makes my stomach flip. "Come to bed, Sloane."

Right. Bed.

He nips lightly at my earlobe.

This is so not fair.

"Ten minutes," I say, proud that my voice sounds almost normal. "I just need to finish this one thing."

"Ten minutes," he agrees, straightening up. His fingers trail across my shoulders as he steps away. "Then I'm coming back to get you."

I nod, not trusting my voice. He turns and leaves, and I collapse back in my chair.

I catch my reflection in the design mirror—flushed cheeks, bright eyes, that look that says I'm absolutely going to allow this man to ruin me tonight.

I can always ask the heavy questions tomorrow. Get the real story about Julian, clear up all these ridiculous theories. But tonight? Tonight I think I'll let myself enjoy the mystery. After all, what's one more night of sin with a man who's probably-almost-definitely not a criminal? One more night of loving that dangerous glint in his eye.

Besides, good girls who play it safe don't get to design winter collections worth millions. Maybe it's time I embrace my darker side. Just for tonight.

The cameras blink steadily in each corner, and I smile at my reflection. My mother always said I had terrible taste in men. Might as well prove her right in spectacular fashion.

Nine minutes . . .

Eight minutes . . .

I force my attention back to the necklace. The thorns need to be sharper, more threatening. I adjust one with my pliers, trying to ignore how the shadows make them look like claws reaching for—

Seven minutes . . .

Focus. Work. Deadlines. Very important things that have nothing to do with the way his hand felt on my shoulder or how his voice gets lower when he—

Six minutes . . .

I actually manage to make progress on the piece, right up until I remember how his fingers trace my designs the same way they trace my skin and—Damn it.

Five minutes . . .

"Screw it." I set down my tools with maybe a little too much force. The gems scatter across my workspace like drops of frozen rain, but I'm already standing, already moving.

Bad decisions never looked so good in Tom Ford.

I hit the studio lights on my way out, leaving the winter collection sleeping in darkness. Only the cameras stay awake, their red lights steady and watchful.

Chapter Twenty-Three

SLOANE

I push open the door to Cole's bedroom. The room is dim, lit only by the city lights streaming through the floor-to-ceiling windows. He's waiting for me, standing in the center of the room, his posture rigid with tension.

His eyes lock onto mine—dark, predatory, possessive. Without a word, he crosses the space between us in three long strides. Before I can even speak, his hand is at my throat, not squeezing but asserting control as he backs me against the door, slamming it shut with my body.

"I've been waiting," he says, his voice tight with restraint.

I can't breathe, not from his grip but from the intensity radiating from him in waves. This isn't the Cole from the workroom. This is something else entirely—something primal and unleashed.

"I'm sorry I made you wait," I manage, my voice barely a whisper.

His thumb traces my lower lip, rough. "Time is valuable to me, Sloane. When I want something, I don't like waiting." His eyes darken further. "And right now, what I want is you."

He rips my blouse open, buttons scattering across the hardwood floor. I gasp at the sudden violence of it, electricity shooting through my veins. His mouth is on my neck, biting hard enough to mark me, his hands tearing at my clothes with a desperation that matches the desire building inside me.

"Making me wait has consequences," he growls against my skin. "Tonight, I own every second of your time to make up for it."

I surrender completely, letting him strip me bare in the entryway. His hand tangles in my hair, yanking my head back to expose my throat to him. The pain transforms into pleasure as his teeth graze my pulse point.

"Say it," he demands.

"You own me," I breathe, and something feral flashes in his eyes.

He lifts me, my legs wrapping instinctively around his waist as he carries me to the bed. The sheets feel cool against my back as he throws me down, but my skin is burning everywhere he's touched me.

"Don't move," he commands, and I freeze, watching as he strips, revealing the hard planes of his body, the evidence of how much he wants me.

His eyes never leave mine. There's something different about him tonight. Something dangerous that should terrify me but only makes me want him more. All I can think about is Cole.

His touch, his taste, the way he's looking at me like he wants to devour me whole.

From a hidden panel in the wall, Cole removes what looks like a leather case. His movements are deliberate, almost ritualistic as he opens it on the nightstand. I catch glimpses of metal and leather before he turns to me, something glinting in his hand.

"Stand up," he orders, voice leaving no room for argument.

I rise on shaky legs, my nakedness making me feel vulnerable. He circles me slowly, appraising, before stopping behind me.

Cold metal touches my spine, making me gasp. "Do you know what this is?" he asks, tracing the object down my vertebrae.

I shake my head, unable to form words as anticipation twists inside me.

"It's a Wartenberg wheel," he explains, voice clinical yet somehow deeply erotic. "Used to test nerve responses." He rolls it across my shoulder blade, the tiny spikes sending electric sensations through my body without breaking skin. "Every nerve ending . . ." he continues, bringing it around to trail across my collarbone, ". . . awakened."

My breathing becomes shallow as he traces it down between my breasts, the pinpricks of sensation making me arch toward him involuntarily.

"Pain and pleasure," he murmurs, "separated by the thinnest of lines."

The wheel travels lower, circling my navel, then along the sensitive skin of my hip. I'm trembling now, not from fear but from a desire so intense it's overwhelming me.

"This tool," he says, rolling the wheel in slow patterns across my abdomen, "allows me to map every sensitive spot on your body. To learn exactly where"—he drags it lightly across my inner thigh, making me gasp—"you respond most intensely."

He continues his meticulous exploration, the pinwheel creating trails of sensation across my skin. When he brings it to the curve where my thigh meets my hip, I can't suppress a moan.

"Interesting," he murmurs, returning the wheel to the same spot, applying slightly more pressure. The sensation intensifies, making me jerk. "The body remembers. Every nerve ending I awaken becomes more responsive."

He moves behind me again, running the wheel across my shoulders, down my spine, over the curve of my ass. Each path leaves a trail of tingling awareness in its wake, as if he's drawing a map of my sensitivity.

"On the bed," he commands. "On your back."

I comply instantly, positioning myself as ordered. Cole returns to the leather case and produces what looks like leather cuffs attached to a long metal bar.

"Do you know what this is?" he asks, his voice a low rumble.

I shake my head, though I have some idea.

"A spreader bar," he explains. "It keeps you open for me. Available."

He fastens the leather cuffs around my ankles, the bar between them forcing my legs apart. I've never felt so exposed, so completely vulnerable.

"Perfect," he murmurs, standing back to admire his work. His gaze is possessive as it rakes over my displayed form. "Now you can't close your legs, no matter how intense the sensations get."

The implication of his words causes my stomach to clench. He returns to his case of implements and comes back with the Wartenberg wheel. The metal catches the dim light as he approaches.

"Now," he says, his voice thick with desire, "we continue our exploration."

He starts at my ankle, just above where the cuff holds me open, and slowly, methodically works his way up my calf. The pinpricks of the wheel are more intense now, as if my skin has become hypersensitive to his touch. When he reaches my inner thigh, he slows even further, making smaller patterns, working inward with agonizing precision.

"Please," I gasp, my body straining against the spreader bar, desperate for relief.

"Please what?" he asks, pausing the wheel's movement.

"I need more," I whisper, not even caring how desperate I sound.

"More of this?" He presses the wheel slightly harder into the tender skin of my inner thigh, making me cry out. "Or something else?"

"You," I manage. "I need you."

He shakes his head slowly. "Not yet. I'm not finished learning your body."

He continues his torturous exploration, bringing the wheel to places that make me writhe—the crease where thigh meets body, the sensitive skin below my navel, circling but never quite touching where I need it most. By the time he reaches my breasts, I'm panting, my body slick with sweat, trembling with need.

"The most fascinating aspect of this tool," he says, rolling it around my nipple without quite touching it, "is how it heightens sensitivity. Every place I've touched"—he finally grazes the wheel across my nipple, making me arch and cry out—"becomes more responsive to other stimulation."

To demonstrate, he sets the wheel aside and lowers his mouth to the path he just traced. The sensation is overwhelming—his tongue following the same path as the wheel, but now every nerve ending is awake and screaming for more.

"See?" he murmurs against my skin. "Your body remembers."

He returns to the leather case and brings back what looks like a thin metal rod with a rounded tip.

"And now for something different," he says, plugging it into a socket beside the bed. "The violet wand." He flicks a switch, and the metal tip glows with a purple light. "Electricity," he explains. "Controlled. Precise."

The air around us seems to crackle with tension as he approaches. He doesn't touch me with it immediately, instead hovering it near my already sensitized skin. I can feel the static electricity making the fine hairs on my body stand on end.

"This works especially well," he says, his voice thick with desire, "on skin that's already been awakened by the wheel."

He demonstrates by bringing the wand near my inner thigh, where the wheel had traced its path minutes before. The static discharge makes my muscles contract involuntarily, sending a jolt of sensation through me that's neither pain nor pleasure but somehow both at once.

"Please," I gasp, not even sure what I'm begging for anymore.

"Not yet," he says, his voice strained with his own restraint. "I want you desperate for me."

He continues his methodical exploration, using the wand to follow the paths the wheel created. The electrical current dances across my skin, making my muscles twitch and spasm, drawing sounds from me I didn't know I could make.

When he finally brings the wand near where I need him most, I'm nearly sobbing with need. The proximity of the current makes me buck against the spreader bar.

"Cole, please," I beg. "I can't take any more."

His eyes are nearly black with desire as he sets the wand aside. "Do you understand now?" he asks, his voice rough. "What happens when you make me wait?"

"Yes," I gasp.

"And will you ever do it again?" he demands, positioning himself between my forcibly spread legs.

"No," I promise, though part of me thinks I might, just to experience this again.

A knowing smile crosses his face, as if he can read my thoughts. "Liar," he says, but there's something like approval in his voice.

Without warning, he thrusts into my pussy in one powerful stroke. I cry out, my body arching against the restraints, the sudden fullness from his cock both shocking and exactly what I've been craving. He doesn't give me time to adjust, setting a punishing rhythm that has the headboard slamming against the wall.

"Every nerve ending I awakened," he growls, his hand finding my breast, pinching the nipple he'd sensitized with the wheel, "remembers my touch."

The dual sensation is overwhelming—the fullness of him inside me combined with the heightened sensitivity of my skin. I'm nothing but sensation, consumed entirely by what he's making me feel.

"Look at me as I fuck you," he commands, and I force my eyes open to meet his intense gaze. "Who owns you?"

"You do," I gasp as he drives deeper. "Only you."

His rhythm falters for just a moment, something flashing in his eyes that looks almost like vulnerability before it's gone again, replaced by raw possession. His hand slides between us, finding the bundle of nerves he'd so carefully avoided with his tools.

"Come for me," he commands, his voice strained with the effort of holding back his own release. "Now, Sloane."

My body obeys instantly, convulsing around him as waves of pleasure crash through me. I scream his name, pulling against the spreader bar as my vision whites out from the intensity.

He doesn't slow, prolonging my orgasm until I'm sobbing from overstimulation. Only then does he allow his own release, his rhythm faltering as he groans my name, his body shuddering against mine.

For a moment, the only sound is our ragged breathing. Then Cole reaches down, carefully removing the spreader bar from my ankles. There's an unexpected tenderness in the way he massages feeling back into my legs, checking for any marks from his tools.

"Are you okay?" he asks, his voice gentler than it's been all night.

I nod, unable to form coherent words yet. My body feels completely spent, every nerve ending still tingling from his attention.

Cole pulls me against him, tucking my head under his chin. His heartbeat thunders against my ear, gradually slowing to a steadier rhythm. His fingers trace patterns on my back, soothing now rather than arousing.

"You were perfect," he murmurs against my hair.

I manage to find my voice at last. "I didn't know it could be like that."

He shifts to look down at me, something almost vulnerable

flashing in his eyes before his usual mask returns. "There's a lot you don't know about me yet, Sloane."

The words hold a promise and a warning, but all I can think about is the "yet." The implication that there will be more of this, more of us. I should be frightened by how completely I surrendered to him, by how much I want to do it again. Instead, I feel oddly safe in the arms of the most dangerous man I've ever known.

"Good," I whisper, meeting his gaze steadily. "I want to learn everything."

A slow smile spreads across his face, darkly satisfied. He pulls me closer, his lips brushing my ear. "Next time," he murmurs, "don't keep me waiting."

I don't know what I've gotten myself into with Cole Asher, and in this moment, I don't care. All I know is that I'm completely, irrevocably his. And I've never wanted anything more.

Chapter Twenty-Four

SLOANE

I'm at my worktable early, still buzzing from last night. God, I should be exhausted, but I can't stop designing. My fingers keep touching the spots where the wheel traced over my skin—still sensitive, still tingling. It's like Cole rewired something in me. The chains and metal pieces I've been using in my collection suddenly feel different. Before, they were just cool design elements. Now? They remind me of how it felt to be under his control, to surrender. I'm seeing my own work through new eyes.

I can't explain it, but I'm working faster, everything flowing out of me like I've tapped into something I didn't know was there. Like last night unlocked some creative door I didn't even realize was closed.

Knox's voice startles me out of my focus. "Ms. Whitmore, your guests, Chloe Hallman and Hailey Parker, have arrived."

I hear Chloe's laugh before I see her. When I turn, Knox is already handing out security badges with his usual efficiency.

"Temporary access cards," he explains. "The elevator won't operate without them. Studio and bathroom access only." He gives Chloe a pointed look. "These need to be returned at the end of the day."

"So serious," Chloe says, dangling her badge. "What, afraid I'll throw a wild party up here?"

I hide my smile as Knox ignores her, tapping something on his iPad. "Basic security protocols. Wear these where they're visible. Sign in, sign out. Don't wander." He pauses. "That means you, Ms. Hallman."

"You're no fun at all," Chloe sighs dramatically. "Not even a tiny tour?"

"In case of emergency, follow the exit signs. Fire escape is through there, stairs are that way." He points to each location, deliberately moving past Chloe's request. "Any questions?"

"Actually," I say, catching Knox's eye, "Hailey might be around a lot more. I'm hoping she'll consider taking a position as my assistant for the collection." I glance at Hailey. "If you're interested, that is. Cole gave me the green light earlier. The timeline's tight, but with your expertise . . ."

Knox's posture shifts slightly—barely noticeable, but I've learned to read his subtle changes. He studies Hailey with new attention, probably already mentally updating security protocols.

Hailey is nothing like I expected. I'd pictured all-black clothing and heavy gothic makeup, but she walks in wearing a crisp white shirt and tailored pants like she just stepped out of a business meeting. It's her jewelry that gives her away—an oxidized silver choker with black diamonds, multiple rings climbing up her fingers, and these wicked silver earrings that curve up her ears into points. The contrast shouldn't work, but it does. Her whole look is a master class in making edge look expensive.

She takes one look at my latest designs and gets it immediately. "You're not making jewelry," she says, picking up one of the sharp-edged pieces. "You're making armor."

Something clicks in my mind. That's exactly what I've been trying to do.

"Finally!" Chloe claps her hands together. "Two of my favorite people in the same room. Sloane, this is Hailey Parker. She did that incredible black diamond collection I showed you last month. Hailey, this is Sloane Whitmore, who's about to shake up the entire jewelry world if I have anything to say about it."

"And there's the Chloe Hallman hype machine," Hailey laughs, already moving closer to examine one of my pieces.

"For once, Chloe's not exaggerating," she says. "You understand that beauty doesn't have to play nice."

I grab my sketchbook, then pointedly look at each security camera in the corners of the room. "So, before we get started . . . full disclosure: We have an audience."

Hailey follows my gaze, her smile faltering slightly. "Ah. Right. The cameras."

"Don't worry," I assure her quickly. "He only watches when—" I stop. "Actually, I have no idea when he watches."

"All the time," Chloe says with unholy glee. "He's probably watching right now. Hi, Cole!" She waves at the nearest camera.

"That's . . . comforting?" Hailey shifts in her chair. "I think?"

"You get used to it," I say, then realize that probably doesn't help. "I mean, not in a creepy way. Just in a . . . security thing. Though maybe we keep certain topics off-limits?"

The morning passes in a blur of creative energy and girl talk. While we work, Chloe demands details about living with Cole. "So does he like . . . watch you sleep through the cameras?" she asks.

"Of course not," I say quickly. "No cameras in private spaces. Bedrooms and bathrooms are completely off-limits."

"And here I was hoping to give Cole's security team a show," Chloe says, examining her reflection in one of the display mirrors.

Hailey glances toward the door where Knox had disappeared. "Speaking of the security team . . . is he always so—"

"Intense?" I smile. "He's actually pretty nice once you get past the whole military-precision thing. Just very . . . dedicated to protocols."

"Super dedicated." Chloe wiggles her eyebrows at Hailey. "Did you see how he kept looking at you during that security briefing?"

The morning settles into a rhythm after that. Hailey proves to have an incredible eye for detail, while Chloe moves around the workspace with her phone, documenting everything. She has a gift for finding the perfect angle, the way light catches each stone. "This is going to break Instagram," she says, zooming in on a particularly intricate piece. "We should do a whole series of teaser posts leading up to the show." She's already wearing one of the tiaras—at completely the wrong angle, but somehow she makes it work for the photos.

"This design is amazing," Hailey says, examining one of the new pieces. "Did it come to you last night? The metalwork looks fresh."

Chloe keeps eyeing the cameras while we work, practically vibrating with unasked questions. Finally, she cracks. "Okay, this is torture. We need a camera-free zone." She looks at me meaningfully. "Like, say, your bedroom?"

I know exactly what she's after, but honestly, I need to talk about it too. "Break time?" I suggest, and Chloe's already heading for the door.

The moment my bedroom door closes behind us, Chloe whirls around. "Spill it! Is he with the mafia or not? Serial killer? What deep dark secrets did you learn last night?"

I sink onto my bed, Hailey perching beside me while Chloe paces excitedly. "I . . ." I twist my hands in my lap. "I didn't ask."

"What?" Chloe stops pacing. "You were alone with him all night and you didn't ask about Julian?"

"I meant to!" I protest. "But last night he was . . . very convincing about other topics." I feel my cheeks flush at the memory. "And then this morning he's just . . . This morning he already had coffee waiting—that expensive stuff I love. And breakfast from Le Petit, which I swear I only mentioned once last week. Then he sat there asking about every piece in the collection like he actually cares about the creative process. How am I supposed to bring up potential criminal activities when he's being so . . ."

"Suspiciously perfect?" Chloe supplies with a grin.

"I'm going with genuinely thoughtful," Hailey says, but she's watching me carefully. "Though it might be good to get some answers about the other stuff. Eventually."

"I mean, there has to be something wrong with him, right?" I glance between them. "Nobody's this perfect."

"Tell us everything," Chloe demands, settling cross-legged on the floor. "Start with the date. Hailey hasn't heard about the rooftop yet."

I can't help smiling at the memory, as I tell them every detail.

"Wait," Chloe interrupts as we discuss the rooftop date, "he has heating lamps AND fur blankets? That's not surveillance, that's romance novel hero territory."

We're so caught up in our increasingly inappropriate discussion of Cole's . . . assets . . . that we don't hear him enter. It's only when Chloe asks, "But seriously, what's he like in—" that I notice him leaning in the doorway, eyebrow raised.

The silence is deafening. Then Cole, perfectly deadpan: "Please, don't let me interrupt what I'm sure is a fascinating technical discussion about jewelry design."

I want to die. Chloe, naturally, just grins wider.

"We were just taking a break," I manage, standing up quickly. "Getting back to work now." I clear my throat. "Cole, this is Chloe Hallman—I'd like her to handle all the marketing for the collection if possible. And Hailey Parker, who might be joining us as my assistant."

"A pleasure to meet you both," Cole says with that smile that makes my stomach flip. "I'll have lunch sent up later. Don't work too hard."

The moment he's out of earshot, Chloe fans herself dramatically. "Oh my god," she mouths. I catch Hailey's eyes roll, but even she's smiling. I can't blame them—in that perfectly tailored suit, with his dark hair slightly messy like he's been running his hands through it, Cole looks like he just stepped out of a magazine. The kind you hide under your mattress.

Back in the studio, the afternoon is intensely productive. With Hailey's guidance, I refine three pieces that had been giving me trouble. The collection is taking shape—no longer just pretty winter-inspired jewelry but statements of power and protection. Each piece tells a story of transformation.

As they're packing up for the day, Hailey helps me organize the pieces into a cohesive collection story. "These aren't just accessories," she explains, laying them out in sequence. "They're weapons disguised as beauty. Every woman who wears them will feel invincible. Like an Ice Queen."

Hailey pauses, then turns to me. "Listen, about the assistant position . . . I'd love to take it. After today, I can see exactly where you're going with this collection, and I'd be honored to help bring it to life. If you think we'd work well together?"

"Are you kidding?" I grin. "You've already helped solve three design problems I've been stuck on for days. When can you start?"

Plans are made for Hailey to return tomorrow. Knox arrives to escort them out, and I don't miss how Hailey lingers a bit, or how he stands just a fraction closer to her than strictly necessary in the elevator.

After they leave, I settle back at my worktable, taking out fresh materials for one final piece. The design has been forming in my mind all day—a choker that reflects these new sensations of yielding and taking control. I work methodically, positioning each crystal with precision, creating clean lines that follow the natural curve of the throat. The metalwork is delicate but sturdy, the crystals arranged to refract light in sharp, controlled patterns. As I work, I think about last night, about the way Cole's firm touch made me feel both protected and dangerous. This piece needs to do the same thing—to make the wearer feel secure while serving as a subtle reminder of their own power.

Hours pass as I perfect every detail. When I finally set down my tools, my hands are steady but my neck and shoulders ache from hunching over the workbench. The choker sits complete on my work surface, exactly as I'd envisioned it. Each crystal catches the late afternoon light streaming through the windows, creating small points of brightness on the table. It's more than just a piece of jewelry—it's a statement about choice and control, about finding strength in surrender.

My phone buzzes just as I'm stretching out the knots in my shoulders. A text from Cole: Wear it to dinner.

Chapter Twenty-Five
COLE

'm not a man who celebrates. Celebrations invite chaos, mess, sentiment. But tonight I want to give her something different than our usual perfect dinners.

Earlier, I'd insisted Sloane take a long bubble bath to unwind from her day at the studio. "Take your time getting ready for dinner," I'd told her, kissing her neck. "I have some work calls to handle." The lie came easily—I needed those two hours.

Now I check my watch while directing the last of the decorating crew. They're efficient, I'll give them that—in just under two hours they've transformed the dining room exactly as I'd specified. Crystal strands catch the light from thousands of tiny LED bulbs we've strung across the ceiling. The effect reminds me of ice forming on tree branches after a storm. White flowers cover every surface— lilies, roses, orchids—arranged in crystal vases that echo the pieces in Sloane's collection.

"The temperature control is set," my head of household staff confirms. "The flowers will stay fresh all evening." She hands me the remote for the lighting system. "Will you need anything else, Mr. Asher?"

I'm about to dismiss her when I hear Sloane's bedroom door open. "That's all. Thank you." The staff file out quietly through the service entrance as I turn toward the main hallway.

The sight of her stops me mid-motion. She's wearing a white dress that seems to float around her, but it's the collar that draws my attention—her newest creation sitting perfectly against her throat. The crystals catch the light as she moves, creating small flashes of brilliance against her skin.

Her steps falter when she sees the dining room. For a moment she just stands there, taking it all in—the lights, the flowers, the way everything sparkles. Then her face breaks into a smile that makes my chest tight.

"Cole . . ." She walks slowly into the room, reaching up to touch one of the crystal strands. "This is incredible."

"I wanted it to complement your collection." I move behind her, running my fingers along the collar. "Though this piece outshines everything else."

She leans back against me, and I can feel her pulse quicken under the collar. "I still can't believe you did all this." Her fingers trail over the tablecloth where I've had dinner set up—fine China, crystal glasses, silver that catches the light from above.

"Dinner should be perfect—the chef's preparing everything fresh." I guide her to her chair, pulling it out for her. The sommelier I hired for the evening steps forward to pour the first wine, a rare vintage I've been saving. I watch Sloane's face as she takes her first sip, the way her eyes close briefly in appreciation.

The first course arrives—a delicate creation of winter vegetables and fresh truffle that looks like frost patterns on glass. It's theatrical without being pretentious, exactly what I'd specified. Sloane takes a bite and makes a small sound of pleasure that sends heat down my spine.

"Tell me about your day," I say, partly because I want to know and partly because I love watching her talk when she's excited about something. The collar shifts with each animated gesture, drawing my attention back to her throat.

"Well, Chloe nearly gave Knox an aneurysm," she says, taking another sip of wine. "She kept trying to convince him to give her a full tour of the security setup."

"I saw the footage. I particularly enjoyed when she tried to convince him she needed to inspect the roof for 'marketing purposes.'"

"Of course you saw that." She grins. "Do you just sit in your office watching security feeds all day?"

"Only the entertaining ones." The chef appears with our second course—butter-poached lobster with champagne sauce. "Though I have to admit, your friend Hailey surprised me. She has good instincts."

"About my designs?"

"About security. She noticed the camera blind spots within ten minutes of arriving. Knox was impressed."

"Is that why he kept hovering around while giving her the security briefing?"

I raise an eyebrow. "You noticed that too?"

"Please. Even Chloe noticed, and she was too busy trying to sneak into restricted areas to notice much of anything." She takes a bite of the lobster and closes her eyes. "Oh my god, this is incredible."

"Thibeaux studied in Paris for fifteen years." I watch her savor another bite. "But you're changing the subject. Tell me more about what you're working on with Hailey."

She launches into an explanation of her latest designs, pausing only when the next course arrives—a small plate of perfectly seared scallops with winter citrus. Her enthusiasm is contagious. I find myself asking questions about the creative process, genuinely interested in how her mind works.

"You actually care about all this, don't you?" she asks suddenly.

"Of course I do. Why do you sound surprised?"

"Most people's eyes glaze over after about thirty seconds of jewelry talk. Even my family starts checking their phones when I get going."

"I'm not most people." I signal for more wine. "Besides, I like watching you talk about things you're passionate about. You get this look in your eyes . . ."

"What look?"

"Like you're seeing something no one else can see yet. It's . . ." I search for the right word. "Compelling."

A slight blush colors her cheeks. "Now you're just trying to charm me."

"Is it working?"

"Maybe." She eyes the next course as it arrives—venison with roasted root vegetables. There's a moment of hesitation before she speaks. "So . . . about earlier today . . ."

"When I walked in on what was clearly not a jewelry design meeting?"

"Did you hear . . . ?" She trails off, unable to finish the question.

"Just the sudden silence." I take a sip of wine, watching her. "Though the looks on all three of your faces were quite telling."

She pushes her food around her plate, clearly wrestling with something. "We were talking about you, actually." Her voice is careful, measured. "About some things Hailey's heard. About you and your ex-partner . . . Julian Voss." She shifts in her seat. "And how he was married to Claire."

I keep my expression neutral, though my grip tightens slightly on my wineglass. "And what exactly has Hailey heard?"

"That Julian . . ." She hesitates, then takes a long sip of wine. "That he's involved in some pretty dark stuff. Underground crime rings. The kind of business deals that don't end with lawyers but with . . ." She trails off, clearly uncomfortable with finishing that sentence.

"I see." My voice gives nothing away.

"But I need to know, Cole. About Julian and Claire. About you."

The question hangs in the air between us. I consider my next words carefully, watching the collar shift against her throat as she swallows. "Some questions are better left unasked, Sloane."

"And some answers I need to hear." Her voice is quiet but firm. "If we're going to . . ." She gestures between us, at the romantic setup I've created, at everything unsaid.

I consider my wineglass for a moment. "Julian does business with bad people. Yes." I watch her process this. "And no, I don't. Though I'm sure there are plenty of rumors suggesting otherwise."

Sloane remains quiet, but I can tell that she's not satisfied with my answer. She needs more.

"I made choices I'm not proud of. When you're young and ambitious, it's easy to justify certain decisions. To tell yourself the end justifies the means." I meet her gaze directly. "Until one day you realize you've become something you never meant to be."

"What changed?"

"Power is seductive. The more you get, the more you want. And when you're good at taking what you want . . ." I pause, choosing my words carefully. "Julian and I, we were very good at it. Every victory made the next one easier to justify. Every compromised deal made the next compromise smaller. You tell yourself it's just business, just strategy. That fear is more efficient than trust."

I take a slow sip of wine, feeling the weight of her gaze.

"Julian thrived on it. The more brutal the strategy, the more he enjoyed the execution. He started attracting attention from people who appreciated his methods. People who saw violence as a business tool." My jaw tightens. "I was no better, for a while. Until I realized we weren't climbing to the top anymore. We were sinking."

"That's why you ended the partnership?"

"I forced him out. Made it clear he had no choice. Then I redirected the company, cut ties with certain clients. Julian didn't take it well. He thought I was betraying everything we'd built." I watch her face carefully. "He wasn't entirely wrong. I did betray his vision of what we could become. I just couldn't be that person anymore."

"And Claire? Was she part of all this?"

I feel my expression darken. "Claire was his wife, but she was never part of his methods. She was a brilliant jewelry designer who believed in ethical sourcing. When I discovered Julian was using blood diamonds and smuggled gems in some of the pieces, I felt she deserved to know."

"So you told her," Sloane says softly.

"I did. She was devastated. Planned to leave him, take her designs with her. She gave me her portfolio for safekeeping. The last collection she designed before . . ." I trail off, the memory still raw.

"Before her accident," Sloane finishes for me.

"That wasn't an accident." The words come out harder than I intended. "Julian found out she was leaving. That she knew everything. Her car going off that cliff was too convenient, too clean. The investigation found nothing, but I know Julian was behind it."

"You have proof?" Her eyes are wide now.

"Nothing concrete. Just a lifetime of knowing how he operates." My voice drops. "If I'd known what he was planning, I would have done anything to stop it. Anything to save her. By the time I realized what happened, it was too late."

She's quiet for a moment, absorbing this. "Is that why there's all this security? Because of him?"

For a moment, I debate telling her the whole truth about the cameras. That while Julian may be the catalyst *now*, I've found other . . . benefits. Like watching her work in her studio, completely lost in her creative process. Or catching the way she dances around her kitchen making coffee in the morning. I decide that admitting to what amounts to high-tech voyeurism might not be the best move over a romantic dinner. Some conversations are better saved for . . . never.

"Julian isn't the type to let go of grudges. Or power." I gesture to one of the cameras. "Knox's protocols might seem extreme, but they're necessary. Julian's made it clear he hasn't forgotten what he considers a betrayal."

"Do you think he's dangerous?"

"I think he's patient. And well-connected." I watch her hand move unconsciously to the collar at her throat. "Having something to lose makes you more careful."

The weight of that statement settles between us. She takes a long drink of wine, then sets the glass down with surprising firmness. "Well, I hope he knows I don't respond well to intimidation."

The unexpected steel in her voice catches me off guard. I feel something in my chest tighten—pride mixed with concern. "No," I say softly, "you certainly don't."

She straightens in her chair. "So what now? We just . . . keep having these perfect dinners while waiting for your ex–business partner to cause trouble?"

She's accepting the sanitized version of my past, not pushing for details I'd rather not share. The exact nature of those "business deals," the lengths Julian and I went to. The things I justified in the name of power.

"Well, we should probably discuss contingency plans," she says, pouring more wine down her throat. "You know, in case Julian ever goes full movie villain, and I end up tied to a chair in some warehouse. I'm thinking I'll distract him with a kick to the balls, and you can handle the rest."

I try not to smile. "You've given this some thought."

"I mean, clearly not enough, since my plan starts and ends with kicking him in the balls. But it's a work in progress."

Her attempt at humor hits its mark, but I can see the tension in her shoulders, the way her fingers keep tracing the rim of her wineglass. She's processing everything I've told her, trying to reconcile the man who arranged this evening with the one who used to work with Julian. I understand her need to make sense of it all, but I didn't create this night to dwell on the past.

I lean back in my chair, studying her face in the crystalline light. "I think we've given Julian enough of our evening." My tone softens. "Besides, the pastry chef will be devastated if we let his creation get cold."

On cue, servers appear with covered silver dishes. They lift the lids to reveal delicate chocolate soufflés, still warm and gently rising. The rich scent of dark chocolate fills the air.

"You planned this timing perfectly, didn't you?" Sloane picks up her spoon.

"Breaking into the soufflé while it's still warm is essential." I watch as she takes her first bite. Her eyes close briefly.

"This might be better than the lobster," she says, going back for another spoonful. "Though I'm starting to think you're trying to spoil me."

"Is that a complaint?"

We finish dessert in comfortable silence. When she sets down her spoon, I stand and offer my hand.

"Dance with me?"

She raises an eyebrow. "There's no music."

I pull out my phone and tap the screen. The opening notes of "Have Yourself a Merry Little Christmas" drift through the room, slow and sultry.

She looks up at me, a smile playing at her lips. "Someone's feeling festive."

I draw her close, sliding one hand to the small of her back. "Not normally," I admit. "But you seem to bring it out in me." Her hand settles on my shoulder, and I can feel the warmth of her skin through my shirt.

We move together, and I'm struck by how perfectly she fits against me. The crystal collar gleams at her throat, but it's the curve of her smile that holds my attention. Her fingers trace small patterns on my shoulder as we turn, and I find myself following her lead as much as she follows mine.

The music shifts to "The Christmas Song," and the familiar opening line about chestnuts roasting on an open fire fills the room. Sloane hums along softly. I press my cheek against her hair, breathing in her scent. For someone who's built his life on control and precision, this feeling is dangerous—this urge to forget everything but the woman in my arms.

"Cole?" she murmurs against my chest.

"Mm?"

"Thank you for tonight," she murmurs. "For telling me about Julian." Her lips quirk up. "Not every romantic dinner includes an interrogation."

I tilt her chin up, caught between amusement and something deeper. "Not exactly the conversation I planned when I had them string up all these lights."

"No?" Her eyes meet mine, gentle but unflinching. "I'm glad you told me anyway."

Looking at her now, I realize she's the first person I've wanted to be honest with in years. The first person who's heard the truth about Julian and is still here, swaying in my arms, looking at me like I'm someone worth trusting. Someone worth loving.

The music shifts to "Winter Wonderland," and Sloane laughs softly against my chest. "You know, for someone with such a carefully maintained reputation, you can be surprisingly sentimental."

"Don't tell anyone." I draw her closer as we turn. "I have an image to maintain."

She lifts her head, meeting my gaze. "Your secret's safe with me." There's something in her eyes that makes my chest tighten—trust, despite everything I've told her. Or maybe because of it.

I brush my thumb across her cheek, and she leans into my touch. When I kiss her, she tastes like chocolate and wine, and I feel her smile against my lips. For once in my life, I stop analyzing, stop planning, stop thinking about what comes next. There's just this—Sloane in my arms, snow falling outside, and Christmas jazz playing softly in a room full of lights.

Chapter Twenty-Six
SLOANE

The soft jazz fills Cole's penthouse as we sway together by the fireplace. His hand rests lightly on my lower back, warm through the thin fabric of my dress. After our intense dinner conversation about Julian and Claire, this feels like needed relief—a moment to breathe, to be normal. But my mind is racing faster than my heart as we sway to the music.

When the song ends and the room becomes silent, I step back, needing some space. My gaze wanders to the grand piano in the corner, gleaming in the low light. I walk over, drawn to it almost unconsciously.

"Do you play?" Cole asks, following me.

"Badly." My fingers ghost over the keys without pressing them. "Though this is nicer than the upright I learned on."

"Play something," he says.

I shake my head. "I told you, I'm terrible."

"Play anyway." He sits on the bench, leaving space for me. "I promise not to judge. Much."

I hesitate, then join him. My shoulder brushes his as I position my hands. The moment my fingers touch the keys, something shifts in my posture. I start with what I know are the opening bars of Beethoven's "Moonlight Sonata"—precise, controlled, technically correct—before abruptly switching to a jazz rendition that would no doubt have given my old piano teacher a heart attack. There's this mischievous little smile on my face as I move further away from Beethoven.

My hands move with surprising confidence, like they've been waiting for permission to break the rules. I catch him staring, and my smile fades a bit—like I just remembered I'm showing him a side of myself most people don't get to see.

"My mom used to play the piano," he says quietly. "Every Christmas Eve. She believed she wasn't very good either, but she loved it. Said music didn't have to be perfect to be beautiful."

My hands still on the keys. "My mother was the opposite." Something in my voice makes him turn to study my profile. "Everything had to be perfect. Piano lessons, skating, grades . . ." I press a key softly. "She meant well, I think. Wanted me to have every advantage she didn't. But nothing was ever quite good enough."

"Is that why you stopped playing?"

"No. Well, maybe." My fingers start dancing across the keys again, this time playing fragments of Christmas carols that dissolve into improvised melodies that have nothing to do with the original tune. "I had this teacher, Mrs. Caldwell. Ancient woman, smelled like mothballs. She'd rap my knuckles with a ruler when I tried adding my own flourishes." I laugh softly. "My mother was horrified when I quit formal lessons at sixteen. Even more horrified when she caught me playing pop songs by ear."

"And now?"

"Now I rarely play at all." I glance down at the keys. "Though she still asks me to play for family gatherings. I usually find an excuse."

"Let me guess. She wants Chopin, and you want to play Chappell Roan?"

"It drives her absolutely insane. She calls it 'noodling around.' "

I trail off, my expression distant as my playing softens. The melody becomes almost melancholy. I recognize that look in his eyes.

The weight of expectations never quite met.

"What excuse did you use for not going home for Christmas this year?" he asks.

"Work." A faint smile touches my lips. "Which isn't exactly a lie now, is it?"

"She's still waiting for me to follow a more traditional path," I continue quietly. "Dad's a surgeon—the practical choice was always very clearly marked. She keeps sending me job listings for corporate design firms. Places with 401(k)s and dental plans."

"Not exactly what you're looking for?" he asks, watching how my fingers still move restlessly across the keys, unable to stay within the lines even in conversation.

"God no," I say with a laugh that's laced with half frustration. "My mom's all about structure and planning. Like, her entire life is color-coded in her planner. Meanwhile, I'm over here with fifty browser tabs open and my best ideas scribbled on coffee-stained napkins." I hit a discordant note deliberately. "She nearly had an aneurysm when she saw my apartment. Called it 'chaotic' like it was the worst insult she could think of. Calls *me* chaotic."

"And are you? Chaotic?"

"Totally. But that's where all the good stuff happens. In the mess, you know? My brain just doesn't work in straight lines." I shrug. "I just want to create something that matters." My fingers trace the edge of a key. "Something that's mine."

I play a final chord that lingers in the air between us. The vulnerability of the moment suddenly feels too intense, so I stand from the bench and move toward the living area.

"Your turn," I say, curling into the corner of the sofa. "Tell me about your first business deal."

He settles beside me, his laugh low and self-deprecating. "It was a complete disaster."

"How bad?"

"I tried to negotiate a software contract thinking I knew everything about everything. I was twenty-two, arrogant, and completely out of my depth." He shakes his head. "Lost the deal and nearly bankrupted my first start-up in the process."

"What happened?"

"I learned. Quickly." His eyes fix on the city below. "Started over. Built something stronger." He turns to me with that hint of a smile. "What about you? First real heartbreak?"

"Oh god." I take a sip of wine. "Junior year of college. He was in the business program, very practical, very focused. Told me my jewelry was 'too artistic' for his taste. That I should consider something more . . . commercial."

"Please tell me you didn't."

"Better. I designed an entire collection inspired by how much I wanted to strangle him. Won my first major award with it."

Cole's laugh echoes against the windows. "Of course you did."

"What about you? First million?"

His expression shifts to something more contemplative. "By twenty-five. Lost it all by twenty-six."

"What happened?"

"Market crash. Bad investments. Every mistake you can make when you think you're invincible." He takes a slow sip of wine. "Made it back triple by twenty-seven."

"Just like that?"

"Nothing worth having comes 'just like that.'" The city lights catch in his eyes. "But yes. Once I understood what I'd done wrong, the path back was clear."

"Failure teaches you more than success?" I guess.

His smirk returns, wolfish in the dim light. "But success is significantly more comfortable."

Something clicks into place as we talk. The drive I see in him, the relentless pursuit of excellence—it mirrors my own. We're both self-made, both pushing against the world's expectations. No wonder he understands my late nights in the studio, my need to prove myself. He's lived it too, just on a different scale.

A comfortable silence falls between us as we watch the snow drift past the windows, coating the city in white. I find myself shifting closer, drawn to his warmth, and Cole lifts his arm in silent invitation. I curl against his side, feeling the steady rise and fall of his chest.

"This view never gets old," I murmur, watching the flakes swirl in the lights from surrounding buildings.

"Mm." His fingers find their way into my hair, absently playing with the strands. After a moment, he speaks again, his voice softer than before. "My first Christmas in the city, I was sixteen."

Something in his tone makes me stay quiet, waiting.

"I bought myself a tiny plastic tree from a drugstore," he continues, his voice distant with memory. "It was hideous. Perfect act of rebellion."

I glance around at the crystalline winter wonderland he's created. "Guess your war on real Christmas trees started early."

"We've been through this," he says, his tone gentle but firm.

"I know, I know. The mess." I sigh, unable to let it go. "But imagine it, Cole. Right there." I point to the empty corner by the window. "A seven-footer with that perfect pine smell. My mom always said a real tree brings the whole room together."

"And brings half the forest floor with it," he counters, but his eyes soften slightly.

"I'd clean up every single needle myself," I promise. "And we wouldn't do anything fancy—just some colored lights. Not white, they're too sterile. And a few special ornaments. Nothing matching or coordinated." I can picture it so clearly: "Like this glass star my grandmother gave me before she died, and this ridiculous wooden moose my brother made in shop class."

He raises an eyebrow. "Sounds like you've thought about this."

"Maybe a little," I admit. "Or a lot."

"It still doesn't change the fact that—"

"That you're impossibly stubborn?" I cut him off with a small smile.

His laugh is soft and warm, and as he draws me closer, I realize something that probably should terrify me but doesn't: I'm falling for him. Not despite his revelations about his past, but partly because of them. Because he's trusted me with the truth, even knowing it might change how I see him.

What does that say about me? That I'm sitting here in the arms of a man who's just admitted to a past that should send me running, and all I can think about is how much I want to stay?

Maybe I'm crazy. Maybe this whole situation is crazy. But as Cole's fingers trace patterns on my skin and the snow falls outside in silent swirls, I can't bring myself to care.

"So what would you have done?" he asks suddenly, and I can hear the hint of amusement in his voice. "If I had turned out to be a serial killer?"

"Well," I say, shifting to face him better, "I've never had sex with a serial killer before, so that would have been interesting."

"That you know of." His voice drops lower.

"True story." I let my fingers trail along his arm. "Though I have to say, you're doing pretty well in the dark and mysterious department without the murder."

His eyes darken as his grip tightens slightly. "If you want dark," he murmurs against my ear, "I don't have to kill anyone to make that happen."

The promise in his voice sends heat racing through me. "Prove it."

His response is to pull me fully into his lap, one hand tangling in my hair while the other finds the zipper of my dress.

"I have something for you," he says, licking my collarbone. "A gift."

"A gift?" I murmur, tilting my head to allow him better access.

"Something I want you to wear tonight."

His lips find mine in a searing kiss, stealing my breath. I melt into him, fingers pulling on his hair to pull him closer. Need coils tight and hot in my core.

When we finally break apart, his eyes are molten, burning with intensity. He starts by removing my necklace and setting it down on the table next to me. Slowly, deliberately, he stands and walks over to a table drawer and withdraws a box wrapped in crimson paper.

My heart pounds as he places the small gift in my hands. I tear off the wrapping paper to reveal a black velvet box. Lifting the lid, I gasp at the exquisite necklace nestled inside . . . a collar, much different than the one I was wearing. Metal and slick. My fingers tremble as I lift the collar from the box.

"A collar?" I begin. "You know . . . jewelry designers shouldn't wear another designers work," I tease, still trying to process exactly what it is he gave me and the possible meaning.

"*I* designed it," he says. "For you."

"You?"

He nods but says nothing more.

"Is this a—" I swallow. "*Collar* collar. Like the ones submissives wear—"

My voice catches in my throat as the realization dawns. The necklace is no ordinary piece of jewelry, but a collar. Sleek and uncompromising, forged from gleaming steel. My fingers trace the cool metal links.

Cole watches me with heated intensity, his eyes dark with desire. "Put it on for me," Cole rasps, his voice rough with need.

"What does this mean? What—" I pause, fingers tracing the cool metal. "Do we need to sign some kind of contract? I mean, I've read . . . things." I feel my cheeks heat. "About collars and BDSM agreements."

A hint of amusement crosses his face. "I thought one contract between us was enough." His thumb traces my bottom lip. "But if you want something more formal . . ."

"God no." I laugh softly. "The merger paperwork was painful enough." I swallow hard, trying to remember how to form words as his mouth moves against my skin. "Don't we need . . . um . . . a safe word?"

He pulls back slightly, eyes dancing with wicked amusement. "Do you want one?"

"I mean . . . isn't that how this works?" I'm blushing furiously now. "Though I refuse to use 'red.' That's so . . . basic."

"Basic?" His laugh is low and dangerous. "All right then, creative one. What would you prefer?"

"Cryptocurrency?"

He arches an eyebrow. "You want to yell 'cryptocurrency' in the middle of sex?"

"It's definitely a mood killer," I point out. "Which is kind of the point, right?"

"Fair enough." His fingers trail down my neck. "If you say 'cryptocurrency,' I stop."

I laugh, the awkward, not pretty-sounding laugh.

His expression turns serious as he cups my face. "But this isn't about rules, safe words, or contracts, Sloane. It's about trust. About you surrendering control to me, and me taking care of you. Just for tonight . . ." His eyes search mine. "At first."

My breath catches at the promise in those last two words. His fingers brush my cheek, igniting sparks beneath my skin. "You're mine," he murmurs, his voice a low rumble that sends tremors down my spine. He leans forward and traces his tongue along my neck where the collar will rest. "And I protect what's mine."

I should be afraid, alarmed by the promise of such complete domination. But as I gaze into the depths of Cole's eyes, I see only scorching desire and a silent plea—trust me. My hesitation melts away, replaced by a yearning so primal it steals my breath.

With trembling hands, I fasten the collar around my neck, the metal cool against my feverish skin. As the final link slides into place, I feel the weight of Cole's possession settle over me, binding me to this man in a way I can't fully comprehend yet. But I don't need to understand, not right now. All I know is that I'm his, utterly and completely.

"Good girl," Cole growls in approval, and the praise sends a jolt of pleasure straight to my core. He pulls me flush against his hard body, claiming my mouth in a searing kiss that leaves me dizzy. His hands roam hungrily, possessively, leaving trails of flame in their wake as he maps every curve, every inch of his new territory.

When he finally releases me, I'm panting and aching for more. Cole's eyes blaze with raw hunger as he takes in the sight of me wearing his collar. "On your knees," he commands, his voice laced with dark promise.

I sink obediently to the plush carpet, the collar feeling impossibly tight and deliciously restraining as I gaze up at him. Cole's fingers trace the line of the collar almost reverently before gripping my hair, tilting my head back to expose the line of my throat.

Cole's eyes burn with primal hunger as he takes in the sight of me kneeling before him, collar gleaming against my skin. His grip on my hair tightens, holding me immobile as he leans down to trail scorching kisses along my neck.

"Mine," he growls against my pulse point, teeth grazing delicate flesh. "As long as you wear this collar, you are mine. In every way."

Chapter Twenty-Seven

SLOANE

Mine.

The weight of his words settles over me like a physical force. Desire floods through me at the thought of belonging to this man so completely—even if it's just for tonight. For now, that feels like enough. More than enough, actually; it feels like everything I never knew I needed until this very moment.

Cole must sense my acquiescence because he rewards me with another fierce kiss before stepping back and beginning to undress slowly—almost tauntingly so—revealing inch after tantalizing inch of tanned skin and solid muscle beneath his clothes as I watch breathlessly from my submissive position on the floor at his feet.

He stands there, completely bared to me, and I can't help but stare. He is magnificent, every inch of him radiating power and confidence. A bead of sweat trickles down my spine as I anticipate what's to come.

"You're overdressed," Cole says, extending a hand toward me. I take it, allowing him to help me to my feet. His other hand reaches for the zipper of my dress, pulling it down the rest of the way slowly, revealing more skin with every inch. The fabric falls away, leaving me standing in nothing but my lingerie.

Cole's eyes rove over my body, taking in every curve, every line. "Perfect," he murmurs, almost to himself. He steps closer, his bare skin brushing against mine, making me shiver with anticipation. His fingers trace the edge of my panties, then slip inside, finding me already wet for him.

"Good," he growls, his breath hot against my ear. "You're always ready for me." He pulls away abruptly, leaving me wanting. "But not yet," he adds, a wicked glint in his eyes.

He picks me up as if I weigh nothing, carrying me to his bedroom. Cole lays me down on his large, four-poster bed, the velvet comforter soft against my skin. His eyes never leave mine as he climbs onto the bed, settling between my legs. He trails a hand up my thigh, slow and teasing, before hooking a finger under the edge of my lace panties and pulling them down.

"Cole," I breathe, my voice barely above a whisper. I feel vulnerable, exposed, but also incredibly desired. It's intoxicating.

"I want you in nothing but my collar." His eyes burn with lust as he tosses my panties aside.

Cole's hands slide up my body as he unhooks my bra and tosses it aside. Now I'm completely naked except for the cool metal collar encircling my throat. His eyes roam over me hungrily.

"Beautiful," he murmurs. "And all mine."

He lowers his head, trailing hot kisses along my collarbone and down to my breasts. I arch into him as he takes a nipple into his mouth, swirling his tongue around the sensitive peak. His hand kneads my other breast, thumb brushing over the hardened bud.

I moan softly, threading my fingers through his hair. Cole nips at my breast in response, the sharp sensation making me gasp.

"Hands above your head," he commands. "Don't move them unless I say so."

I obey, gripping the headboard as Cole continues his sensual assault on my body. His mouth blazes a trail of fire down my stomach, tongue dipping into my navel before moving lower. My hips buck involuntarily as he settles between my thighs.

"Stay still," he orders, voice rough with desire. His breath ghosts over my most sensitive area. "Or I'll have to punish you."

The threat sends a jolt of arousal through me. Part of me wants to test his resolve, to see what punishment he might dole out. But a larger part craves his approval, wants to be good for him.

So I force myself to remain motionless as Cole's tongue finally makes contact with my aching center. He licks a long, slow stripe up my slit before focusing his attention on my clit. I bite my lip to stifle a moan as he alternates between broad strokes and quick flicks of his tongue.

One of Cole's hands grips my thigh, holding me open for him. The other slides up to squeeze my breast, pinching and rolling my nipple between his fingers. The dual sensations are overwhelming.

I struggle to keep still, my fingers clenching and unclenching around the headboard as waves of pleasure wash over me. Cole's talented mouth works me relentlessly, bringing me closer and closer to the edge. Just when I think I can't take anymore, he slides two fingers inside me, curling them to hit that perfect spot.

"Cole!" I cry out, unable to hold back. "Please, I need—"

A slow, wicked smile spreads across his face. "Not yet." He stands from the bed and walks over to his bedside table and says, "Do you need some help being a good girl and keeping your hands above your head?"

I nod, my body thrumming with anticipation. Cole opens the drawer and pulls out a length of silky black rope. He returns to the bed, his eyes dark with desire.

"Wrists together," he commands.

I comply immediately, holding my arms out in front of me. Cole's fingers brush against my skin as he winds the rope around my wrists, creating an intricate pattern. The knots are tight enough to hold me securely but not so tight as to be uncomfortable. When he's finished, he guides my bound hands back above my head, securing them to the headboard.

"Perfect," Cole murmurs, running his hands down my now-restrained arms. "Now you can't touch, even if you want to."

He resumes his position between my legs, his hot breath fanning over my sensitive flesh. I whimper in anticipation, tugging lightly at my bonds.

"Remember," Cole says, his voice low and commanding, "you don't come until I give you permission."

With that, he dives back in, his tongue working me with renewed vigor. I cry out, my back arching off the bed as pleasure courses through me. The inability to touch him, to run my fingers through his hair or grip his shoulders, only heightens every sensation.

Cole alternates between long, slow licks and quick flicks of his tongue against my clit. His fingers pump in and out of me, curling to hit that spot that makes me see stars. I'm writhing beneath him, desperate for release but determined to obey his command.

"Cole, please," I gasp, my voice ragged with need. "I'm so close."

He lifts his head, his eyes meeting mine. "Not yet," he says, a wicked glint in his gaze. "I want to be inside you when you come."

Cole moves up my body, positioning himself at my entrance. He teases me, rubbing the head of his cock along my slick folds. I strain against my bonds, desperate to touch him, to pull him closer.

"Please," I beg, beyond caring how needy I sound. "I need you."

"What do you need?" Cole asks, his voice rough with desire. "Tell me."

"You," I gasp. "I need you inside me. Please, Cole."

"Ask the right way . . . like the good little submissive you are."

I swallow hard, my cheeks flushing with a mix of embarrassment and arousal. But the desire coursing through me overpowers any hesitation.

"Please, *please*," I whisper, my voice trembling. "Please fuck me. I need you inside me."

Cole's eyes darken with lust. "Good girl," he growls, and with one powerful thrust, he buries himself inside me to the hilt.

I cry out at the sudden fullness, my back arching off the bed. Cole pauses for a moment, allowing me to adjust to his size. Then he begins to move, setting a slow, torturous pace that has me writhing beneath him.

"You feel so good," he murmurs against my neck, nipping at the sensitive skin there. "So tight and wet for me."

I wrap my legs around his waist, urging him deeper. Cole responds by picking up the pace, his hips snapping against mine with increasing force.

The room fills with the sounds of our heavy breathing and the slap of skin on skin. I strain against my bonds, desperate to touch him, to pull him closer. The frustration only adds to my arousal, pushing me closer to the edge.

"Cole," I pant, feeling my climax building. "I'm close. Please, can I come . . . please?"

Cole's eyes lock onto mine, burning with intensity. "Not yet," he growls, his hips never slowing their punishing rhythm. "I want you right on the edge."

I whimper in frustration, my body trembling with the effort of holding back my release. Cole's hand snakes between us, his thumb finding my clit and circling it mercilessly.

"Please," I beg, my voice breaking. "I can't . . . I need . . ."

"You can and you will," Cole commands, his voice leaving no room for argument. "You're mine, remember? Your pleasure belongs to me."

His words send a fresh wave of arousal through me. I clench around him, drawing a groan from his lips.

"That's it," he murmurs approvingly. "Feel how perfectly you take me. How well your body responds to mine."

Cole shifts slightly, changing the angle of his thrusts. The new position has him hitting that perfect spot inside me with every stroke. I cry out, my back arching off the bed as much as my restraints will allow.

"Cole!" I gasp, teetering on the brink of orgasm. "Please, I need to come. Please let me come."

He studies my face for a moment, his eyes dark with desire. Then, finally, he nods. "Come for me, Sloane. Now."

The permission is all I need. With a final, deep thrust, I shatter, waves of pleasure crashing over me. I cry out Cole's name as my body convulses around him. He groans, his rhythm faltering as my inner walls pulse around him.

"Fuck, Sloane," he grunts, his hips snapping against mine with increased urgency. "You're so fucking perfect."

A few more powerful thrusts and Cole follows me over the edge, burying himself deep inside me as he comes with a low, guttural moan. He collapses on top of me, both of us breathing heavily.

After a moment, Cole lifts his head, pressing a surprisingly tender kiss to my lips. He reaches up and begins to undo the knots binding my wrists to the headboard. As soon as I'm free, I wrap my arms around him, pulling him close.

Cole gently massages my wrists, his touch soothing the slight marks left by the rope. His eyes meet mine, a mix of passion and concern in their depths.

Cole's fingers trace the edge of the collar, his touch sending shivers down my spine. "How does it feel?" he asks softly.

I take a moment to really consider the question. The metal is cool against my skin, a constant reminder of his claim on me. It should feel constricting, but instead, I feel . . . safe. Protected. Cherished, even.

"It feels right," I whisper, meeting his intense gaze. "Like it belongs there."

A slow smile spreads across Cole's face. He leans down, pressing a gentle kiss to the hollow of my throat, just above the collar. "Good," he murmurs against my skin. "Because I don't plan on taking it off anytime soon. And only I can take it off."

I run my fingers through Cole's hair, savoring the closeness. "I don't want you to take it off," I admit softly.

Cole's eyes darken with possessive desire. He trails his fingers along the collar, then down my neck and over my collarbone. "Good," he murmurs. "Because you're mine now, Sloane. In every way."

"I don't think I truly understand what this all means," I say, touching the collar around my neck. "But I'd like to find out."

Cole's expression softens, a tender smile playing at his lips. He pulls me closer, his strong arms enveloping me in a comforting embrace.

"We'll figure it out together," he murmurs, his breath warm against my ear. "This is new for both of us, in a way. I've never felt this . . . connected to someone before. And I've never wanted to use jewelry as a way to show it. But with you, it feels right to have a necklace represent this . . . us."

I nestle closer to Cole, his words warming me from the inside out. The weight of the collar around my neck feels comforting now, a physical reminder of the connection we share.

"I've never felt this way either," I admit softly. "It's intense and a little scary, but . . . I don't want it to stop."

Cole's hand comes up to cup my cheek, his thumb gently stroking my skin. "It won't," he promises. "I meant what I said, Sloane. You're mine now. And I take care of what's mine."

Chapter Twenty-Eight
COLE

From my office in the penthouse, I watch Sloane pace her studio through the security feed, her movements growing more agitated with each pass. She's been working with Hailey for days straight, their winter collection taking shape in gleaming black metals and crystalline accents. But even through the grainy footage, I can see the tension building in her shoulders, the way her usual fluid grace has become sharp and brittle.

Knox appears in my doorway, leaning against the frame with barely contained amusement. "Your girlfriend attempted to leave the building this morning. Alone."

"For?"

"Christmas shopping, apparently," Knox says. "Said something about gifts for her entire family back in Montauk. She wasn't happy when we redirected her back inside." There's a pause. "She's getting restless."

I watch the feed again, seeing the way she moves from workbench to window and back, like an animal testing the limits of its enclosure. The security measures necessary to keep her safe are clearly starting to wear on her. And, watching her now, I'm struck by the irony of trying to protect something wild by caging it.

"Set up everything I asked for earlier," I tell Knox. "The works."

When I enter the kitchen twenty minutes later, Sloane is already there, stabbing at her phone with more force than necessary. She's wearing one of my sweaters over her workout clothes, her hair a mess of tangles, and my collar still gleaming at her throat. The sight of it—of her marking herself as mine even while bristling against my constraints—does something to my chest.

"I tried to find online shopping options," she says without looking up. "Did you know your security team has actually blacklisted my favorite stores from delivering here?"

"Sloane—"

"I'm starting to feel trapped. Every time I try to step outside to get a breath of fresh air—"

"Sloane—"

"I can't keep living in a gilded cage, Cole." She finally meets my eyes, and the frustration there is edged with something deeper. "Even if it's the most beautiful cage in Manhattan." She holds up her hand before I can speak. "I know, I know, I have an intense deadline. And Hailey and I have made huge progress—we're actually ahead of schedule. But Christmas is coming, and I haven't gotten a single gift for my family." Her voice softens. "I already can't be there with them . . . the least I can do is send something thoughtful." Her lips quirk despite her frustration. "I mean, I hear there's a whole city out there somewhere. With stores full of Christmas gifts and everything."

Instead of arguing about security protocols and Julian's latest movements, I study her for a moment. "Get dressed," I say finally. "Wear something warm."

Her eyes narrow. "Why?"

I let myself smirk. "Because I'm about to be extremely extra, as your friend Chloe would say."

"What does that mean?"

"It means dress warm. We leave in thirty minutes."

She studies me for a moment longer, then shakes her head and heads for her room. I hear her mutter something about "cryptic billionaires" as she goes, and I allow myself a small smile. Knox has already set everything in motion—the rink, the decorations, the security preparations. Time to remind her that even a gilded cage can have its doors opened.

When we pull up to Fifth Avenue an hour later, Sloane's suspicion has shifted to excitement. I lead her toward the first store, watching her face light up at the holiday displays and twinkling lights adorning every storefront.

"You're really going to help me shop for every single Whitmore?" she asks, eyebrows raised.

"From babies to grandparents," I confirm. "Though I confess I know nothing about what your teenage nephew might want."

"Cole . . ." She turns to face me, her expression softer than I've seen in days. "This is . . . thank you."

"Wait for it." Right on cue, Knox appears with a team of discreet security personnel dressed as holiday shoppers. "You pick the items, they'll handle the bags, and everything gets delivered to the penthouse for wrapping before shipping to Montauk."

"Of course you turned Christmas shopping into a military operation," she says with a laugh.

We spend the next few hours moving from store to store. I watch Sloane carefully select each gift—cashmere for her mother, a rare first edition novel for her father, custom jewelry for her sisters, and an assortment of toys and clothes for the children. She tells me stories about each family member as we shop, bringing them to life through her clear affection. I find myself making mental notes, storing away the details of these people who matter to her.

As we're walking between stores, Sloane suddenly stops, her attention caught by something across the street. I follow her gaze to a mobile pet rescue van parked near the curb, its side decorated with holiday wreaths and photos of animals needing homes.

"Can we look?" she asks, already moving toward it. "Just for a minute?"

Before I can object, she's crossing the street, Knox and his team adjusting their positions with practiced ease. Inside the van, various dogs and cats are housed in temporary enclosures, volunteers managing the steady stream of interested passersby.

Sloane gravitates immediately to a pen containing a golden retriever puppy with oversize paws and soulful eyes. The volunteer explains that the puppy was found abandoned just a week ago.

"Look at him," Sloane coos, scratching behind the puppy's ears as it leans blissfully into her touch. "He's perfect."

She looks up at me, her eyes soft. "I grew up with them. We always had at least two goldens at the house in Montauk." Her expression grows wistful. "My last one, Sailor, died right before I moved to the city. I've never gotten another one because . . ." She gestures vaguely. "Small apartment, crazy schedule, no yard."

The puppy paws at the edge of the pen, trying to get closer to her. I check my watch, already calculating how this detour will affect our schedule.

She lifts the puppy up, cradling him against her chest. He immediately starts licking her chin. "Oh my god, you're the sweetest thing."

I take a step back when the puppy's enthusiastic movements send a few golden hairs floating toward my custom suit. "These things shed everywhere," I observe, brushing at my sleeve with mild distaste.

Sloane rolls her eyes. "He's not a 'thing,' Cole. He's a puppy."

The volunteer approaches, smiling. "He seems to really like you. He was found taking his chances crossing the highway."

"You're kidding," Sloane says, her eyes widening. "He was on the highway?"

"A truck driver saw him and stopped traffic. Brought him to us." The volunteer shrugs. "Christmas miracle, I guess."

"He deserves a good home," Sloane says softly, nuzzling the puppy's fur.

"You sure you don't want to fill out an application?" the volunteer asks. "He'll go fast."

Before Sloane can answer, I interject. "We're not looking for pets." My tone is polite but firm, leaving no room for discussion.

Sloane's face falls slightly, but she hands the puppy back to the volunteer. "Thank you for letting me hold him."

"Knox," I say, checking my watch again. "We're running behind schedule."

As we exit the rescue van, Knox falls into step behind us, but not before I catch his eye and give him a subtle nod toward the rescue van—a silent instruction he acknowledges with the barest tilt of his head. I notice Sloane looking back once more at the van, but I say nothing as I guide her to the waiting car.

After completing our shopping, with gifts selected for every Whitmore family member, I direct the driver to our final destination of the day.

When we pull up to Central Park, Sloane's expression shifts from wistful to curious.

I lead her toward Wollman Rink, watching her face as we round the final bend. The entire rink has been transformed—ice sculptures of winter animals catch the morning light, while thousands of crystal strands create a shimmering canopy overhead, catching and fracturing the winter sun into rainbow prisms across the ice. A custom hot chocolate bar has been set up in one corner, complete with every topping imaginable.

"You didn't," she breathes.

"I did." I gesture to the empty rink. "It's ours for the day."

"The whole thing?"

"Including the very discrete security team disguised as rink staff." I nod toward Knox, who looks decidedly uncomfortable in his bright red jacket with WOLLMAN RINK emblazoned across the back.

"Cole . . ." She turns in a slow circle, taking in the decorations. "This is insane."

"Wait for it." Right on cue, a woman in a Team USA jacket approaches. "Sloane, meet Jessica Martinez. She won silver in figure skating at the last Olympics, and she's going to teach us how not to fall on our asses today."

"Speak for yourself, Mr. Asher. This is right in my wheelhouse," Sloane says with a grin.

Jessica's eyes light up when Sloane mentions she skated competitively as a kid. They immediately launch into a conversation about edges and jumps that might as well be in another language. I watch as Sloane steps onto the ice with practiced ease, muscle memory taking over despite the years away. Within moments, she's gliding backward, testing old moves as if reacquainting herself with an old friend.

I, on the other hand, approach the ice with all the confidence of someone who's never so much as seen a skating rink outside of television. My feet seem to have their own agenda, completely disconnected from what my brain is telling them to do.

"Keep your knees soft," Jessica calls out, demonstrating with the same irritating ease as Sloane. "And remember to bend slightly at the waist."

Sloane circles back to where I'm clinging to the wall, executing a graceful stop that sends a spray of ice in my direction. "You know," she says, eyes dancing with amusement, "for someone so obsessed with control, you're remarkably bad at this."

"I'm strategizing," I say with all the dignity I can muster while essentially hugging a wall.

She laughs, the sound echoing across the ice. "Is that what we're calling it?" She spins in a lazy circle around me. "Come on, Cole. Let go of the rail."

"I'm good here."

"The great Cole Asher, afraid of a little ice?" Her eyes sparkle with mischief as she demonstrates another perfect figure eight. "What would your board of directors say?"

"They'd recommend a thorough risk assessment before proceeding." But I find myself loosening my grip anyway, drawn by the challenge in her voice.

My first step away from the wall is . . . less than graceful. Sloane's laugh turns wicked as she watches me wobble, my usual poise absolutely useless while she glides around me like some kind of winter spirit.

"Not so perfect at everything, are you?" she calls, executing a wobbly but passable turn.

I watch her hair catch the light as she moves, the way her cheeks have flushed with cold and joy. "I don't need to be perfect," I tell her honestly. "I just need you."

The words surprise even me—I'm not a man who admits to needing anything. Or anyone. Sloane freezes mid-glide, her eyes finding mine across the ice. For a moment, everything stills—the gentle scrape of blades, the winter wind, even my carefully maintained control.

"Cole . . ." Her voice is soft as she skates back to me. When she reaches for my hand, I realize I'm no longer gripping the rail. "That's good," she says, threading our fingers together, "because all I need is you too."

The raw honesty in her voice catches me off guard. We stand

there, both a little stunned by the weight of what we've admitted, until Jessica's voice breaks the spell.

"All right, Sloane—show me what you've got. Those edges are looking pretty sharp for someone who claims to be rusty."

Sloane's eyes light up at the challenge. She squeezes my hand once before letting go, then pushes off with newfound confidence. I make my way back to the rail—somewhat less shakily than before—and watch as she picks up speed, her movements becoming more graceful with each pass. When she launches into a spin, her body a perfect silhouette against the winter sky, I'm reminded that she's always had this kind of grace. I've just never seen it quite like this.

"Not bad," Jessica calls out. "Want to try a jump?"

Sloane's answering grin is all the response needed.

The afternoon becomes something I didn't know I was missing—the two of us stealing kisses in the middle of the rink, drinking hot chocolate spiked with peppermint schnapps, falling more times than I care to admit. For a few precious hours, we're just a couple enjoying Christmas in New York. No deadlines, no threats, no constant surveillance.

As the winter sun starts to dip, I find myself settled on one of the benches, nursing aching muscles I didn't even know I had. I've long since admitted defeat to the ice, content to watch Sloane continue to practice moves with Jessica. She's been relentless, making up for lost time, each successful jump bringing back more of her old confidence.

When she finally skates over to join me, her cheeks are flushed with exertion and joy. She sits beside me, leaning into my shoulder despite my wincing.

"Thank you for this," she says softly. "For knowing what I needed before I did." Her eyes meet mine, clear and certain. "About this morning . . . I know the security is necessary, and I want you to know . . . I choose this, Cole. I choose you."

I've spent my life maintaining absolute control over everything and everyone around me. But her choice—her willing acceptance of my protection rather than fighting against it—affects me more deeply than I expect. For a moment, I can't find words.

Later, back in the penthouse, I watch her practically skip to her studio, full of renewed energy while I contemplate whether crawling to my office would be less dignified than my current attempt at walking. As soon as her door closes, I pull out my phone, trying not to wince as I shift in my chair.

"Knox. The plans we discussed for Christmas. Make sure that happens. She'll be ready." I pause, watching Sloane through the cameras as she begins sketching with renewed vigor. "And I know you disagree about tomorrow night, but I've decided. We're going. It's time to show the world exactly who my Ice Queen is."

No more hiding. No more cages. Just her, brilliant and fierce, wearing my collar and choosing to stay. Julian and his threats be damned—I'll give her the freedom she needs while keeping her safe. It's long overdue for me to show her off.

She's mine, and I want everyone to know it.

Even that fucking bastard, Julian.

Chapter Twenty-Nine
SLOANE

I can't stop working. After yesterday at the rink, everything feels clearer, sharper. My hands remember the feeling of cutting across ice, that perfect edge between control and freedom. I translate it into metal and stone, working through the night, trying to capture that crystalline moment when sunlight hit the rink's surface.

The cold has always inspired me, but yesterday reminded me why. There's beauty in winter's bite, in the way frost transforms ordinary things into something magical. I shape delicate silver strands into patterns that echo the ice sculptures from the rink, each piece holding that same suspended beauty.

When Hailey arrives early the next morning, she takes one look at my new designs and grins. "Now that's what I'm talking about. Whatever Cole did the other day, it worked."

I run my hands through my hair, looking at all the work still spread across my bench. "We have so much left to do, Hailey. And the deadline's coming up fast."

"Hey." She picks up one of the finished pieces—a bracelet that looks like crystallized snowflakes linked together. "Look at what we've already done. These are incredible, Sloane. And now that you've got your groove back?" She grins. "We'll get it all done. Trust me."

She's right. The sketches and prototypes scattered across my workbench have an energy my earlier pieces were missing. We're discussing setting techniques for the next piece when a stream of deliverymen interrupts us, bringing in dozens of boxes from Bergdorf's.

Inside, I find a collection that takes my breath away—silk and velvet gowns in deep winter colors, each one more stunning than the last. A midnight blue dress with crystals scattered across the bodice like stars. An emerald silk that catches the light like aurora borealis. A deep burgundy velvet that looks like it was made for Christmas at the Met. Between the formal gowns, there are cocktail dresses in blacks and silvers, each one perfectly cut, perfectly chosen. More of Cole's elaborate gifts, but these feel different somehow. Then I find his note tucked into the sleeve of a black gown that makes my heart skip: *Time to show New York their new Ice Queen. First event Friday.*

"Holy hell," Hailey breathes, running her fingers over a silk sleeve. "He doesn't do anything halfway, does he?"

I touch the collar at my throat unconsciously, a habit I've developed whenever I think about what Cole and I are to each other. Not boyfriend and girlfriend—those words seem too small for what we've become. His note says it all. His Ice Queen.

"The man has incredible taste," Hailey says, lifting a midnight blue gown. "Or his personal shopper does." She grins at me. "Makes me think I should reconsider my dating standards."

"Oh?" I look up from the note, grateful for the distraction.

"Let's just say my track record involves a lot of guys who think owning a motorcycle makes up for not having a job." She holds the dress up against herself. "My last date? He told me his band was 'about to make it big' right before asking to borrow rent money." She rolls her eyes. "Maybe it's time to stop falling for guys whose only investment portfolio is their vinyl collection."

I laugh despite my nerves. "To be fair, I wasn't exactly looking for a billionaire."

"No," she says softly. "You just found someone who sees you exactly as you are." She puts down the dress.

"We need to call Chloe—right now," I tell Hailey, grabbing my phone. She follows me to the bedroom, where I know there are no cameras. We settle on the bed and I FaceTime Chloe with shaking hands. "He wants me to go public? Like, *public* public."

"Finally!" Chloe's face fills my screen, beaming. "I've been dying to post about you two on Instagram!"

"Chloe, this is serious. I'm about to become . . ." I swallow hard. "I'm about to be seen publicly with Cole Asher."

"You're about to become a lot more than that," Hailey says. She lifts the black gown, letting the fabric catch the light. "You're debuting one of the most anticipated jewelry collections of the season. Own it."

She's right. Again.

With my phone propped against the bedroom mirror, we start the fashion show for Chloe, pulling gowns from their boxes and tissue paper. The butterflies in my stomach settle a bit with each dress, replaced by my friends' running commentary.

"Okay, but did you ever actually ask him if he's in the mafia?" Chloe asks as I emerge in the emerald silk. "Because the whole mysterious billionaire thing is very Godfather-adjacent."

"Chloe!" But I'm laughing. "Yes, I asked. He's not in the mafia."

"And you believed him?" Hailey asks, adjusting the dress's shoulder. "Just like that?"

I think about the bits and pieces I've learned about Cole's past. "He's not mafia," I say slowly. "But his past is . . . complicated. Dark, even." I smooth my hands over the silk. "Maybe I should have asked more questions, but I've been taking it one revelation at a time."

"Baby steps," Chloe agrees. "Though I have to say, the whole security detail thing does seem a bit intense."

My smile fades slightly. "That's because of Julian." Both girls go quiet.

"Hey." Hailey squeezes my shoulder. "Cole's got you covered. And this dress? This is definitely the one for making dramatic entrances at fancy galas while being surrounded by security."

"Try the black one next," Chloe calls from the phone. "I need to see if it lives up to Cole's note. Ice Queen vibes only, please!"

After we say goodbye to Chloe, Hailey and I get back to work. She moves through the studio with practiced efficiency, her hands steady as she sets stones and shapes metal. I've never seen anyone work with such precision and speed—she can execute a design faster than most jewelers can read the blueprint.

I lose myself in the delicate work of setting tiny diamonds into the frost-inspired patterns, watching each piece transform from concept to reality. Hailey works beside me, offering quiet suggestions that always make the piece stronger, her expertise making our process seamless. By late afternoon, we've completed three new pieces and have two more in progress. The collection is really coming together—elegant and fierce, exactly how I want to feel on Friday night.

When Cole comes home, I'm wearing the black dress Hailey declared perfect, paired with a set of earrings I just finished—delicate cascades of metal and crystal. Cole goes still in the doorway, his expression making me forget every insecurity.

"Too much?" I ask, but I already know the answer from the way he's looking at me.

He crosses the room, touches one earring with reverent fingers. "Perfect."

"The gala on Friday," I say, touching the delicate bracelet I'm wearing—another of my pieces. "It's not just a charity event, is it?"

"No. Bergdorf is hosting. They want to debut part of your collection—give everyone a sneak peek of what's coming."

The announcement should terrify me. Instead, I feel ready. More than ready.

Chapter Thirty
COLE

7 days until . . .

"Y ou're making a mistake." Knox stands in front of my desk, arms crossed. He's been at it for twenty minutes.

I continue reviewing the security plans for tonight. "We've been over this."

"The moment you step into that ballroom with her, Julian will know she's the chink in your armor."

I look up from the papers, meeting his gaze. "No. He'll know she's my strength. And if he so much as looks in her direction, I'll burn his empire to the ground with him in it."

Knox's laugh is sharp, humorless. "Listen to yourself. You're getting arrogant, Cole. Maybe you can afford to be. Hell, maybe you are fucking invincible at this point." He plants his hands on my desk, leaning forward. "But is she? Because Julian doesn't play fair. He doesn't come at you directly—he finds what matters and he breaks it. You know this. You've seen him do it."

I feel my jaw tighten. "That was before."

"Before what? Before you became New York's golden boy? Before you thought you could control everything?" Knox straightens, shaking his head. "I've known you fifteen years. I've watched you build all this. But I've never seen you this blind."

"I'm not blind." My voice is quiet now. Dangerous. "I see everything. Every angle, every threat, every possibility. That's why we're doing this. Because hiding her away, treating her like she's fragile—that makes her a target."

"So what's your alternative? Parade her around at every society event? Make her New York's newest sensation?" Knox watches me carefully. "And then what, Cole? What happens when the jewelry line launches? When the excitement dies down? You going to keep her locked in that penthouse like a bird in a gilded cage?"

The question hits harder than I want to admit. I turn to look out the window at the city below, my city, where I've always been able to control every moving piece. "You think I haven't asked myself these questions?"

"Have you found any answers?"

"She's not meant for cages." The words come out before I can stop them. "You've seen her work. Her mind. The way she creates beauty from nothing, transforms raw materials into something impossible . . ." I stop, realizing how much I'm revealing.

"Then what?" Knox's voice is quieter now. "Exactly, then what?"

I don't have an answer. For the first time in years, I don't have the next ten moves mapped out. I know how to protect her from Julian, from my enemies, from the press. But how do I protect her from the life I've built? From what loving me means—the constant security, the scrutiny, the knowledge that every move is watched and analyzed. The reality that she'll never have a normal life again, never be able to just walk down a street alone or open her studio to the public without a threat assessment. From the fact that loving me means living in a world where even the smallest decision becomes a strategic calculation, where trust is a luxury we can rarely afford, where every person who approaches her might have an agenda. How do I protect her from that?

The weight of Knox's stare tells me he sees right through me, sees every doubt I'm trying to bury. He's known me too long not to recognize when I'm wrestling with something I can't control.

"Just . . . tell me you've considered all the angles."

"Every single one." I stand, grabbing my jacket. "Double the security detail tonight. I want eyes on every entrance and exit."

"Already done." Knox follows me to the door. "Teams are in position at the venue. Additional surveillance is set up. But Cole—" He pauses. "Julian's not the only threat. Everyone's going to be watching, analyzing. You sure you want to put her in the spotlight like this?"

"It's not just about her, Knox. It's about everything the collection represents." I check my watch. "When Bergdorf's announces Sloane's line as their exclusive New Year's launch—"

"Julian's house of cards collapses," Knox finishes, finally understanding. "His fake Claire collection becomes worthless overnight."

"Exactly. Making her public doesn't just protect her—it ensures the collection gets the attention it deserves. The attention that will destroy Julian's plans completely."

"But when he realizes you don't plan on using Claire's designs for the launch, he'll still want them for himself. Even more so."

"That's why we have contingency plans." I straighten my tie. "That's why every member of the security team has been briefed on Julian's previous tactics. And that's why, after tonight, he won't dare touch her. Not when the entire luxury world is watching."

Knox sighs. "I hope you're right. For both your sakes."

"Making her public makes her untouchable." My voice is cold, certain. "After tonight, hurting her would be an open declaration of war. Not just against me, but against every power player in that room who wants a piece of her collection. Julian's smart enough to understand that."

"I think you're giving Julian too much credit. He's not rational," Knox presses. "Never has been."

"I know Julian. I know how to control this situation."

Knox nods but doesn't look convinced.

I head home early to get ready, though my mind's still running through contingency plans. The press will have a field day with this—Cole Asher, finally claiming someone publicly. They've documented all my carefully curated appearances over the years: models, socialites, daughters of business partners. Beautiful women who understood their role was temporary, who played their part in maintaining the image I needed. Three hours maximum at any event, a few practiced photographs, then separate cars home. Clean. Controlled. Forgettable.

This is different. There will be pictures of us all over social media. The way I keep her close, how my hand lingers on her back, the possessive edge to my smile when someone stares too long. The collar at her throat—to most, just another piece of exquisite jewelry. A lover's gift. But certain members of New York's elite will know better. The ones who frequent more exclusive circles, who understand the weight of such symbols. They'll recognize it for what it is—a mark of ownership, elegant and absolute. No one will speak of it, of course. Not in polite society. But in their private clubs, their whispered conversations, they'll know exactly what it means that Sloane wears my collar to her own debut.

She's not just another pretty distraction. She's an artist about to take over their world, and she's unmistakably mine.

When Sloane emerges from the bedroom, everything else falls away. The black dress fits her like it was sculpted onto her body. Her jewelry catches the light—frost-etched pieces that seem alive against her skin. The earrings cascade like icicles, and her wrists shimmer with interwoven silver that mimics winter's first frost across glass. But it's my collar at her throat that makes my pulse quicken—platinum and diamonds forming an elegant chain of possession, marking her as mine even as she stands ready to claim her own power. She's transformed herself into something ethereal, untouchable.

I was right. She doesn't belong in the shadows.

"You look . . ." I step closer, touching one of her earrings. They're new—she must have just finished them. The metal work is intricate, precise. Like her.

"Acceptable for my debut as the mysterious woman who's caught Cole Asher's attention?" There's a hint of teasing in her voice.

"Perfect for your debut as the artist who's about to take New York by storm."

Her smile tells me she's ready for this, even if she won't say it out loud. We head down to where Knox is waiting with the car, the winter air sharp against our faces. Sloane slides into the back seat, her dress whispering against the leather.

The city lights flash across Sloane's face as our car moves through Manhattan traffic. Before we reach the Met, there are things she needs to know. I pull out my phone, showing her a photo from last month's charity auction.

"Diana Winters. Art critic for the *Times*. She can be ruthless, but she respects technical skill above all else. Show her the inner mechanisms of your frost series—she'll appreciate the engineering behind the aesthetics."

Sloane studies the image of a sharp-featured woman in her fifties. "I've read her reviews. She destroyed the Wilson exhibit last spring."

"Because his work was derivative." I swipe to the next photo. "James Morton. Old money, major collector. He funded three of the biggest jewelry exhibitions at the Met in the last decade. He'll try to lowball you through intermediaries, but he always pays full price for pieces he really wants."

"The one who outbid everyone for the Cartier archives?"

"You've done your research." I pause at a photo of a younger man with cold eyes. "Richard Kane. My biggest competitor in Asian markets. He's been trying to expand into luxury goods. Don't accept any private meetings if he offers."

She nods, then reaches up to adjust one of her bracelets, making minute adjustments that probably only she can see.

"Nervous?" I ask.

She meets my eyes. "No. I'm ready."

The moment we step into the Metropolitan's grand ballroom, the buzz of conversation falters. Crystal chandeliers cast golden light across marble floors and velvet gowns, highlighting the cream and gilt molding that frames the soaring ceiling. Heads turn in waves—first those near the entrance, then rippling outward like stones dropped in still water.

I note with satisfaction the models I'd arranged for—three willowy figures in white silk sheaths that serve as perfect backdrops for Sloane's pieces. They move through the crowd with practiced grace. One wears a suite of white gold and diamonds that traces the elegant line of her spine. Another displays an intricate collar of silver filigree and moonstones that draws every eye in the room. The third wears a convertible piece that transforms from bracelet to necklace, demonstrating its mechanics to a captivated audience. Every movement is choreographed to ensure the jewelry catches the light just so.

I keep my hand on Sloane's lower back as we descend the curved staircase. Her black dress moves like liquid shadow, making the diamonds at her throat and ears seem brighter, more alive. Against the sea of bright colors—emerald silks, ruby satins, sapphire chiffons—she stands out like a perfect black diamond.

The crowd parts and re-forms around us. Women in designer gowns pause mid-conversation, champagne flutes forgotten in their hands. Men in tailored tuxedos track our movement across the floor, their usual carefully maintained expressions slipping. Within minutes, we're surrounded by New York's elite, all vying for introductions. Diamond-draped socialites lean in close, openly staring at the delicate silver pieces adorning Sloane's neck and wrists. A well-known fashion editor actually reaches out to touch one of her earrings before catching herself.

Sloane handles it perfectly. She's gracious but not eager, elegant but approachable. When asked about her collection, she speaks with quiet confidence about her inspiration, her techniques. She doesn't oversell—she doesn't need to. The pieces speak for themselves.

"Cole." A familiar voice cuts through the crowd. Alexander Pierce, one of New York's biggest collectors. "Aren't you going to introduce me to your lovely companion?"

I make the introduction, watching as Sloane charms yet another influential figure in the art world. But I'm also scanning the room, noting who's watching, who's making calls, who's trying to get closer.

Let them watch. Let them see exactly who she is. What she's capable of.

Let them all see that she's not just mine. She's a force of her own.

After an hour of introductions and carefully navigated conversations, I notice her fingers drifting to her collar more frequently—a habit she only falls into when she's feeling overwhelmed. I lean close, my lips near her ear. "Come with me."

I guide her through a hidden door behind a tapestry, into one of the Met's private galleries. Here, the noise of the gala becomes distant, muffled. Ancient artifacts rest in glass cases, bathed in soft light. Sloane's shoulders relax as she takes in our surroundings.

"How did you know I needed this?"

"You were starting to fidget with your collar." I run my finger along its edge, feeling her pulse quicken. "You've been perfect out there. Every person in that room is either envying you or wanting to own a piece of what you create."

She turns to face me, and in the dim light I see something fierce in her eyes. "I saw the models wearing my pieces. That was your doing?"

"You can't wear everything you've created." I trace the line of her jaw. "And I want them desperate to see the full collection. The convertible piece on Isabelle has three society wives plotting how to get first dibs. The spine necklace on Sofia had Diana Winters taking notes. And that moonstone collar?" I smile. "I've watched at least five women try to get James Morton's attention, hoping he'll buy it for them."

"You're teasing them."

"I'm creating demand. By the time we reveal the full collection, they'll be ready to kill each other for it." My thumb brushes her bottom lip. "Besides, you chose which pieces to wear tonight. The ones that matter most. The ones that show exactly who you are."

"Tactical marketing through strategic torture? How very you."

"Having second thoughts about any of this?"

"No." She reaches up, adjusting my tie with familiar precision. "But I keep waiting for someone to see through it all. To realize I'm just a girl from Montauk who—"

I cut her off with a kiss, harder than I should in such a public setting, but I need her to feel the truth of it. When I pull back, my hand tightens on her waist. "You're exactly who you're meant to be. The girl from Montauk who's about to have half of Manhattan fighting over her jewelry."

"Only half?" One eyebrow arches as she smooths my lapel. "I must be losing my touch."

"I saw three society wives ready to steal that convertible piece right off the model."

"Careful." Her lips curve into a smile against my jaw. "A girl could get used to this kind of power."

"Good." I trace the edge of her collar. "Because watching you own that room is incredibly attractive."

"Is that why you dragged me into a dark corner of the Met? To tell me how attractive I am?"

"Actually, I dragged you into a three-million-dollar gallery of ancient artifacts." I glance at the cases around us. "Much more dignified."

She turns to one of the displays, her fingers hovering over the glass. "The craftsmanship in these pieces . . ." Her eyes light up the way they do when she's studying something that inspires her. "I could spend hours in here."

"Now who's avoiding the party?"

"Says the man who orchestrated this escape." The smile she gives me over her shoulder is pure temptation.

"That, and you look absolutely sinful in that dress."

She brushes her thumb across my bottom lip, removing a trace of her lipstick. "We should get back. I have a room full of potential clients to seduce."

"Should I be jealous?"

"You started it with those models in white." She steps toward the door, then glances back over her shoulder. "Coming?"

I lead her back toward the noise and light of the gala, but not before catching the way she touches her collar, a gesture of confidence now rather than anxiety. Let them see that too—how thoroughly she belongs to me, even as she conquers their world.

We've barely rejoined the crowd when I spot Jasmine Walsh approaching, looking expensive but trying too hard in a dress that screams new money. The owner of Moth to the Flame, where she'd spent two years trying to break Sloane's spirit with manipulation and stolen designs. The woman's smile is sharp as cut glass.

"Sloane, darling." Her air-kiss misses Sloane's cheek by design.

"Who would have thought you'd end up here?" She gestures broadly at the opulent ballroom.

My jaw tightens, but Sloane's hand finds my arm, a subtle request to let her handle this.

"Jasmine." Sloane's voice is warm honey over steel. "I was just telling Diana Winters about my time at Moth to the Flame. How it taught me exactly what I didn't want my brand to be."

Jasmine's perfectly lined eyes narrow. "Oh? And what's that?"

"Delicate. Girly. Lacking edge." She pauses deliberately. "Derivative." Sloane takes a sip of champagne. "But you've seen the pieces on the models. I'd love your professional opinion on how they compare to your current collection. The one inspired by Van Cleef's 1950s archive?"

I hide my smile behind my glass. The woman's latest line is a blatant copy of the classic jeweler's work, and everyone in the industry knows it.

"I see success hasn't improved your attitude." Jasmine's voice has lost its fake warmth. "I hope you remember who gave you your first real experience in this business."

"Of course." Sloane's smile is radiant. "Your company taught me everything I needed to know about what sells . . . and what deserves better." Her eyes flick meaningfully to the models displaying her work. "Something original."

I watch Jasmine's face flush as she realizes she's not dealing with the same young woman she once lorded over. My possessive pride wars with the urge to step in, to put this woman in her place. But Sloane doesn't need my protection. Not anymore.

"Well." Jasmine clutches her clutch tighter. "I suppose we'll see how the market responds to your . . . unique perspective." She turns to me, desperation making her bold. "Cole, I don't suppose you'd be interested in discussing some investment opportunities in established brands?"

"Actually"—I keep my tone pleasant even as I shift closer to Sloane—"I'm exclusively focused on supporting genuine innovation in the industry. Speaking of which—Diana's waving us over." I touch Sloane's back. "Jasmine, if you'll excuse us."

As we walk away, I lean down to murmur in Sloane's ear. "That was impressive."

"The part where I eviscerated my former boss or the part where I didn't let you do it for me?"

"Both." I press my lips to her temple, not caring who sees. "Though watching you destroy her while smiling was incredibly arousing."

She laughs softly. "Down, boy. We still have a room full of much more important people to impress."

"I don't think that's going to be a problem." And it isn't. Because the woman beside me isn't just wearing confidence like her jewelry—she's earned it.

Chapter Thirty-One
SLOANE

My feet are killing me, but I've never felt more alive. Three hours of handshakes, subtle politics, and thinly veiled social warfare have left me exhausted and exhilarated in equal measure. I catch Cole's eye across a cluster of aging socialites who've been debating the merits of my spine necklace for twenty minutes, wondering if he'd notice if I kicked off these heels under my dress.

Probably. He notices everything.

I make my way to him, searching for a tactful way to suggest we leave without seeming ungrateful or overwhelmed. Maybe I could fake a headache? Though knowing Cole, he'd have a doctor here in ten minutes. Perhaps I could—

Cole's entire demeanor shifts. The change is subtle—most wouldn't notice—but I've learned to read him. His hand slides to my lower back, fingers pressing slightly harder than usual. His stance widens, angling his body partly in front of mine.

That's when I see them. Three men in impeccable suits that somehow look wrong here, too sharp-edged for the polished wealth around us. They move through the crowd with practiced ease, but there's nothing social about their approach.

"Ms. Whitmore." The one in front smiles without warmth. "Quite a debut."

Cole's fingers flex against my back. His eyes are scanning the room, and I follow his gaze just as it lands on Knox, who's already moving toward us with controlled urgency.

"Cole . . . Julian sends his regards," another one says, his accent vaguely Eastern European. "He wasn't aware you had *another* designer . . . for your line."

My spine stiffens at his tone. Did Cole have another designer besides me at one point?

"To think," the man continues. "Julian thought you were going to try to launch Claire's designs this entire time. Instead you brought in"—he looks me up and down—"a body double."

Cole remains quiet, but I can nearly feel the rage sizzling off his skin.

"I particularly admire that piece." The first man gestures to my collar, his eyes lingering too long. "Is the line your design alone, Ms. Whitmore?"

"Why would you ask that?" I keep my voice steady, even as Cole's hand tightens possessively at my waist.

Knox arrives just as the third man steps forward, speaking softly. "Julian just wanted to remind you that in this industry, the right connections are everything. And some connections"—his eyes flick to Cole, then back to me—"can become quite dangerous. For everyone involved."

They melt back into the crowd before Cole can respond, leaving behind a chill that has nothing to do with the winter air outside. Knox moves closer, his expression grim.

"Time to go," Cole says, and for once, I don't argue about being protected.

The look in Cole's eyes is murderous, but his touch remains gentle as he guides me toward the exit. Knox flanks us, speaking quietly into his comm unit. I notice how the security team materializes around us, a choreographed dance I'm starting to recognize. I think of Chloe trying on gowns in my bedroom, teasing me about whether I'd actually asked Cole if he was in the mafia. The memory almost makes me laugh. Almost.

"Cole?" I keep my voice low, steady despite the rapid beating of my heart.

"It's fine." His response is automatic, practiced. But I catch the way his eyes keep scanning our surroundings, the slight tension in his jaw. "Just a precaution."

Right. Because everyone leaves their own gala with a small army of security. Just another casual Friday night at the Met. I want to make a joke about sleeping with the fishes, but the steel in Cole's expression stops me.

"Car's ready," Knox murmurs. "Thompson caught them heading east on Eighty-Second."

Cole's jaw clenches. "And?"

"Two black SUVs. Diplomatic plates." Knox's voice drops lower. "Russian."

I feel Cole's entire body tense against mine. There's an undercurrent to their exchange I don't fully understand, but I recognize enough to know this wasn't just a casual threat.

We emerge into the bitter night air, and I'm grateful for both Cole's warmth and the armed men surrounding us. The exhaustion from earlier has transformed into something else—a humming awareness of danger that makes every shadow seem deeper.

"I'm sorry," Cole says once we're in the car. "We should have stayed longer. It was your night, and I had to cut it short—"

"What was that all about?" I turn to face him, sudden anger flaring. "Tell me the truth. All of the truth."

Something shifts in Cole's expression.

I fold my arms. "And what line are you talking about—his or mine? Because it sounds like there's a race happening and I'm just now being told I'm in it."

"Sloane." Cole's voice drops, his hands reaching for mine. "Let's not do this now. You've had an amazing night. Your collection was incredible—"

"Don't change the subject." I pull my hands away. "What did he mean about another designer?"

Cole runs a hand through his hair, his eyes darting to Knox, who's pretending not to listen from the front seat.

"It's complicated," he says finally.

"Uncomplicate it," I snap.

"Not here." He glances meaningfully at the partition between us and the driver. "Not like this. When we get home—"

"No." My voice is steel. "Now."

"I'm handling it—"

"You're not handling anything! You're sitting here refusing to tell me why I just got menaced by what I can only guess is the Russian mob at my own fashion debut!"

I narrow my eyes.

"Was I a pawn? My line—"

"Is going to be the best we've seen in a very long time," Cole cut in. "You are not a pawn. Yes, I brought you in to beat Julian's line, but it's because of your skill. Your talent. Only your designs can beat what he's trying to fake and pass off as Claire's. The minute I saw your work, I knew how truly talented you are."

"Why is he trying to do this? Why try to fake her designs?"

"Because Julian doesn't want her remembered for what she actually was. He's been rewriting the story—trying to frame his new line as the continuation of her legacy."

"And mine gets in the way."

"Yes." Cole doesn't sugarcoat it. "If your line comes first—if it's better—then everything he's built falls apart."

I stare at him, pulse ticking in my throat. "You brought me in to stop him."

He hesitates. Then nods. "You're not the kind of talent you can fake. And that's all he has—smoke and mirrors and stolen stories. I knew if you launched something real before he did, he wouldn't recover."

My breath catches. "So that was the plan all along."

"Not all of it," he says, softer now. "It started that way. But then you became . . . more."

I cross my arms. "You could've told me."

He sighs, and I can see the weight in it. "I didn't want to put that pressure on you. Or that target."

"Too late," I whisper. "The Russians at the Met? The cameras everywhere? I've been in actual danger this entire time? I think it's fair to say I'm a target."

He doesn't answer. He doesn't have to.

"Wait—" I put up my hands as realization crashes over me. "That night we met. The party. You approaching me wasn't random, was it? You were fucking *stalking* me!"

Cole's jaw tightens. "I was looking for you, yes."

"So everything—" My voice catches. "Everything was calculated from the beginning." Each word feels like I'm spitting out glass. "You needed someone to beat Julian, and I was the perfect candidate. Young. Hungry. Naive."

"It wasn't like that—"

"Then what was it like, Cole?" I don't try to hide the tremor in my voice now. "Did you even like my designs? Or was I just convenient? The right skill set with the right desperation to meet your timeline?"

"Of course I liked your designs—"

"Or was I just the closest thing to Claire you could find?" The question hangs between us, sharp and dangerous.

Cole flinches. "That's not fair."

"None of this is fair!" My voice rises. "You've had me working around the clock to beat some deadline to piss off a rival, for a battle I didn't sign up for, against people who apparently have no problem threatening me in public!"

"I was protecting you—"

"No." I shake my head fiercely. "You were using me. There's a difference."

Knox shifts uncomfortably in the front seat, but I'm beyond caring who hears this.

"Sloane." Cole reaches for my hand. I pull away. "I admit I wasn't completely transparent about why I needed your line to launch so quickly. But everything else—us—that was real."

"Real?" I laugh, the sound hollow even to my own ears. "You had me followed. You had security on me before I even knew I needed it. Our entire relationship has been built on things you decided I didn't need to know."

"To keep you safe—"

"To keep your plan intact," I correct him. "I wasn't your partner. I was your weapon against Julian. I need to know—are Hailey and Chloe safe? My family?"

Something flickers in Cole's eyes. He glances at Knox, who's already pulling out his phone.

"They're safe," Cole says. "But if it would make you feel better, Knox can arrange—"

"Security on them?" The words taste bitter. "Eyes on their homes? Tracking their movements?" I run a hand through my hair, reality crashing in. "Jesus. This is insane. A week ago I was worried about meeting collection deadlines, and now I'm standing here discussing putting surveillance on my best friends because some psycho with Russian mob connections—" I break off, my throat tight.

"This isn't the life I signed up for," I continue, my voice steadier now. "I wanted to design jewelry, not get caught in some vendetta between billionaires with dangerous friends."

"I wouldn't have let anything happen to you—"

"You don't get to make that call!" I'm shouting now, weeks of stress and exhaustion fueling my anger. "You don't get to decide what risks I take, what battles I fight. That was my choice, and you took it from me."

"Sloane, please—"

"No." I shake my head, tears threatening. "I'm done being a pawn in your game."

"Sloane." Cole reaches for me, and this time I let him. "They're safe. Julian won't—"

"You don't know that." I press my face into his chest, breathing in his familiar scent. "I don't want them followed. I don't want any of this. I just want him to go away."

His arms tighten around me. "I know."

But I can hear what he doesn't say: wanting something doesn't make it happen. And this isn't going away.

I should protest. Should insist my friends don't need to be dragged into this world of shadows and threats. But all I can think about is Chloe's bright laugh, Hailey's fierce loyalty, my mother's quiet strength. And I know—if anything happened to them because of me . . .

The thought stops me cold. Because of me, and my choices. Because somewhere between his first arrogant smile and this moment, I've fallen in love with Cole Asher. The realization hits me like a physical force. Love. When did that happen? And of course it would dawn on me now, discussing Russian mobsters and surveillance teams.

I pull away from him suddenly, like his touch burns. The cruel irony isn't lost on me—realizing I love him at the exact moment I can't trust him anymore.

"I need to go." My voice is surprisingly steady. "Take me to Chloe's place."

"Sloane, it's late, and after what just happened—"

"Take me to Chloe's." I don't phrase it as a request this time. "Or I'll call a cab."

"Be reasonable," Cole says, frustration edging into his voice. "It's not safe for you to be alone right now."

"I won't be alone. I'll be with Chloe." I meet his gaze defiantly. "And I'm pretty sure I'm safer away from you at this point."

I see the hurt flash across his face, but I'm too angry to care. Too scared. Too everything.

"We'll drive you," Cole says finally, his voice tight.

"Fine." I turn toward the window, watching the city lights blur as tears fill my eyes.

The rest of the ride passes in tense silence. I can feel Cole watching me, can sense the words he wants to say building in the air between us. But he doesn't speak, and neither do I.

What could he possibly say now that would make any of this okay?

I think about the collection waiting in my studio, all those hours of work, the joy I felt creating each piece. Was any of it real? Or was I just playing my part in Cole's revenge story all along?

Was I just Claire Voss 2.0?

When the car finally stops outside Chloe's house, I don't wait for Knox to open my door. I reach for the handle, then pause, still facing forward.

"I need time," I say quietly. "Don't call me. Don't send security. Don't do anything."

"Sloane—"

"I mean it, Cole." I finally turn to look at him, hating the way my heart still lurches at the sight of his face. "It's my turn to decide what happens next. I'm the one in control. Not you."

I don't wait for his response. I slip out of the car and into the cold night air, not looking back even when I hear his door open, even when I hear him call my name. I keep walking until I reach Chloe's door, until I'm safely inside the house, until I can finally let the tears fall.

Chapter Thirty-Two

SLOANE

I reach across the bed, half-asleep, my fingers searching for warmth. For Cole. The space beside me is empty, and reality crashes back like a bucket of ice water. I'm not in the penthouse. I'm at Chloe's house, in her guest room with its pastel blue walls and framed motivational quotes. Last night's fight with Cole replays in my mind, his face when I demanded to come here instead of home.

I rub my eyes, which feel raw and puffy. My phone shows it's almost ten. I never sleep this late, but then again, I don't usually cry myself to sleep either.

The smell of coffee drifts in, along with something sweet. Not Chloe's usual breakfast smoothie concoction. I drag myself out of bed, pulling on the oversize NYU sweatshirt I borrowed from her last night after showing up at her door with nothing but my purse and a broken heart.

"Morning, sunshine!" Chloe chirps when I shuffle into her kitchen. She's wearing a red-and-green apron with tiny elves prancing across it, her hair piled on top of her head.

"Morning," I mumble, eyeing the chaos spread across her normally pristine countertops. Bowls of colored icing. Cookie cutters. Sprinkles in little dishes. "What's all this?"

"Emergency Christmas therapy." She hands me a giant mug of

coffee, exactly how I like it. "I figured you needed this more than avocado toast today."

I take a grateful sip, the caffeine beginning to cut through the fog in my brain. "You're decorating cookies at ten in the morning?"

"*We're* decorating cookies at ten in the morning," she corrects, sliding a plate of bare sugar cookies shaped like snowflakes and stars toward me. "Sometimes a girl needs frosting for breakfast."

Despite everything, a small smile tugs at my lips. "You're ridiculous."

"I'm a genius. Sit." She points to a barstool. "Doctor's orders."

I do as I'm told, wrapping my hands around the warm mug. "I don't know if even Christmas cookies can fix this, Chlo."

"Try me." She slides into the seat beside me, pushing a piping bag of green icing into my hand. "Create something beautiful. It's what you do."

I stare at the plain cookies, then at the icing bag. Muscle memory takes over as I begin to pipe a delicate pattern along the edge of a snowflake.

"So," Chloe says, carefully casual as she floods a star with red icing, "you want to talk about it?"

"Not really." The design flowing from my hands is intricate, delicate. Even heartbroken, I can't help being meticulous.

"Okay." She nods, focusing on her cookie. "Then I'll talk. You'll listen."

I roll my eyes but don't stop her.

"You love designing jewelry. It's your thing. Your passion. Your superpower."

"I know that."

"And this collection you've been working on? It's incredible. Not because Cole asked you to make it. Not because it's for some fancy Asher brand launch. Because *you* created it."

I swallow hard, moving to the next cookie. "It doesn't matter. The whole thing was built on a lie. He didn't believe in me. He just needed someone to design his precious collection, and I was convenient."

"Bullshit." Chloe never sugarcoats anything. It's why I love her. "He invested in you because your work is amazing. Maybe his timing was questionable, and yeah, he should have told you about the Julian/Claire drama sooner. But that doesn't change the fact that your designs are brilliant."

I focus on the intricate latticework I'm creating on a particularly large snowflake, not wanting her to see how her words affect me. "I just feel so stupid."

"For falling for him or for believing in yourself?"

My hand jerks, smearing the design. "That's not fair."

"Life isn't fair. Christmas cookies for breakfast is what we get instead." She reaches for the silver sprinkles, dusting them over her finished star. "Look, I don't know what's going on with Cole. Maybe he's as big a jerk as you think right now. Or maybe he's a guy who made a mistake. Either way, this jewelry line isn't about him."

"It feels like it is."

"Only if you let it be." She points her piping bag at me. "You designed those pieces. They came from your heart, your talent. Are you really going to throw that away because some guy hurt your feelings?"

"It's more than hurt feelings," I protest, but even to my ears, it sounds weak.

"I'm sure it is. But my point stands." She slides another cookie my way. "You owe it to yourself to finish what you started. Not for Cole. Not for Midnight Frost. For Sloane Whitmore, the most talented jewelry designer I know."

I'm quiet for a long time, decorating cookies and drinking coffee, letting her words sink in. The rhythm of creating, even with something as simple as icing, steadies me. Reminds me who I am.

"What if I can't be around him?" I finally ask, voicing my biggest fear.

"Then you be professional. Cold as ice if you have to." She smirks. "You're good at icy when you need to be."

"Thanks a lot."

"It's a compliment! Ice is beautiful. Powerful. And damn hard to break." She reaches over and squeezes my hand. "Just like you."

By the time we've decorated two dozen cookies and consumed at least that many ounces of coffee, I've made my decision. I shower, borrow some of Chloe's clothes that don't scream "walk of shame," and call a rideshare.

"You sure about this?" Chloe asks as she walks me to the door.

"No," I admit. "But you're right. I need to finish what I started."

She pulls me into a hug. "That's my girl. Call me later?"

"Promise."

The ride to Cole's building feels both too long and too short. My stomach knots as the elevator climbs to the penthouse. I still have the key he gave me, but using it feels wrong now. I knock instead.

When he opens the door, he looks as terrible as I feel. Dark circles under his eyes, hair rumpled like he's been running his hands through it. Something inside me aches at the sight, but I steel myself against it.

"Sloane." My name on his lips is almost my undoing. "I—"

"I'm here to finish the jewelry line," I say, cutting him off, my voice as professional as I can make it. "As I promised. Nothing more."

His jaw tightens, but he steps back to let me in. "Of course."

I walk past him, not allowing myself to breathe in his scent, not letting myself remember how it felt to be held by him in this very spot. I head straight for the studio space he set up for me, removing my coat with mechanical precision.

"The deadline's still the same?" I ask, not looking at him.

"Yes." His voice is equally cool now, matching my tone. "New Year's."

"Fine. I'll need to work late tonight. And probably tomorrow."

"Whatever you need."

I finally turn to face him. He's watching me with those dark eyes that see too much, but his expression gives nothing away. Two can play at this game.

"What I need," I say, "is space to work. Alone."

He nods once, then turns and walks away, leaving me with my designs, my tools, and a heart that refuses to freeze over no matter how much I wish it would.

Chapter Thirty-Three
COLE

I check my phone again. No messages from Sloane. I scroll through our text history, stopping at the last exchange before everything fell apart. Her excitement about decorating for Christmas jumps off the screen.

The perfect tree isn't perfect at all, she'd written. It needs character. A wonky branch or two, maybe even a bald spot. That's how you know it has a story.

I slip my phone back into my pocket and stare at the rows of Christmas trees in front of me. The lot owner hovers nearby, clearly wondering why this guy in an expensive coat has spent forty-five minutes examining every single tree without buying one.

"Looking for something specific?" he asks.

"Something imperfect," I say. "Something with character."

His eyebrows shoot up, but he nods.

I follow him to the back corner of the lot, where several neglected trees lean against the fence. One catches my eye immediately. A six-foot spruce with a dramatic curve in its trunk and a sparse patch on one side that gives it a lopsided appearance. It's exactly the kind of tree Sloane would love.

"That one," I point, already pulling out my wallet.

The lot owner looks skeptical. "You sure? Got some much nicer ones up front."

"This is the one." I'm certain. "It's perfect because it's not."

Twenty minutes later, I'm strapping the tree to the roof of my car, mentally checking off the first item on my "Win Sloane Back" list. Next stop: decorations. She'd spent an entire evening telling me about her family's Christmas traditions—handmade ornaments, popcorn garlands, multicolor light strands, and the ceramic star her grandmother had given her that always tops the tree.

I drive to three different stores before finding everything I need, including a ceramic star that's a decent stand-in if the original isn't at the penthouse. My final stop is the most important . . .

Knox's apartment is quiet when I knock, which means he's either not home or ignoring me. I'm about to call him when the door swings open, and he stands there with a knowing smirk.

"About time," he says, stepping aside to let me in. "The little monster's been driving me crazy."

As if on cue, a ball of golden fur comes tumbling around the corner, all paws and floppy ears. The golden retriever puppy skids across the hardwood floor before colliding with my shoes, immediately attacking my shoelaces with fierce determination.

"Jesus, Knox. What have you been feeding him?" I crouch down, and the puppy abandons my shoes to lick my face enthusiastically.

"The usual. Kibble, water, the occasional shoe." He crosses his arms. "So you're really doing this? The whole Christmas miracle thing?"

I scoop up the puppy, who settles against my chest with surprising contentment. "I don't have a choice. I screwed up."

"Yeah, you did." Knox disappears into his kitchen and returns with a bag of puppy supplies. "I'm not going to say I told you so." Knox hands me the puppy's leash. "He's already house-trained. Mostly."

"Mostly?"

"Nah, I'm kidding. You're screwed. Good luck."

An hour later, I'm juggling a squirming puppy, carrying bags of decorations, and attempting to maneuver the Christmas tree into the elevator of our building. The doorman tries to hide his amusement as he helps me.

I've timed this carefully. Sloane gets so absorbed in her work that she loses track of everything else. If I'm lucky, I can get the tree set up before she realizes I'm home.

The puppy, thankfully, seems to understand the mission. He sits quietly in the kitchen with a chew toy while I wrestle with the tree stand. It takes nearly an hour to get the tree balanced—the crooked trunk making it a challenge—but finally, it stands proudly in the corner of the living room by the floor-to-ceiling windows that overlook the city.

I string the lights carefully, just as Sloane described. The ornaments go on next, a mix of store-bought ones and the few I found tucked away in a box labeled "Christmas" in her closet at her old apartment. I make a popcorn garland too, though it looks nothing like the neat strands Sloane had described from her childhood. Mine has gaps where I broke the thread and pieces that are clearly mangled from my clumsy fingers.

Just as I'm placing the ceramic star on top, I hear the faint sound of her workshop door opening down the hall.

Quickly, I dim the other lights in the apartment and grab the puppy, who's fallen asleep on the couch. He blinks drowsily as I hold him against my chest, positioning myself next to the tree.

"Cole?" Sloane's voice carries from the hallway. "Is that you?"

"In here," I call back, my heart pounding.

She appears in the doorway, still wearing her work clothes—jeans and an oversize sweater, red hair piled messily on top of her head. There's a smudge of something on her cheek, probably silver dust from the piece she's been working on. She's never looked more beautiful.

For a moment, she just stares at the tree, her expression unreadable.

"What is this?" she finally asks, her voice quiet.

"It's a tree," I say lamely. "You said you wanted one."

"That was before—" She stops, noticing the puppy in my arms for the first time. Her eyes widen. "Cole . . ."

I step forward, the puppy now fully awake and wiggling. "I know I messed up. I know I should have told you the full truth from the beginning." I take another step. "Your work is brilliant, Sloane. I knew it the moment I saw the first piece you created. Yes, initially I thought your line would be a perfect way to fuck over Julian and protect Claire's legacy. I was using you as a tool. I can't deny that. But you've created something beyond what I could imagine. Something that stands entirely on its own merit. You aren't Claire. You have something far darker, edgier, and completely your own."

She doesn't move, but her eyes remain fixed on the puppy.

"I never meant to put you in danger. I let my arrogance get in the way of thinking I was more powerful than Julian. Knox tried to warn me, and I didn't listen. I also should have never stalked you. Because you are right. That's exactly what I was doing. No excuse."

"A tree and a puppy," she says softly. "That's how you think you'll fix this?"

"No." I shake my head. "Nothing fixes what I did. But I'm hoping it's a start. I'm hoping you'll let me spend every day showing you how much I believe in you. In us."

She looks up at the tree, taking in the crooked trunk, the sparse patches, the messy popcorn garland. Her eyes linger on the ceramic star.

"You bought a star," she notes.

"I wasn't sure if you had your grandmother's."

The puppy yawns dramatically, making Sloane laugh despite herself.

"Cole . . ." she whispers, reaching to take the puppy. It immediately starts covering her face in enthusiastic kisses. "This is the puppy from the rescue van. You adopted him? I thought—"

"I know it's crazy," I say quickly, my words tumbling out. "I know puppies are messy and unpredictable and completely against everything I usually—" I break off as the puppy wriggles free from Sloane's arms and bounds over to me, attacking my tie with delighted ferocity. I can't help but smile. "But when I saw the way you looked at the little guy . . ."

Sloane watches me as I gently detangle my silk tie from the puppy's mouth, and I'm acutely aware of how undignified I must look—Cole Archer, CEO, completely undone by a handful of fur and enthusiasm. But somehow, I don't care.

"When did you do this?" she asks, moving closer, taking the puppy into her arms.

"Knox went back for him. He's been hiding at his place, which has not been good for Knox's reputation with his security team." I feel my expression turn serious, the weight of what I've done settling in. "I know it's a big step. A puppy isn't just a gift, it's—"

"A commitment," she finishes. "A responsibility. A complete disruption to your perfectly ordered life."

"Our life," I correct her softly. "And maybe it needs disrupting." The puppy is licking her face and squirming all around. She catches him just before he face-plants. "I've spent my whole life thinking I needed to control everything. Then you came along . . ." I look down at the puppy, now contentedly chewing her finger. "I thought I was giving you a gift, but really . . . I think I'm giving us both permission to make a mess. Create something new."

She takes a deep breath, and I can see the walls she's built around herself starting to crumble. Carefully, she sets the puppy down on the floor, where he immediately begins investigating his new surroundings.

Sloane steps toward me until we're just inches apart. Her eyes search mine, and I force myself to stay still, to let her see everything—my regret, my hope, my love.

"I was so angry," she whispers. "Not just because of what happened, but because I was afraid of my worst fear. That you never really believed in me."

"I believe in you more than I've ever believed in anything," I say, my voice rough with emotion. "And I swear I'll spend the rest of my life proving it to you."

She reaches up, cupping my face in her hands. "You found a crooked Christmas tree."

"I found the perfect tree."

A smile breaks across her face, this one reaching all the way to her eyes. "Yes, you did."

And then she's rising on her tiptoes, her lips meeting mine in a kiss that feels like coming home. I wrap my arms around her waist, pulling her closer, feeling the tension of the past days dissolving as her body melds against mine. The kiss deepens, filled with forgiveness and promise.

A crash from the kitchen interrupts us, followed by the sound of scampering paws. We break apart and turn to see the puppy streak past the doorway, a dish towel clutched triumphantly in his mouth.

Sloane laughs, a real laugh that makes her eyes crinkle at the corners. She walks over and kisses me. Her lips are soft against mine, and something in my chest unravels.

"You're really saying yes to shoes being chewed and perfectly arranged pillows being knocked over?" she asks, pulling back with a smile that makes my heart skip.

"I ordered protective covers for all the furniture," I admit. "And puppy-proofing consultants are coming tomorrow."

She laughs, the sound filling the space between us as she picks up the puppy again. "Of course they are." The puppy has discovered her hair and is treating it like the world's best toy. "I love you," she says, still smiling as she tries to free her hair from tiny teeth.

The words hang in the air, and I feel my breath catch. She goes very still, clearly realizing what she's just said—what she's never said before.

"I—" she starts to say, but I cut her off with a kiss that pours every ounce of what I'm feeling into her. My hands find her face, cradling it like something precious.

"I love you too." My voice comes out rough with emotion. "God, Sloane, I've been trying to find the perfect moment to tell you, and here you are, just saying it while a puppy uses you as a chew toy."

She lets out a shaky laugh that I feel against my lips. "That's us, isn't it? You planning everything to perfection, and me just blurting things out between catastrophes."

"I wouldn't have it any other way." I brush her hair back from her face, my fingertips lingering on her skin. "And for the record, this actually might be the perfect moment."

"Better than whatever elaborate scenario you had planned?" Her eyes are teasing now, the green in them bright with happiness.

"Way better," I admit. "I was thinking about renting out The Pierre. I had a whole speech prepared. But this . . ." I glance around at our living room—the crooked tree, the messy decorations, the puppy chewing everything it sees. "This is us. Real. Messy. Perfect."

"Yeah?" She leans in to kiss me again, but the puppy chooses that moment to let out an indignant yip, clearly feeling ignored. "Does he have a name?"

"I thought we could figure that out together." I watch her untangle her hair from tiny puppy teeth, her fingers nimble against the golden fur. "Though given his clear disregard for proper order and expensive accessories, might I suggest Havoc?"

Sloane's smile widens as she lifts the puppy higher, holding him at eye level. "Havoc," she says as she tests the name. "I like it."

"Welcome to our beautiful mess," she tells him, and my laugh joins hers as Havoc suddenly wriggles free and makes a beeline for the Christmas tree, immediately batting at a low-hanging ornament.

I pull Sloane against me, arms wrapping around her waist as we watch our new puppy circle the tree with boundless enthusiasm. Her body fits perfectly against mine, and when she tilts her head back to look at me, I see everything I've ever wanted reflected in her eyes.

"I love you," I say again, because now that I've said it, I never want to stop.

Her answer is a kiss that starts soft but quickly deepens, her fingers threading through my hair. Havoc is completely forgotten as I lift her into my arms, her legs wrapping around my waist. I carry her toward our bedroom, leaving a trail of decorations and puppy toys in our wake.

For the first time in my life, I don't care about the mess.

Chapter Thirty-Four
COLE

Sloane's been living in her studio lately, consumed by this collection. The security feeds show her working until dawn most nights, though she thinks I don't know. I've been working long days as well, but all I want to do now is be tangled in her arms with our puppy at our sides.

Knox meets me in the parking garage. "She's been pacing for the last hour," he says as we step into the private elevator. "Whatever she's finished, it must be good."

The elevator opens directly into our penthouse, and I hear music drifting from the direction of her studio. Following the sound, I find her in her workspace, surrounded by scattered sketches and tools. Her hair is pulled back messily, and there are dark smudges under her eyes from too many late nights. Havoc dozes in his bed in the corner, having learned that the studio means "quiet time."

"Look." She lifts a piece from her workbench.

The crown seems to capture moonlight, black diamonds set in darkened platinum. No excess ornamentation, just pure, clean lines that draw the eye.

"This is the centerpiece?" I ask, though I already know. I've watched her work on it through the security feeds, seen her obsession grow with each passing night.

"Try to tell me this isn't exactly what the collection needed." Her eyes sparkle with pride and exhaustion.

She sets the crown down carefully, her hands trembling slightly. For a moment, she just stares at it. Then I see the tears forming in her eyes.

"It's done," she whispers, like she can hardly believe it. Her voice gets stronger. "Cole, it's done. The collection is truly and finally done!" She lets out a sound between a laugh and a sob. "Hailey just left after finishing the final bracelet, and now with the crown . . ." She spins in a circle, gesturing at the pieces arranged around her studio. "I've been working toward this for so long, I almost can't believe it's real."

She stops spinning, bracing herself against her workbench. "When you gave me that deadline, I thought you were actually insane. One month for an entire collection? But I did it." She shakes her head in disbelief. "I actually did it."

"I never doubted you would." I move closer, brush a strand of hair from her face. "You've exceeded every expectation I had, and trust me, they were high."

"Holy shit." She looks around her studio again, like she's seeing it with new eyes. "Now what?"

"Now," I say, pulling out my phone, "you need to eat actual food. And leave the penthouse for the first time in what, three days?"

I send a message to Gloria Ashworth. She'd turned down three billionaires this week alone, but she still keeps a table for me at her restaurant. Twenty years of running the most exclusive supper club in the city has made her particularly skilled at knowing which of her wealthy patrons actually matter.

"Has it been three days?" She glances down at herself, at the work apron covered in metal dust. "Oh god."

"Go get changed," I tell her, nodding toward her bedroom. "Dinner reservations at eight."

She looks up, finally seeming to notice how long she's been in the studio. "I probably look like a disaster."

"You look like an artist." But I can see the fatigue around her eyes, the way she's been running on nothing but creative energy for days. "Take a break. Celebrate."

Two hours later, Knox drives us to an unmarked door in the Financial District. Gloria's is the type of place that doesn't officially exist unless you know the right people. Sloane's black dress makes the diamond studs in her ears stand out like ice as we step into the private entrance. The exhaustion from earlier is gone—she looks energized, ready to celebrate.

The maître d' recognizes me immediately, guiding us through a dark wood-paneled corridor into the main dining room. The space feels more like a private manor than a restaurant—all coffered ceilings and vintage crystal chandeliers casting warm light over intimate alcoves. Each table is separated by strategic distance and clever architectural details, ensuring absolute privacy. The room holds perhaps twelve tables total, though you'd never see them all at once.

Gloria has preserved the building's prewar details—the original herringbone floors, hand-carved moldings, brass fixtures that have aged to a perfect patina. But she's modernized in subtle ways: temperature-controlled wine walls behind antique glass, state-of-the-art kitchen equipment glimpsed through discrete passthroughs, lighting that makes everyone look ten years younger.

My preferred alcove is ready, with its leather banquette and views of both the room and the city lights beyond the centuries-old windows. A bottle of champagne is already breathing in an antique silver bucket.

"I didn't even know places like this existed," Sloane whispers as we're seated, her fingers trailing over the leather upholstery. "How did you find it?"

"You don't find Gloria's," I tell her, watching her take in every detail with wide eyes. "Gloria finds you."

She studies the room, then leans closer. "That's the CEO of Richmond Tech at the corner table, isn't it? And I swear I just saw Senator Matthews walk by."

"The interesting ones are the people you don't recognize," I say, nodding toward a quiet man in the far alcove whose hedge fund could buy Richmond Tech ten times over. "The ones who prefer to stay out of the spotlight."

The sommelier pours our wine, and Sloane immediately relaxes into the evening, the tension of the past month melting away. Between bites of her scallop appetizer, she can't stop talking about the crown.

"You should have seen Hailey's face when we tried the new setting technique." Her eyes light up. "Everyone said black diamonds were too risky at that size, that they'd shatter, but—" She leans forward, lowering her voice like she's sharing a trade secret. "We found a way to distribute the pressure points so perfectly that—"

She breaks off as our entrées arrive, the waiter setting down her duck with a flourish. I've never seen her this animated, this proud of solving what everyone said was impossible.

She breaks off as voices from the next alcove grow louder, cutting through the usual quiet murmur of the room.

"—completely unexpected. The whole company."

"Moth to the Flame? I thought they were stable."

"Complete collapse. Bankruptcy filing this afternoon. My broker called to warn me to dump the stock, but it was already too late."

Sloane's fork pauses halfway to her mouth as the conversation from the next alcove registers. She sets it down slowly. "Did they just say Moth to the Flame filed for bankruptcy?"

I meet her eyes. "I heard about it this afternoon."

"And you didn't tell me?"

"Tonight was about celebrating you. Your collection. Your achievement." I lean back, studying her reaction. "I was going to tell you tomorrow."

She's quiet for a moment, processing. Then she grabs her phone and starts typing rapidly.

"What are you thinking?" I ask, though her intense focus tells me she's already forming plans.

"Marcus." Her fingers keep moving across the screen. "And Sarah. The whole platinum workshop team, really. They're artists, Cole. The best I've ever worked with, and now they'll be scattered to whatever corporate jewelry chain will take them."

I watch her add another name to her list. "You want to hire them."

"I want—" She looks up suddenly, eyes bright with possibility. "I want to build something real. Not just my private studio but a proper workshop. A place that values craft over quarterly profits. Where talented people can actually create, not just churn out whatever tests well in focus groups."

Watching her plan her next venture over a plate of duck confit at Gloria's feels exactly right. She's always ten steps ahead, seeing possibilities where others only see rubble.

"I have real estate holdings that might interest you," I say casually. "A few historic buildings with good natural light."

She pauses mid-bite, eyes narrowing. "How long have you been waiting to mention these buildings?"

"About thirty seconds." I take a sip of wine. "Though there might be some equipment from a recent acquisition that could be useful too."

A slow smile spreads across her face. "Are you trying to be my angel investor, Mr. Asher?"

"I know a good investment when I see one." I meet her gaze. "And you've more than proven your return potential."

She traces the rim of her wineglass, and I catch a flicker of something in her expression. "If the collection is a hit." Her voice is quieter now. "The reveal is in nine days and—"

"Stop." I lean forward. "I've watched women's faces when they try on your pieces. That crown alone . . ." I shake my head. "Every woman who sees this collection is going to want to wear it. Not just own it—wear it. Make it part of who they are."

The confidence returns to her eyes, along with something fiercer. She picks up her wineglass again, a slight smile playing at her lips.

"You know," she says, setting the glass down again, "for all their faults, Moth to the Flame had some incredibly talented people. I can't save everyone's job, but . . ." She starts counting on her fingers. "Marcus's metalwork, Sarah's stone setting, Jenna in procurement who somehow found the impossible . . ." She stops suddenly. "Oh god, Chloe. I need to text her. Moth to the Flame was her biggest contract. All those sponsored posts, the events—"

"Chloe," I say, "is about to be very busy as the face of your collection. And as for the others . . ." I gesture to her phone. "Make your list. Anyone you vouch for, I'll make sure they land somewhere. If not with your new venture, then with one of my subsidiaries."

She looks at me for a long moment. "Just like that?"

"Just like that. Talent is talent, and I trust your judgment."

The waiter clears our dinner plates and presents the dessert menu. Sloane's been quieter for the last few minutes, turning her wineglass by the stem.

"So," she says, not quite meeting my eyes. "Tomorrow's Christmas Eve."

I look up from the menu. In the whirlwind of the past month—her moving into the penthouse, getting Havoc, decorating that ridiculous tree—we somehow never discussed our first Christmas.

"Your mother's still upset you're not going to Montauk?" I ask, though I already know the answer from the heated phone calls I've overheard.

"She'll survive." Sloane takes a sip of wine. "I told her I'm not spending Christmas watching her drink too much wine and make passive-aggressive comments about my life choices."

"And what are those life choices?" I set down the menu. "Getting your CEO to buy a crooked Christmas tree? Letting a puppy chew up my Italian leather shoes? Or is it the part where you're building an empire while your mother thinks you should be in Montauk drinking white wine and discussing tennis lessons?"

"The shoes were Havoc's choice, not mine," she says primly, but I can see her fighting a smile.

"All of the above." She grins, but then it falters slightly. "We are spending tomorrow together, right? I mean, I just assumed, with the tree and everything . . ."

I reach across the table and take her hand. "I should warn you—I haven't done a real Christmas since I was a kid. I might be terrible at it."

"Good thing you have me then." Her fingers lace through mine. "One month to master a jewelry collection, remember? I'm excellent at impossible tasks."

Looking at her across the table in the warm light of Gloria's, I see the woman who changed every plan I thought I had. Who made me want something more than just success.

First Christmas Eve. Then her empire. But tonight, we're having dessert. And for the first time in my life, I'm not thinking about what comes next. I'm exactly where I want to be.

Chapter Thirty-Five

SLOANE

I wake to the sound of Cole having what appears to be a very serious conversation with our puppy.

"The tree is not a bathroom," he's saying in the same tone he probably uses for hostile takeovers. "We discussed this."

Havoc's response is the scraping sound of another ornament being batted across the floor.

I slip out of bed and peek around my bedroom door. Cole's in his usual impeccable suit—he has a morning meeting he couldn't reschedule—but he's on his knees trying to extract a silver ball from under the couch while Havoc helpfully pounces on his tie.

"That's Hermès silk you're treating like a chew toy." But he's scratching behind Havoc's ears even as he says it.

"Your tie collection was doomed the day we got him," I say, and Cole looks up, caught in the act of baby-talking to a puppy. "I have photographic evidence of the mighty CEO on his hands and knees at seven in the morning."

"Delete it."

"Not a chance." I snap another picture as Havoc successfully steals the tie. "This is definitely becoming my Christmas card next year."

Cole stands, abandoning the tie to its fate. His eyes do that slow sweep that makes my skin heat. I'm wearing one of his dress shirts that I stole weeks ago, and his gaze lingers on my bare legs.

"I'm only going to be gone two hours," he says, stepping closer. "Three at most."

"We have all day." I straighten his collar, deliberately brushing my fingers against his neck. "Go be a CEO. Havoc and I need to wrap your presents anyway."

"About that." He glances at the pile of wrapped gifts under the tree. "You do realize there are significantly more packages there than last night."

"Knox helped me hide them in the garage. And before you say anything about excessive gift-giving, I saw your security team trying to be stealthy all week. They're terrible at it, by the way. Even Havoc noticed them sneaking around with those giant boxes."

"I have no idea what you're talking about." But the slight quirk of his mouth tells me otherwise. "Three hours," he says again, and kisses me in a way that makes me seriously consider making him late for his meeting.

The moment he's gone, I race to the kitchen. I have precisely two hours and fifty-eight minutes to attempt something I've never done before—make Christmas Eve dinner. Well, attempt to make Christmas Eve dinner. I've got backup reservations at three different restaurants, but I'm determined to at least try the whole domestic goddess thing.

How hard can it be?

Two hours later, I've learned several important life lessons:

Cooking videos make everything look deceptively easy.

Setting off the smoke alarm once means Knox will appear in full tactical gear.

Setting it off twice means the entire security team will be hovering nervously in the hallway.

Setting it off three times means Knox will gently suggest ordering takeout while confiscating your oven privileges.

Knox clears his throat from the doorway.

"The cleaning service is here," he says with admirable professionalism. "And may I suggest a cooking class for the new year?"

"That obvious?"

"Let's just say I've seen less destruction in active war zones."

The cleaning crew works miracles. By four, there's no evidence of my culinary disaster, and Gloria's team has transformed the dining room into something straight out of a magazine. The whole penthouse smells like roasting turkey instead of burning . . . everything.

Knox does a final sweep of the floor before his shift ends. "You're all set. New team's coming up in five minutes for the night shift." He pauses at the elevator. "I'm heading home. Merry Christmas."

"Merry Christmas, Knox. I'm sorry for all the commotion today."

He grins. "Maybe stick to jewelry design."

I'm still laughing as the elevator doors close. I head to my room to change—I bought a new red dress for tonight, wanting to look festive for our first Christmas Eve.

That's when I hear the elevator again. Too soon for the new security team.

Too soon for Cole.

When I step into the hallway, it's not Cole's security team waiting for me.

I freeze in the hallway, my hand instinctively reaching for my phone before I remember it's still in the kitchen. The space suddenly feels too small, too confined, as I recognize the two broad-shouldered men flanking a third figure—the Russians from the Met gala, their expressions as cold and impassive as I remember.

But it's the figure between them who holds my attention. He's a slight man, dressed in an impeccable charcoal suit that seems to absorb the light around him. His silver hair is perfectly styled, his smile pleasant and practiced—like a politician's, or a shark's. Everything about him screams old money and influence, right down to the signet ring on his right hand.

"Hello, Sloane," he says, his voice carrying a slight accent I can't quite place. "I'm Julian Voss."

My throat goes dry. I've imagined this moment so many times, played out countless scenarios of finally meeting the man who's been haunting the edges of my life. But standing here now, I realize none of my imagined confrontations prepared me for the reality of him.

"I must say," he continues as he bends down to scoop up Havoc, who had bounded over to investigate the newcomers, "what a delightful puppy." His manicured fingers scratch behind Havoc's ears, the gesture almost gentle. The sight of my dog in his arms makes my stomach turn.

Something in my expression must show, because his smile widens slightly. I glance toward the security panel near the elevator, its light blinking red instead of the usual green. Somehow, they've disabled it.

"The new security team won't be joining us," Voss says, reading my thoughts. "I hoped we could have a private conversation.

"You remind me of Claire, you know. She had the same . . . fire." His gaze drops to my throat. "Your designs are so close. Not exact, but close."

One of the Russians steps forward, grabbing my arm with bruising force. I struggle instinctively, managing to land one solid kick to his knee before the second man pushes me against the wall, hand at my throat.

"Careful," Julian says sharply. "She needs to be intact."

I think of Knox, already headed home, and Cole, stuck in his meeting across town. My mind races, trying to calculate options, escape routes, anything.

I see the movement too late. The Russians step forward in perfect synchronization, and before I can scream, one of them presses a cloth against my face. The world begins to blur at the edges.

The last thing I see is Voss carefully setting Havoc down, the puppy's tail still wagging as my vision goes dark.

Chapter Thirty-Six

SLOANE

The first thing I notice when I regain consciousness is that my captors have excellent taste in furniture. The chair I'm tied to is Danish modern, all sleek lines and butter-soft leather. The room itself could be featured in *Architectural Digest*—if you ignored the whole "hostage situation" vibe.

My heart is trying to punch through my ribs, and there's a scream building in my throat that I refuse to let out. Fear claws at my insides—raw, primal terror that threatens to shatter my carefully maintained composure. But I can't fall apart. Not now. Not when my life depends on keeping my wits about me.

One of the Russians checks the restraints, his grip bruising as he yanks the silk rope tighter. My wrists burn from the friction, but I bite back a whimper. The other one—I've mentally named them Boris and Vladimir—sets up a sleek laptop on the desk, connecting it to some kind of strange device with a camera lens and what looks like a hand scanner.

A hysterical laugh bubbles up as I realize this is exactly like one of those mafia romances I pretend not to read. Except this isn't fiction, and there's no guarantee of a happy ending.

Deep breath. Channel your inner femme fatale, Sloane.

I've managed to kick off my heels, partly out of spite, partly because if I'm going to die, it's not going to be in four-inch Loubou-tins. The rope around my wrists is silk. Because of course it is.

"The facial recognition system is ready," one of the Russians says, his accent thick.

"Good." Julian's voice comes from the doorway. "That's why we're keeping her face pretty. For now."

When Julian walks in, I raise an eyebrow. "Do all corporate megalomaniacs take interior design classes? This is very 'serial killer chic'—very Martha-Stewart-meets-Hannibal-Lecter."

His perfectly controlled expression twitches. Just slightly. Good.

"I see why he likes you," Julian says, settling into an armchair across from me. "You share his . . . particular sense of humor."

"If this is where you launch into your villain origin story, can we skip to the highlights? The chloroform gave me a headache."

My pulse quickens at my own daring. Every word is a gamble—too submissive and he'll know he has power over me, too defiant and he might decide I'm not worth keeping alive. I can feel the silk rope digging into my wrists, and the urge to struggle against it is almost overwhelming. But I force myself to stay still, to keep my breathing even. Show no weakness. Give him nothing.

He studies me for a long moment, and I see something flicker in his eyes—something that makes me think of a cobra sizing up its prey. "Did Cole ever tell you how we met?"

I keep my voice steady, neutral. "No. He hasn't."

"I found him," Julian continues as if I hadn't spoken, "fresh out of business school, brilliant but raw. Unpolished. I saw myself in him—that same hunger, that same drive." His voice takes on an almost wistful quality. "He was like a son to me."

"And Claire?" I ask, the name slipping out before I can stop myself. "Did you 'find' her too?" His face darkens instantly, and I know I've struck a nerve.

"I *invented* Claire," he seethes. "She was nothing before me."

"Really? Because I was under the impression you were nothing without *her*."

Julian's hand moves so fast I barely see it before his palm connects with my cheek. The sting brings tears to my eyes, but I refuse to let them fall.

"Don't speak unless I ask you to," he hisses. "Learn your place."

Motherfucker, that hurt! But I refuse to show it. I refuse to give the man the power even though I'm damn near panicked right now.

"Why don't we skip to the part where you explain why I'm here?" My voice is quieter than I intend, but steady. "Why you took me from my home on Christmas Eve."

His smile is cold, precise. "Christmas Eve. I chose it carefully. Five years ago, it was Christmas Eve when Cole destroyed everything." His voice drops lower, almost intimate. "I thought it fitting that he should lose something precious on the same night." He stands abruptly, pacing the room.

I keep my expression neutral. I'm not going to give away anything more than I have to.

"Claire was my *wife*." He spits the words like they taste bitter. "We could have made so much money if it wasn't for Cole." He practically sneers the word.

I remain silent, watching the way his composure cracks when he speaks about her. Each word reveals more about Cole's past, about the darkness that still haunts him.

Julian's pacing brings him to a wall safe I hadn't noticed before. He opens it with practiced movements, removing something wrapped in black velvet.

"Look at this craftsmanship," he says, unwrapping what I now see is a necklace of such intricate detail it takes my breath away. "Claire's signature. The way she layered metal and stone . . . no one could match her vision." His fingers trace the delicate metalwork with an unsettling intimacy. "She created pieces for the most exclusive clients. Never asked questions about where the diamonds came from. Until . . ."

His voice hardens. "Do you know what happens to profits when someone starts asking inconvenient questions about diamond origins?" He folds the velvet around the necklace like he's wrapping a wound. "Cole filled her head with noble ideas about right and wrong. Made her forget about loyalty."

He moves to the window, staring out at the snow that's started to fall. "I tried to reason with her. Told her to think about everything we'd built together." His hand presses against the glass. "The night she tried to leave, it was snowing. Just like this."

The temperature in the room seems to drop as he turns back to me. "A tragic accident. Black ice on a mountain road. No guardrail. They found the car three hundred feet down." He gives a sad smile but his eyes are chips of ice. "Leaving behind a heartbroken husband."

I feel a fierce pride in Cole, in the man he chose to become. "That's when it started, isn't it? Cole's 'war' against you. He knew what you'd done."

"He blamed me for her death. Said I'd killed her as surely as if I'd pushed the car off that cliff myself." Julian carefully rewraps the necklace. "That's when he made it his mission to dismantle everything I'd built. With her blood money, he called it."

I shift in my chair, testing the ropes. Still secure. But for the first time, I'm grateful for every paranoid security measure Cole ever insisted on. The cameras I complained about, the trackers I teased him for, Knox's constant surveillance that used to drive me crazy—it all means something very different now. They'll have footage of Julian's men. They'll know exactly who took me, how many there are, what they're driving.

And Cole . . . Cole who plans for every contingency, who has backup plans for his backup plans, who has built his empire on being three steps ahead of everyone else—he has to know by now. Has to be moving pieces into place, making calls, mobilizing whatever network of resources he has for exactly this kind of nightmare.

Every second Julian talks is another second bringing Cole closer. Because Cole is coming. Not if, but when. And god help anyone who stands in his way.

Julian moves to a leather briefcase I hadn't noticed before, and my breath catches as he starts laying out familiar pieces on his desk. My pieces. The ones his men must have taken when they grabbed me.

"Beautiful work," he says, arranging them with disturbing care. "Perhaps not quite Claire's level, but . . . promising." His fingers trail over my designs. "Tell me, Sloane, would you like to know what I have planned for you?"

The casual way he asks sends ice through my veins, but I force myself to meet his eyes. "Isn't that the part where the villain traditionally monologues about his grand plan?"

"Ah, but that would spoil the surprise." His eyes drift to the collection pieces arranged on his desk. "I suppose I could share that your designs—your exquisite, innovative designs—will make the perfect addition to Claire's collection. The collection Cole has kept hidden away in this case. The one you *will* be opening for me. Otherwise . . . well, let's just say I'll need to make your disappearance as convincing as your former assistant's."

My blood turns to ice. "Maya? What did you do to her?"

Julian ignores me, turning to the Russians. "Get her to the scanner. We need her biometrics to access the case. Cole set it up so only Claire, himself, or his designated successor could open it." He smiles coldly at me. "Congratulations, Ms. Whitmore. You're the successor."

What the fuck is he talking about? *Biometrics?* But my thoughts quickly return to Maya.

"Maya was working for you, wasn't she? That's why she disappeared, isn't it? She found something while working on your fake Claire collection."

Julian's laugh is cold, empty. "Smart girl. Yes, she was quite talented. Not as good as you, but she had potential. Until she started asking the wrong questions. Looking through the wrong files." He shrugs, the gesture casual, chilling. "She lacked . . . staying power."

Oh my god. Maya is dead. Because of what she knew, what she saw.

One of the Russians drags my chair toward the biometric device. I struggle against the restraints, but it's useless. His fingers dig into my scalp as he forces my face toward the scanner, and I think of Maya, of what they might have done to her before the end. I squeeze my eyes shut, twist my face into the most grotesque expression I can manage, anything to prevent the scan from working.

"Nyet. Stop this," the Russian growls, gripping my jaw harder. "Face normal."

"Sorry, this IS my normal face," I reply, then cross my eyes and puff out my cheeks like a demented chipmunk. The scanner beeps in protest.

"It needs neutral expression!" he barks, shaking me slightly.

I immediately switch to an exaggerated smile that would make the Joker proud. "Is this better? I'm being very cooperative." The scanner flashes red again.

Julian sighs heavily. "Ms. Whitmore, childish antics won't help you. That system needs to verify your identity to access Cole's case where Claire's final collection is stored."

"Oh, is THAT what we're doing? Why didn't you say so?" I ask innocently, before launching into a series of rapid-fire expressions—

duck lips, nostrils flared, eyebrows waggling independently, and what I hope is a passable impression of a constipated walrus.

The Russian curses in his native tongue, while his partner snickers despite himself. Julian's perfect composure finally cracks.

"Enough!" he snaps. "Hold her properly. I want access to those jewels NOW."

The first Russian clamps my head in a viselike grip while the other produces a small spray bottle. "This make eyes open," he warns, positioning it uncomfortably close to my face.

Great. Threats of chemical warfare. That's totally going to make me cooperate.

"You won't win," Julian says calmly, watching my desperate attempts. "Everyone breaks eventually. Maya did. Even Claire did, in her way."

He pulls out his phone, smile widening. "Besides, I think Cole should be here for this conversation. I'm sure he's wondering where you are by now." He smiles, all predator, as he pulls out his phone. "Why don't we give him a call?"

Chapter Thirty-Seven
COLE

Something's wrong.

I feel it the moment the elevator doors open. The penthouse is too quiet, too still. No Christmas music drifting from the kitchen where Sloane had insisted on attempting to cook. No sound of Havoc's nails clicking across the hardwood as he races to greet me.

"Sloane?" My voice echoes in the silence.

A whine draws me to the living room. Havoc sits alone by the Christmas tree, tail thumping weakly against the floor. An ornament rolls beneath the couch, city lights from the window catching the silver ball.

The security panel by the elevator glows red instead of green.

I scan the room, cataloging details with growing dread. A half-empty wineglass on the coffee table. The faint scent of something burnt from the kitchen. A cold mug of coffee on the counter, a perfect red lipstick print on the rim.

My feet carry me to her workspace before my mind fully processes why. The display cases are empty. Not just one or two pieces—all of them. Every prototype, every finished design. Gone.

I reach for my phone just as Knox bursts through the stairwell door, tactical gear still on, face grim.

"They took her." His words hit like bullets. "Didn't even try to hide it. Left the cameras running. They wanted us to see."

My phone starts vibrating. Julian's name lights up the screen.

"Don't." Knox's command is sharp. "That's exactly what he wants. He's expecting you to answer, to come charging in. He's got a trap laid out, just waiting for you to spring it."

The phone keeps buzzing. Each ring feels like a year of my life.

"Trust me on this, Cole." Knox steps closer, his voice low and intense. "I've seen this playbook a hundred times in the field. The staged scene, the obvious breadcrumbs, the perfectly timed call. It's Psychological Warfare 101. He's counting on you to be emotional, to rush in without thinking."

"To hell with that." My voice is razor-sharp. "I'm not leaving her with that psychopath for one more second."

"Listen to me." Knox's eyes lock onto mine. "The moment you answer that phone, he owns you. He'll have his threat ready—his 'do what I say or else.' And then every minute she's with him becomes another weapon he can use against you. The only way to keep her safe is to take that power away from him."

I grip the phone so hard the case creaks. "If he hurts her—"

"He won't. Not yet. This is about you. About making you suffer. Making you watch." Knox's voice drops lower. "So let's make him suffer instead. Let's make him wait."

The phone stops ringing. Starts again immediately.

"You know what's worse than fear?" Knox continues. "Anticipation. Uncertainty. Let them sit there all night, jumping at every sound, wondering if this is it. Let them stare at the monitors, at the doors, at their phones. Let them get tired. Sloppy."

"You want me to wait until morning." The words taste like ash.

"I want you to be the Cole Asher who built an empire by never doing what anyone expected. The one who wins because he thinks three moves ahead." Knox's eyes are steady. "Julian's got this whole night choreographed in his head. So let's rewrite his script."

The phone rings a third time.

"He took her on Christmas Eve for a reason," Knox says. "Made it personal. So let's return the favor. Let's make him spend his whole night wondering why you're not playing your part in his little drama."

"Do we know where they took her?" My voice is barely controlled.

Knox nods grimly. "Working on it. Pulling surveillance from every street camera in a ten-mile radius. But . . ." He hesitates. "I've got a pretty good idea."

"The estate on Hillcrest." The words taste bitter. Claire's studio is still there, untouched since that night. Julian's been waiting all these years to draw me back to where it started.

"That's my guess. I've got eyes on it now." Knox's jaw tightens. "We'll know for certain soon."

"How the fuck did this happen?" I snap. "How the hell did he get past security?"

Knox sighs. "Everyone wanted to be with their families for the holidays. No fucking excuse, but we became a skeleton crew. And the guard on duty manning the entrance conveniently had a bathroom break at the time. Don't worry, we'll get to the bottom of it and make the responsible party pay."

"Be sure that you do."

Knox nods, already typing on his phone. "I've got teams moving into position. By morning, we'll have options."

The phone starts ringing again.

I silence it without looking, then walk to where Havoc sits anxiously by the tree. He nuzzles my hand as I scratch behind his ears, his whole body trembling slightly.

"I know, buddy," I murmur. "We'll get her back."

The words catch in my throat as reality crashes over me. How could I have been so blind? I'd anticipated Julian's moves like this was still just business—expected him to go after her designs, try to sabotage her work. But kidnapping? I convinced myself he wouldn't dare, that he wouldn't risk something so bold.

And why? Because it didn't fit the pattern? Because it wasn't his style?

This is the man who murdered his own wife. Who orchestrated Claire's "accident" with such precision that even now, five years later, no one can prove otherwise. And I what—thought he'd stop at corporate espionage when it came to Sloane?

I let my guard down. Worse, I let her guard down. Sent the security team home. Ignored the signs. All because I couldn't admit that Julian's obsession with destroying me had nothing to do with business anymore.

"Hold on, Sloane," I whisper to the empty room. The thought of making her wait, of leaving her with him for even one more minute, makes me physically sick. But she's strong—stronger than Julian knows, stronger maybe than I deserve. "Just hold on. Be smart. Be the woman who never backs down, who looks danger in the eye and raises an eyebrow at it. I'm coming. I swear to god I'm coming."

Snow falls steadily outside the windows, each minute feeling like an eternity. But I force myself to stay still, to breathe through the rage burning in my chest. Because Sloane's life depends on me being smarter than my instincts right now.

Julian wants me desperate. Wants me reckless.

He'll have to settle for ruthless instead.

Chapter Thirty-Eight
SLOANE

Where. The. Hell. Is. He?

I stare at the ornate clock on the wall, forcing my breathing to steady. The silk tie around my wrists is tight enough to remind me of my situation but not enough to cut off circulation.

The minute hand moves again. Another fifteen minutes gone. Why isn't he here? What if something happened to him? What if they hurt him? What if this is all some elaborate revenge plot and he's lying somewhere, bleeding out, while I sit here uselessly tied to a chair? What if—

No. Stop it. Think.

Julian stares at the biometric scanner in disbelief, his composure finally shattered as the red warning flashes across the screen: "ACCESS DENIED. MAXIMUM ATTEMPTS EXCEEDED. SYSTEM LOCKDOWN INITIATED."

"What does that mean?" he demands, rounding on the Russian holding the device.

"It's bad," the man says, backing away slightly. "Very bad. System's locked now. We need the override code."

Julian's face contorts with rage. "Override it!"

"I cannot. We need the special code. From him." The Russian looks genuinely afraid now. "From Asher."

I can't help the triumphant smile that spreads across my face, despite the stinging in my cheeks from all their attempts to force me into a neutral expression. My little facial gymnastics routine worked better than I'd hoped.

Julian notices my smile and strikes like a snake, the back of his hand connecting with my cheek hard enough to snap my head to the side.

"You think this is funny?" he seethes. "You knew exactly what would happen."

I taste blood but meet his gaze steadily. "Vault Security 101. Too many failed attempts triggers a lockdown. Pretty standard stuff."

"Boss," the other Russian interrupts, examining the scanner. "System also sent an alert signal. To Asher."

Julian goes utterly still, processing this new information. Then a cold smile spreads across his face. "So he knows we're here. He knows exactly what we want." He runs his fingers through his perfectly styled hair, mussing it for the first time. "And yet he's still not coming. What does that tell you, Sloane?"

This is Cole Asher we're talking about. The same man who had an entire dossier on me before our first meeting. Who knew my shoe size, my coffee order, and somehow even which side of the bed I prefer to sleep on. The man who flew me to Switzerland just to convince me to sign with his company. Who had a contract drafted before I'd even officially said yes.

Cole doesn't do anything without a plan. Everything—every gesture, every word, every seeming coincidence—is meticulously calculated. He's probably known where I am since the moment they took me.

Which means there's a reason he's not answering Julian's increasingly angry phone calls.

"Your little victory means nothing," Julian says, pacing now, his expensive shoes clicking against the marble floor. "All you've done is force a change of plans."

"And what exactly was the original plan?" I ask, trying to keep him talking. Every minute he spends ranting is another minute for Cole to get here. "Profit off the designs Claire never wanted you to have, steal mine while you're at it, and . . . what? Live happily ever after knowing you've finally gotten revenge on Cole?"

"Don't pretend to understand what this is about," he snaps. "This was never just about the designs."

"Then what is it about?" I press. "Because from where I'm sitting—literally—this seems like an awful lot of effort just to steal some jewelry."

His laugh is cold and bitter. "Jewelry? Is that what you think this is? These are more than pretty baubles, Ms. Whitmore. It's about not letting Cole win."

Across the room, Julian paces, phone pressed to his ear. His perfectly tailored suit is starting to show signs of wear, his usual composure cracking around the edges. The two Russians exchange worried glances as Julian's call goes to voicemail for the fifth time.

"Where the hell is he?" Julian snarls, throwing the phone onto an antique desk.

I can't help it. A small laugh escapes me, drawing their attention. "Would now be a good time to tell you that Cole and I had a huge fight right before you came?" I lean back in my chair, affecting a casual pose despite my bound wrists. "Huge. Breakup type of fight."

Julian's eyes narrow as he stalks toward me. "You're lying."

I shrug, ignoring how my heart pounds faster with each step he takes. "Maybe he's just done with all of this." I force my lips into a smirk. "Can't say I blame him."

A muscle twitches in Julian's jaw. "He wouldn't—"

"Ignore you?" I arch an eyebrow at him. "Looks like he already is. I guess neither of us is as important to Cole Asher as we thought we were."

"If he doesn't care about you anymore," Julian says, his voice

dangerously soft, "then perhaps you've outlived your usefulness."
He reaches inside his jacket, pulling out an ornate switchblade. The
blade springs open with a soft click that somehow sounds more
threatening than any gunshot.

"Boss," one of the Russians says nervously, "the plan was—"

"The plan has changed." Julian cuts him off, tracing the knife tip
along my collarbone. "No case access means we need a new incen-
tive for Mr. Asher. Perhaps pieces of his girlfriend delivered one by
one will motivate him to come out of hiding."

I try to lean away from the blade, but there's nowhere to go. A
bead of blood wells up where the knife presses against my skin.

"Let's start with something small," Julian muses, his eyes never
leaving mine. "A finger, perhaps? Or maybe an ear? Artists don't
really need both, do they?"

My heart hammers against my ribs, but I force myself to keep
my voice steady. "You do that, and you'll never get what you want.
Cole won't negotiate if you hurt me."

"Won't he?" Julian presses the blade a fraction deeper. "I think
you underestimate how much he values you. How much he would
sacrifice to keep you whole."

"Exactly. To keep me whole. He doesn't want a mutilated girlfriend."

I watch with satisfaction as uncertainty creeps into Julian's
expression.

"You know him. Has he ever accepted anything less than perfection?"

I think of him decorating a crooked tree. Wrestling his tie out of
Havoc's mouth. He would love me, "mutilated" or not. But that's
not the Cole Julian knows.

The Russians shift uncomfortably, muttering to each other in
low voices.

Julian snatches up his phone again, stabbing at the screen. His composure cracks further with each unanswered ring. Finally, he hurls the device across the room. It hits the wall with a crack that makes me flinch.

"This isn't—" He cuts himself off, taking a deep breath. "Get her designs loaded. All of them. If he won't answer . . ." He turns to me, and the look in his eyes makes my blood run cold. "Then maybe we need to give him a better reason to call back."

The Russians move toward the stack of my prototype cases. My stomach lurches as they start handling my work, my art, like it's nothing more than cargo to be shipped.

Boris—or maybe it's Vladimir—drops one of the cases. The sound of metal hitting marble makes me jerk against the silk tie. "Careful with those," I snap before I can stop myself.

Julian's head whips around. A smile spreads across his face that does nothing to warm his eyes. "Ah. So you do care about something besides making me believe you and Cole are finished."

He walks over to where the case fell, picking up one of my designs. My newest one. The one I hadn't even shown Cole yet.

"Beautiful work." He turns it over in his hands. His fingers trace the edge of the metal with an intimacy that makes my skin crawl. "Perfect, really. Claire's final collection, discovered after all these years."

I force myself to stay still, to keep my voice steady. "What exactly do you think you're going to do with my designs?"

"These?" He lifts the piece to catch the light. "These are *Claire's* designs. Found in her private studio after her tragic accident. Her final collection, never shown to the world." He sets the piece down with exaggerated care. "The art world will be captivated. Her legacy, living on. The press will eat it up."

Ice slides down my spine as I realize what he's planning. Not just theft—complete erasure. He's going to wipe away my name, my work, everything I've created.

"You'll never get away with—"

"Won't I?" His smile is cold. "By the time this hits the press, these pieces will have all the proper documentation. Every sketch, every note, every prototype—all in Claire's hand. It's amazing what money can buy these days. And the best part?" He checks his watch again. "It won't matter that I couldn't access Claire's real work. All this effort to keep them from me won't matter. Cole will have to watch as everything you've created becomes part of her legacy instead."

The calm I've been clinging to starts to crack. These designs aren't just pieces of metal and stone—they're pieces of me. My vision. My soul. Each one represents countless hours of work, of failing and trying again, of finally getting it exactly right. And he's going to erase all of that with a stack of forged papers.

A loud thud from somewhere in the mansion makes everyone freeze. Julian's head snaps toward the door.

"Go check," he orders one of the Russians, who immediately draws his weapon and slips out.

The second Russian looks nervous now, his hand hovering near his holster. "Boss, maybe we should—"

"Keep loading," Julian snaps. "We're not leaving without those designs."

The remaining Russian returns to packing my work, but his movements are hurried now, careless. Another piece clatters against the side of the case.

"If that's Cole," I say quietly, "you should know he won't come alone."

Julian's smile is cold as he turns back to me. "I'm counting on it." He draws the knife again, moving behind me. "In fact, I think it's time we prepared a proper welcome."

His fingers twist into my hair, yanking my head back as the

knife comes to rest against my throat. My pulse throbs against the cold metal.

"This is the oldest story in the world, Sloane," he whispers against my ear. "The hero comes to rescue the damsel, only to walk right into the trap."

Another crash echoes from deeper in the house, followed by what sounds unmistakably like a gunshot.

"Tick tock," Julian murmurs, his breath hot against my skin. "Your knight approaches."

One of the Russians drops another case with a clang. Julian doesn't even flinch at the sound this time, too busy staring at his phone. Seven calls now. All ignored.

"Load them in the van," he snaps suddenly. "All of them. And carefully this time, you idiots. These are priceless pieces of art now." He barks out a laugh. "Worth far more with Claire's name on them than they ever would have been with yours."

I bite my tongue until I taste blood, refusing to give him the satisfaction of seeing me react. But inside, my mind is racing. There has to be something, some detail that would prove these are mine. My signature elements, my techniques . . .

"What about the girl?" one of the Russians asks, his accent thick.

Julian's eyes sweep over me, cold and calculating. "Leave her with me. Mr. Asher and I have some unfinished business to discuss." His lip curls. "When he finally decides to show up."

Something in his tone makes my skin prickle. As the Russians begin hauling out the cases, I watch the last traces of Julian's polished veneer crack away. The man underneath is something else entirely. Something darker.

And suddenly I'm not so sure about Cole's plan anymore.

Chapter Thirty-Nine

COLE

No." Knox's voice is granite. "You're not going in."

"Like hell I'm not." I check my watch again. Five hours. She's been with him for five hours.

"Cole." Knox steps between me and the SUV. "I've got two teams in position. Thermal imaging shows three heat signatures on the main floor. We know the layout. My people can handle this."

"Your people didn't get her into this mess. I did." My voice breaks slightly. "This is my fault. I should have told her everything from the beginning, should have known Julian would come after her."

"Exactly." His jaw tightens. "You're too close. Too emotional. In operations like this—"

"This isn't one of your operations." I step closer, forcing him to meet my eyes. "This is Sloane. And I need to be the one to get her out of there. I need to look her in the eye and tell her how sorry I am."

"And that's why you'll get her killed," Knox retorts. "We just got the alert from your case security system. Multiple failed biometric attempts before a lockdown. What does that tell you?"

"That Julian's getting desperate," I say, a cold satisfaction spreading through me. "And that Sloane is fighting back."

Knox's expression softens slightly. "She's resourceful, I'll give her that. But Julian's unpredictable when he's cornered."

"I've been waiting five years for this," I say, checking my weapon one more time. "Five years of watching my back, of building something Julian couldn't touch, of making sure I was ready when he finally made his move."

"And now he has," Knox reminds me. "With her. The one variable you can't control."

I hate that he's right. Julian knew exactly where to hit me. The one vulnerability I couldn't eliminate.

"Which is precisely why you need to stay back. Julian's expecting you to come charging in. He's planned for it. What he's not expecting is a four-man tactical team that knows every inch of that house."

I look past him to where his team is gearing up, efficient and silent in the predawn darkness. Professional. Skilled. Probably the best chance Sloane has.

And completely fucking irrelevant.

"Five minutes," I tell him. "Give me five minutes alone with Julian before your team moves in."

"Absolutely not."

"You know I'm going in either way. With or without your help." I meet his eyes. "But if you work with me, we can use Julian's obsession to our advantage. He's waiting for me. Let's give him what he wants."

Knox stares at me for a long moment. I can practically see him running scenarios, weighing options. Finally, he mutters a curse.

"Four minutes." He pulls a palm-size device from his vest. "And you wear this. It's a tracker with a panic button. You press it, we come in hot. You don't press it within four minutes, we come in hot anyway."

I take the device. "The Russians?"

"My team will handle them. You just . . ." He shakes his head. "Don't do anything stupid."

"When have I ever?"

"You really want me to answer that?" He signals to his team. "Move into final positions. Radio silence from here on."

He grabs my arm before I can move. "You get her out. That's your only job. You don't try to settle scores, you don't try to be a hero. You get her clear, and my team handles the rest."

I nod, though we both know it's a lie. Five years of waiting, of planning, of building toward this moment . . . Julian and I have unfinished business that goes beyond Sloane, beyond the designs, beyond everything that's happened tonight.

"One more thing," Knox says, his voice dropping. "Julian's men put something in that SUV before you got here. We haven't had time to check what it is."

"Probably her designs," I say, already turning away. "He'll want to take them when he runs."

"Or it's a bomb," Knox says bluntly. "Don't get tunnel vision, Cole. Julian doesn't just want you to show up. He wants you to die doing it."

I watch them disappear into the shadows around the estate. Professionals doing what they do best. But they don't know Julian like I do. Don't know the darkness he's capable of. Don't know how many lives he's destroyed while maintaining that perfect, polished smile.

I check my watch one last time. Almost dawn.

Time to end this.

My earpiece crackles. "Team One in position. First guard neutralized."

"Team Two," comes another voice. "East perimeter secure."

I don't respond. They're not talking to me anyway. I'm already moving toward the house, keeping to the shadows of the manicured garden.

I spot the first Russian before he sees me—a hulking figure patrolling the rear entrance. His partner is nowhere in sight. Sloppy. Julian's standards are slipping.

The man reaches for his radio, probably checking in with his missing comrade. That's when Knox's team strikes—quick, efficient, silent. The man is subdued without a sound. I continue toward the house.

Through the kitchen window, I can see two more of Julian's men hurriedly loading cases into the waiting SUV. Sloane's designs. My jaw tightens, but I force myself to stay focused. The designs can be replaced. Sloane can't.

The first floor is empty except for one guard, who Knox's team has already restrained and secured.

I pause at the base of the grand staircase, listening. There—voices from the study. Julian's voice, then Sloane's. The relief of hearing her alive nearly makes me miss the sound of footsteps behind me.

I spin just as the fourth Russian emerges from the shadows, weapon already raised. I dive for cover as his shot goes wide, splintering the wooden banister beside me. Before either of us can fire again, one of Knox's team appears and subdues the man with a precise takedown. The Russian slumps to the floor, unconscious. I nod gratefully to Knox's team member as I step over the incapacitated guard.

Knox's voice buzzes in my earpiece. "Status?"

"I'm in," I breathe, keeping my voice low. "Proceeding to target."

"We've got movement at the east entrance," Knox reports. "Two more hostiles loading cases into a vehicle."

"Let them," I say. "Sloane first."

I make my way down the corridor, staying close to the wall. The gunshot will have alerted Julian. The element of surprise is gone. But so is his patience. He'll be desperate now, dangerous. And Sloane is caught in the middle.

Drawing a deep breath, I steady myself.

Julian's been waiting all night for this moment, orchestrating every detail. I step into the study, the same one where I first met Claire five years ago. Where I watched her show Julian her latest designs, desperate for his approval. Where I stood, three months later, as the police asked their careful questions about her accident.

"I was starting to think you weren't coming." Julian's voice drifts from the back of the room. Calm. Controlled. A perfect host welcoming an expected guest.

I follow his voice, each step measured. Not rushing. Not giving him the satisfaction of seeing me desperate.

Julian stands by the fireplace, drink in hand, looking for all the world like this is a casual social call. And there, in one of the leather wingback chairs, is Sloane. Her wrists are bound with what looks like one of Julian's Italian silk ties. Her eyes meet mine, and the relief I see there nearly breaks my control.

"Where's the rest of it?" I ask, keeping my voice level.

Julian takes a slow sip of his drink. "The designs? Already gone. Being authenticated as we speak. Claire's final collection . . . it's really quite poetic when you think about it."

I check my watch. Time to stick to Knox's plan.

"You know what's funny, Julian?" I take a step deeper into the room. "You've spent years trying to destroy me. My company. My reputation. But you never quite managed it."

"And now I have." His smile doesn't reach his eyes. "Everything you've built with her—the designs, the publicity, the perfect power couple—it all becomes part of Claire's legacy instead. Fitting, don't you think?"

Three minutes left.

"You still don't get it." I take another step. "You're so focused on the past, on what you think you lost, that you can't see what's right in front of you."

He swirls the drink in his glass. "And what exactly am I missing?"

"How pathetic this is." I watch his fingers tighten on the glass. "You didn't just lose Claire. You lost your talent for this game. Five years of trying to hurt me, and the best you can come up with is stealing some jewelry?"

Two minutes.

"Stealing?" His composure cracks, just slightly. "I'm reclaiming what should have been Claire's. Your little protégée's work will finally serve a purpose. A tribute to real talent."

I catch Sloane's slight head shake. She knows what I'm doing. Keeping him talking. Keeping him focused on me.

"Claire had real talent," I agree, taking another step. "She didn't need you to forge her legacy. To fake her designs. She would have hated this, Julian. But then, you never really knew her, did you?"

His glass shatters in the fireplace.

One minute.

"Don't you dare tell me about my wife." His polished veneer is gone now. "You have no right—"

"I have every right. I was there, remember? Watched you destroy her, piece by piece. Just like you tried to destroy me. Just like you're trying to destroy Sloane." I'm close enough now to see the tremor in his hands. "But here's what you still don't understand."

Thirty seconds.

"What?" he snarls.

"That you've already lost." I smile and watch his expression falter. "Again."

The first flash-bang crashes through the study window behind him.

I'm moving before the blast, tackling Sloane's chair backward as the room erupts in light and sound. Her head tucks against my chest as we hit the floor, my body covering hers from the spray of glass.

Knox's team flows through the window and door like smoke—black tactical gear, precise movements. No hesitation. No warning. I hear Julian shout something, but it's lost in the breach.

I focus on Sloane, working at the silk tie around her wrists. "You okay?"

She nods against my chest, then lifts her head. There's a cut on her cheek from the glass, but her eyes are clear. Steady. "The designs—"

"Knox has another team at Julian's headquarters." I help her sit up as the tie finally comes loose. "They moved in the moment we breached here."

"You let him take them." Understanding dawns in her eyes. "You wanted him to split his men between locations." She gives me a look. "You made me wait five hours with Boris and Vladimir for this plan to work, didn't you?"

"I'm so sorry," I say, my voice rough with emotion. "I should have been here sooner."

"You should have."

I wait for the fury. The rage. But none of that comes.

She touches my face, her fingers gentle against my cheek. "Hey. You came for me. That's what matters now."

But then her eyes narrow, searching mine. "Julian said something earlier. About Maya, my old assistant."

I freeze. "What do you mean?"

"He didn't come right out and say it, but . . ." She swallows. "The way he talked . . . it sounded like she's gone. Like maybe he killed her. Chloe had mentioned that there's no word of her and—"

"Anything's possible with Julian," I say, my voice tight. "But if there's even a chance she's alive, I'll find out. And if she is"—I look her in the eye—"I'll make sure she gets out."

She nods once, but the silence that follows is heavy.

"I was terrified," I admit, the words pouring out now. "When

I realized he had you—" I break off, unable to finish the thought. "I'm sorry, Sloane. For all of this."

"I know. I know this was never your plan." She pauses and appears to shake off any darkness that passed through her eyes. "Are we in agreement that *plans* aren't always the best path?" she teases, clearly trying to lighten the moment.

A crash from across the room draws our attention. Julian's on his knees, Knox's team surrounding him as he spits curses and threats. The perfect, polished mask is gone completely now. All that's left is the raw, ugly truth underneath.

He's not listening anymore, his eyes fixed on the fireplace, on the spot where Claire used to sit and sketch. Lost in whatever twisted version of the past he's created for himself.

Knox appears at my side, offering Sloane his hand. "Building's secure. Medical team's outside if you need them."

She takes his hand, lets him pull her to her feet. "I'm fine. But my designs—"

"Already recovered." Knox's normally stern expression softens slightly. "All of them. Team found them exactly where you said they'd be, Cole. Along with enough evidence of fraud and conspiracy to put him away for a very long time."

I stand, keeping my hand on Sloane's back. She's trembling slightly, though whether from adrenaline or cold, I'm not sure. "Let's get out of here."

I shrug off my jacket, draping it over her shoulders. She leans into me slightly, but her eyes are on the horizon where the sun is just starting to paint the sky in shades of pink and gold.

"Not exactly how I planned to spend Christmas morning," she says quietly, then tenses. "Havoc—"

"Is fine. My assistant is watching him." I pull her closer. "And I still have those breakfast reservations at Rivers."

She looks down at her wrinkled and torn dress, touching a large tear at the hem. "Cole, I can't go to Rivers like this. Let's just go home."

"You haven't tried their cinnamon rolls yet." I can't quite keep the longing out of my voice. After the night we've had, I need something normal. Something good.

She studies my face for a moment, her expression softening. "Pretty sure showing up looking like this violates every dress code they have."

"We just survived our own *Die Hard* Christmas. I think we can get away with being a little disheveled."

That gets a real smile. "Does that make me Bruce Willis in this scenario?"

"Yippee ki-yay," I murmur into her hair, and feel her laugh against my chest.

Behind us, Knox's team leads Julian out in handcuffs. He doesn't look at us. Doesn't say a word. Just stares straight ahead as they put him in the waiting car.

"Come on." I take her hand. "Let's go celebrate our first Christmas together."

Chapter Forty
SLOANE

Leo, Rivers' legendary maître d', actually takes a step back when we walk in. I can't blame him. My Marchesa dress, which started the evening as a masterpiece of red silk, now looks like I've gone three rounds with a paper shredder. Cole's tactical gear is barely concealed by his overcoat, and there's a faint dusting of glass in his hair that catches the light like frost.

Leo opens his mouth—probably to suggest we might be more comfortable somewhere else—but Cole just looks at him. It's not threatening, exactly, but it carries the weight of a man who's spent the night destroying everything Julian built.

"Your usual corner table, Mr. Asher?" Leo asks, already reaching for the menus. Cole nods, and we follow him through the restaurant.

The view of Manhattan stretches out before us, everything dusted in snow and twinkling with Christmas lights. It would be magical if I wasn't so aware of the other diners stealing glances at us.

"Bloody Mary," I tell the waiter before he can even hand me a menu. "Extra bloody."

Cole's lips twitch. "Coffee. And two orders of the cinnamon rolls." He glances at me. "Unless you want your own order?"

"I think I'll start with the vodka and see where that takes us."

The waiter hurries away, probably grateful for an excuse to escape the intensity radiating from our table. Cole's hand hasn't left my lower back since we walked in, and his eyes keep scanning the room in a way that would seem paranoid if we hadn't just survived what we did.

"The police will want statements," he says quietly, thumb moving in small circles against my spine. "Knox is handling the initial reports, but—"

"Can we maybe save the criminal proceedings discussion until after I've had my drink?"

His expression softens. "Of course. What would you prefer to discuss? The weather? The stock market? The fact that you managed to make two trained Russian mercenaries argue about vodka brands for five hours?"

That startles a laugh out of me. "They were very passionate about their opinions. I think Boris is still mad that Vladimir prefers Grey Goose."

"I assume those aren't their real names."

"Probably not. But they seemed to enjoy it when I started using them."

The Bloody Mary arrives, garnished with enough vegetables to count as a small salad. I take a long sip, feeling some of the tension start to ease.

I reach across the table and take his hand. His fingers tighten around mine immediately.

"I thought my surveillance and security measures would be enough." He looks down at our joined hands. "I never imagined he'd be bold enough to take you from our home. That's on me. All of it."

I study his face, seeing the genuine regret in his eyes. The man who plans for every contingency, who anticipates every move, is torturing himself over the one possibility he didn't see coming.

"You're right. It is on you," I agree, my voice firmer than I intended. "You put my face in a biometric system that could access Claire's designs without telling me. You made me Julian's target without giving me the chance to understand what I was walking into."

His face pales. "The biometrics—I never thought he'd try to use you to access the case. That was meant to be a safeguard, a way to protect Claire's legacy by giving access to someone I trusted completely."

"But you didn't trust me enough to tell me about it." The hurt in my voice is clear. "How did you even get my biometric data? When did that happen?"

"The security system in the penthouse," he admits, looking ashamed. "The first week you moved in. I . . . I told myself all the cameras, all the viewing, all the control . . . it was for your protection. To be completely honest . . . I forgot I even did it or I would have told you when I came clean about everything."

I pull my hand back and take another long sip of my drink.

His voice breaks. "There's no excuse. None."

I sit with that for a moment, then sigh. "I forgive you," I say softly, meaning it. "We both made it through. And maybe now we can actually build something with no more secrets between us."

His eyes meet mine, relief washing over his features. "No more secrets," he agrees, his thumb tracing over my knuckles. "I promise."

The cinnamon rolls arrive, still steaming, drowning in icing. Cole's entire focus shifts, and I have to bite back a smile at his obvious delight.

"I'm starting to think you only brought me here for the pastries."

"I brought you here because—" He stops, reaching out to brush something from my cheek. "Because I want us to start a Christmas tradition. Cinnamon Rolls at Rivers."

"Tradition means more than one time, you know . . ." I'm fishing for more. No doubt about it.

"I know exactly what tradition means." He leans back, his eyes serious. "I never want to feel that helpless again. Not being able to reach you, to protect you—"

I offer a soft smile. "Hey. I'm here. We're here."

He presses a kiss to my knuckles, his lips warm against my chilled skin. "You're right. We're here. And I plan on keeping it that way."

I raise an eyebrow, trying to lighten the mood. "Is that your way of saying you're never letting me out of your sight again?"

Cole laughs, a real one that crinkles the corners of his eyes. "I suppose that's too much to hope for."

Cole's cell buzzes and he takes a minute to read the text. A smile on his face tells me he received good news. "Maya's found. She managed to get away and was laying low with her family in Jersey, but she's safe and returning home as we speak."

I release a breath. "Oh thank god." I take another long drink.

"Knox says she's unharmed."

The waiter appears then, refilling my drink and leaving a fresh carafe of coffee for Cole. We place our breakfast orders—Eggs Benedict for me, steak and eggs for him.

As the waiter departs, Cole's gaze turns serious again. He reaches into his coat pocket and pulls out a small box, placing it on the table between us.

"Okay, enough of the dark stuff. We need something lighter."

My heart stutters. "Cole, what—"

"Open it." His voice is soft but insistent.

With trembling fingers, I lift the lid. Nestled inside is a key. I look up at him, unspoken questions in my eyes.

"It's to my place," he explains. "I want you to have it. I want . . ." He takes a breath. "Your collection is complete. New Year's is almost here. And we have never actually discussed what's next. I want you to officially move in. Not because of a contract. But by choice. Both of our choices."

Emotions clog my throat. This man—this strong, brave, cinnamon roll–loving man—is offering me more than just access to his apartment. He's offering me a future. A partnership in every sense of the word.

I slide my hand into his, the key pressed between our palms. "Cole, I . . . I don't know what to say."

He smiles softly. "You don't have to say anything right now. I know it's a big step. I just wanted you to know where I stand. Where I hope we're heading."

I nod, blinking back the sudden dampness in my eyes. "Can I . . . can I think about it?"

"Of course." He squeezes my hand. "Take all the time you need. I'm not going anywhere."

I drink some more of my Bloody Mary, the spice and the vodka bolstering my courage. I set the glass down with a decisive clink.

"Okay, I've thought about it."

Cole raises an eyebrow, a smile playing at the corners of his mouth. "That was quick."

"What can I say? I'm a decisive woman." I lean forward, my eyes locked on his. "Yes, Cole Asher. Yes, I will move in with you."

His grin could light up the entire restaurant. "You're sure? You don't need more time to consider the pros and cons? Make a list? Sleep on it?"

I shake my head, laughing. "Nope. I'm sure. Completely, utterly, one hundred percent sure."

"Well then." He lifts his coffee mug in a toast. "To new beginnings and quick decisions."

The rest of the meal passes in a blur of warm smiles, shared bites, and the occasional brush of fingers. By the time we step out-side, the snow has stopped, leaving the city blanketed in white.

Cole tucks me into his side as we walk, his arm a solid warmth around me. "So, what's the verdict on this new Christmas tradition of ours?"

I lean into him, smiling. "I think it's a keeper. Though next year, I vote we skip the life-threatening situations leading up to it."

He chuckles. "Deal." His car pulls up and he assists me inside. "I have someplace to take you. I want to show you your Christmas present."

As if on cue, a sleek black car pulls up to the curb. Cole opens the door, assisting me into the plush leather interior before sliding in beside me. He leans forward to murmur something to the driver before settling back, his hand finding mine.

I tilt my head, curiosity piqued. "Where are we going? I thought we were heading home."

An enigmatic smile plays at his lips. "I have someplace I want to take you first. Call it one of your many Christmas presents."

I raise an eyebrow. "I think I've had my fill of surprises for the next twenty-four hours, Cole. Between Russian mercenaries and unexpected house guests, I'm not sure my heart can take much more excitement."

He chuckles, bringing our joined hands to his lips for a quick kiss. "I promise, this surprise involves significantly less adrenaline. Trust me."

"Always." The word comes without hesitation, without doubt.

As the city lights blur past the windows, I allow my mind to wander, trying to puzzle out our destination. A new restaurant? A private art showing? With Cole, the possibilities are endless.

Twenty minutes later, we're pulling up to a building I've passed a hundred times—one of those gorgeous old industrial conversions with huge windows and exposed brick. Cole leads me inside, and I'm immediately struck by the light. Even in the early morning, it floods the space, catching on pristine white walls and gleaming hardwood floors.

"What is this?"

"This"—he pulls a set of keys from his pocket—"is your new atelier."

I stare at him. "My what?"

"Come on." He takes my hand, leading me through the space. "Main gallery here. Private showing room through there. Your personal workspace is upstairs, with a view of the park. And here . . ." He opens a door to reveal a series of workstations. "Room for your team. I was going to hire them all too but decided I'd leave that to you. Once your collection is revealed on New Year's, your life is going to change drastically. You're going to have so many orders, demands . . . you're going to need a good team."

"Cole." My voice catches. "This is . . ."

"Yours." He presses the keys into my hand. "The security system is state of the art. Biometric locks, reinforced storage, surveillance—"

I lean into him, my heart so full it feels fit to burst. "This is incredible, Cole. Truly. I don't know how to thank you."

He presses a kiss to my temple. "You never have to thank me. Seeing you happy, knowing you're safe and doing what you love . . . that's all I want."

I twist in his arms to face him, my hands sliding up to cup his face. "I love you, Cole Asher. More than I ever thought possible."

His smile softens, his eyes shining with emotion. "I love you too, Sloane. Now and always."

I spot one of the cameras in the corner and can't help but laugh. "Really? More cameras?"

"What can I say? I like seeing you when you're sleeping . . ." His arms slide around my waist. "Next to me. And I want to know when you're awake . . . when you aren't next to me."

"That's either the most romantic or the most stalkerish thing you've ever said."

Cole's embrace tightens as he chuckles. "I prefer to think of it as romantic, but I suppose there's a fine line."

About the Author

Alta Hensley is a *USA Today* bestselling author of dark romance where the villain always gets the happily ever after. Twisted, clever, and occasionally unhinged, her books deliver morally gray anti-heroes, sharp-tongued heroines, and happily-ever-afters that taste even sweeter after a little ruin. With a signature blend of grit, wit, and heat, Alta's stories prove one thing: Villains deserve love too. Alta lives on the foggy coast of Oregon with her husband, two daughters, and a pair of dogs who think they're in charge. When she's not writing redemption for the irredeemable, she's walking the coastline or sipping craft beer in eccentric little bars that feel like they belong in her books.